Admit One:

10 Steps to Choosing your Acting or Musical Theatre College Program

by Chelsea Cipolla and John West

13-digit: ISBN: 978-1-61364-385-3

Credits
Cover Art: Amanda Sylvester
Editorial and Design: Abella Publishing Services, LLC, www.abellapublishingservices.com
Copy Editor: Lisa Allen
Proofreader: Youn-Joo Park
Design: Amanda Sylvester

Disclaimer
All survey information was provided by the individual schools during the 2010–11 academic year. The authors are not responsible for information incorrectly reported or changes to programs that were made after the information was submitted. Any opinions expressed in a survey belongs to the individual respondents and not the authors.

Descriptions for Summer Programs and Additional Programs to Consider were culled directly from each program's marketing materials.

Contents

Part 1: The Steps

Part 2: The Surveys

Acknowledgments

This book could not have been written without our students. Thank you for continually inspiring and motivating us to be better teachers.

Thank you to the entire staff of *My College Audition* (Grant Mac-Dermott, McCaela Donovan, Justin Stoney, Kevin Michael Murphy, Jonathan Brenner, and Joe Marella) for your dedication and commitment.

Thank you to all of the professors, teachers, assistants, department heads and guidance counselors that helped contribute to our college surveys. We can't express how much we appreciate your support, enthusiasm and cheer while helping us complete this book.

We also want to send a huge thank you to our first, and finest, assistant Lauren Fondren. Without your organization, insight and humor this book would truly not exist.

Thank you to Courtney O'Connor for surpassing your duties as my professor. You are a friend and mentor that I am grateful to know.

A huge thank you goes out to the Abella Team: Belinda Thresher, Lisa Allen, Youn-Joo Park, and Amanda Sylvester. Thank you for taking this project on and for guiding us every step of the way.

To Jon Popp, website designer and computer wizard, thank you for putting up with my constant requests. And, for being the nicest guy I know.

Thank you to M&A for your unwavering support.

Preface
How to Use This Book

You want to be on Broadway . . .

You just finished your star turn as Adelaide in your senior homecoming musical, *Guys & Dolls*; you took a trip to New York City over spring break and saw *Sister Act;* and now you have your sights set on the Great White Way. Obviously you'll *start* by playing Elphaba, and *then* you'll probably get cast opposite Matthew Morrison on *GLEE.*

Or perhaps you're not much for musical theatre, but you *did*, after all, just bring previously unexplored nuance to your portrayal of Leonid in your community experimental theatre's post-apocalyptic version of *The Cherry Orchard* . . . and you are eager to get up to the city for your first audition for The Public.

Your heart feels alive when you're on stage. You watch Kenneth Branagh on your *Hamlet* DVD at least once a month, you listen to *Spring Awakening* every day on the way to rehearsal, and you can *totally* sing it better than Lea Michele!

Perhaps you would rather be a movie star, a renowned designer, an actor who is consistently employed in quality regional productions, or the artistic director of your community theatre. Maybe you'd prefer to be a high school theatre teacher, a stage manager, or the founder of a children's theatre.

But somewhere, and sometime, someone told you getting a college education was a good idea, so you're considering it. Maybe it was your parents, your guidance counselor, a professional actor, or a casting director at a master class.

"Training," they said, "is essential. Go to college."

But . . . should you? For many of you, college is a foregone conclusion. You know you want to experience that part of your life, you know you need time to hone your skills, and obtaining a college degree has been a goal ever since you can remember.

Others reading this may be on the fence: "I'm thinking about school—but I'm *really* talented! Why would I spend four years of my life learning when I can move to one of the big cities and be an actor now?" This is a valid concern, but the majority of high school students who pose this question are guilty of having delusions of grandeur (believe us). Pursuing a career in theatre is absurdly difficult, and many 17 year olds (due to their high school success) presume that Broadway is the next step—no training required.

The reality is that the number of theatre and musical theatre majors in this country has never been larger. *Thousands* of professionals are competing for an increasingly small number of jobs. Broadway legends are at auditions competing against the hundreds of students being churned out of top college programs each year.

You need to be at the height of your game to survive. Most 17 year olds haven't had the training and experience—not to mention the maturity and self-awareness—necessary to compete at the top level. It becomes almost impossible for casting directors or agents to take you seriously if they're looking at you next to a polished graduate from Florida State.

On the other hand, there are many shows these days that *do* use younger actors. For those who consider dance to be their strength, ages 17 to 23 can be considered prime years. And there are those in that .01% who are so obscenely talented that they really *don't* need school to become huge stars. There *are* professional opportunities—and great ones—for young talents.

Even if you're that megastar, though, going to college for training has its advantages. Many people who don't have the "college experience" regret it, and it has always been our position to encourage people to seek training before attempting to pursue a life in the theatre. (Plenty of compromises are available. In the following pages, you will see that a number of schools are located in those big cities and encourage professional auditions.)

So if you want to be on Broadway or anywhere else in the world of theatre, and you've decided college is right for you, you naturally want to attend *the* school that can get you there.

The truth is, however, that even though we've devoted an entire book to that very desire, only *you* can get yourself there. The one thing that *everyone* will tell you about any undergraduate theatre program is, "It's what you make of it." We've heard this phrase about every program in the country—be it Southwest Missouri State, Juilliard, Shenandoah, or AMDA. There are opportunities wherever you go, and it takes a tremendous amount of self-discipline, maturity, and passion to glean the most from what a program can offer you.

A college theatre program is what you make of it.

If you spend time with actors in New York City, you'll see leads on Broadway who went to a state school in Nebraska and plenty of consistently unemployed actors who went to Rutgers. We also know tremendously successful actors who didn't go to college for theatre *at all* or went for an entirely different major. The school in and of itself does not guarantee success or failure.

Talent is talent, and if you're good enough, you can get cast professionally, no matter where you matriculated. Choosing a college is an important decision, but it's not life or death. Honing your talent, no matter where you go to do it, is going to give you a leg up in the real world. Having said that, "all actors are talented," as the saying goes, so it is in your best interest—while you have this time—to look for a program that gives you additional advantages best suited for your goals. Many schools offer not only top-quality training but also access to resources that will provide you with—if you're playing the odds—a greater *chance* at success than others.

With all the choices, not to mention the pressure to pick the best and most appropriate college to meet your needs, where do you start?

It's helpful to think of college selection as a process of elimination. You begin with thousands of schools, and you need to narrow that list to one. In this book, we take you through the steps, one at a time, to help you discover your dream college.

In each step, you'll want to evaluate what your "deal breakers" are. What can't you live without? Think carefully, but it's important that not everything along the way be a deal breaker. Try to balance an open mind with wise consideration and preferences, and only establish a "must have" when you are absolutely certain it's what you want and what you can't live without.

The more open minded you are toward the beginning of the process, the better your odds of finding that gem of a school that is right for you. Don't assume you know the importance of a particular step (for example, "I *have* to have a BFA") until you thoroughly explore its implications. Once you have given serious thought to what you want to do with your life and assess the insight from each step, then begin to make some concrete decisions about what's best for your particular pursuits. After all, at some point, decisions will have to be made. There's always that underlying fear that by eliminating schools at each step, you could be missing out. So carefully consider and evaluate, but then make your criteria elimination decisions and stick to them. The other schools will always be there.

We want to get as many schools out of the picture as possible with each step of narrowing your search. So . . . let's dive in. First things first . . .

Part 1

The Steps

Step 1

My Decision

So . . . you're headed to college next year, and you're thinking about declaring theatre as your major. Is this the right decision for you?

1. Your Motivation

Theatre is an extraordinary discipline, and it can be a tremendous choice for advanced study. The type of world that you'll inhabit as a theatre major is vastly different from any other. It is four years of studying a medium that has the power to inspire, transform, and invigorate the human spirit. There is a familial quality among theatre majors that is rare in other majors. In the typical theatre department, you will live with, go to class with, rehearse with, study with, and socialize with the same core group of people. It's a world full of artists, eccentrics, passion, intelligence, and excitement.

You're probably drawn to study it because of some meaningful involvement you've had with the stage in the past. That experience compelled you to consider spending more time—and perhaps the rest of your life—pursuing this field.

But before we dive into figuring out which school is the best fit for you, now would be a good time to ask yourself if a theatre degree is truly the right path for you.

Notes

Who Should Get a Theatre Degree?

Obtaining a degree in theatre arts is a terrific idea for many people, but it's not for everyone. After all, practically speaking, it doesn't always carry a lot of weight in the job market. A theatre degree is considerably less versatile than a diploma indicating that you're competent at business or science.

The first thing to evaluate is how serious you are about pursuing it as a career. It doesn't mean you have to be 100% certain—that's part of what college is for: figuring yourself out. But the sooner you start to weigh these issues seriously, the better equipped you'll be for your future.

Reasons You Shouldn't

We try to dissuade students from choosing to pursue a theatre degree when one of the following best describe them:

1. You think it will be an easy way to get through college.

2. You've never done any sort of theatre before at all, but you think you'd be good at it. (There are ways to get experience before diving in completely to something you know very little about.)

Reasons You Should

However, if you belong to one of the three basic groups we'll be discussing, theatre could be what you'd want to declare as a major:

1. You were born to play Elphaba . . . and you *will*. Nothing's going to stop you. You are a performer. It's in your blood, and you've never doubted it for a second.

2. You think you're interested in a professional life that involves theatre in some capacity. Not performing, necessarily, but you've been around shows and you love them. If any of the following careers sound appealing, a degree in theatre can help you figure out where you best fit: a stage manager, production designer (do you have an affinity for lighting or costumes?), director, choreographer, artistic director, college professor, high school teacher, general manager, box office supervisor, music director, writer, company manager, agent, casting director, entertainment lawyer . . . the list goes on.

3. You've done some acting, and you could do it as a career . . . maybe? You like it more than anything else, and you're pretty good at it. You're about to go to college, and there's nothing else you're interested in. Your parents are unsure, but you'd like to give it a good try. Who knows, right?

Do you fit into one of these categories? If so, read on!

It's Not Set in Stone

Remember, especially if you're uncertain, this is not set in stone. What you declare as your major can always change. You should give yourself permission to grow and learn more about yourself. Don't feel monumental pressure that you *have* to get this exactly right when you're 17. The goal is simply not to waste your time, and if you gain some skills that you can apply to your ultimate career, all the better. If you can determine that theatre won't be your ultimate career now, it's better than discovering it during your senior year and having to start over again from scratch.

2. Your Future with a Theatre Degree

There's no denying that a theatre degree offers a lot of opportunities for growth and learning (and fun!) during your college years. But what your life will be like as a theatre major *during* college and as a theatre major *after* college are two very different considerations.

 Things to Consider

Can I Make a Living with a Theatre Degree?

Yes. We're not suggesting you can make a good living solely as an actor—that's tough (but possible). There are also countless opportunities in theatre beyond acting. Many actors make their living from voice-over work, the occasional commercial, industrial videos, and trade shows. Having a degree in theatre can also help immeasurably when working toward myriad career tracks, including those listed earlier.

Is a Theatre Degree Useful for Other Careers?

Absolutely! Again, if you already know you want to do something else, then concentrate on that area of study from the get-go. But many students who graduate with degrees in theatre go on to graduate schools or specialized training centers for other disciplines— some of the best lawyers we know have theatre degrees. Our research assistant has a theatre degree, and she is on the fast track to political diplomacy.

Although an undergraduate degree in theatre isn't necessarily the most versatile for employment right off the bat, it's certainly good for getting you into institutions for higher learning. Many law and business schools are intrigued by theatre majors, as the skill set they bring to the table often makes them valuable commodities in their field.

At the end of the day, you can do *anything* with a theatre degree—it's a college degree! A theatre degree can leave you with an immense amount of comfort speaking in front of large crowds, and a greater amount of self-esteem and overall confidence that you can apply to a number of professions. You can choose where to go and what to do after you obtain it. But try to be mindful of being efficient with your time and resources when pursuing higher education.

What if I Want to be Exclusively a Movie Star? . . . or a Dancer? . . . or a Singer?

The great thing about a theatre degree is that you get training in many different areas. If you *know* you have a face for camera, casting directors love seeing people with stage training. A degree in theatre certainly would be a great first step. Choose a school such as UCLA or Wright State that has a strong film-training component. If you are certain that you want to be a ballerina, opt for a dance major. Want to sing opera professionally? Venture over to the voice department and commit to being a vocal performance major. If you enjoy acting, though, and are open to the possibility of being a more versatile performer, a theatre or musical theatre degree may be the way to go.

3. Doubts: Yours and Your Family's

Having to decide what you want out of the next four years is no easy task, and having to juggle your own desires and the expectations of your family can seem downright impossible. Never fear! You are not alone. The best things you can do are to be honest with yourself and your family and keep the channels of communication open.

Can I Declare Myself a Theatre Major if I'm Not 100% Sure?

Yes. Let us reiterate: You can always change your major. The point is, think as hard as you can about it now. College costs a ton of money these days, so you want to be as efficient as possible with your study and cash. The hope is that even if you do change your mind halfway through, you won't view your theatre classes as a waste of time. Besides, if you're getting a number of your general education credits out of the way in your first couple of years (as you should), those will be applicable to any degree.

My Family Is Not Supportive

This may be one of the biggest hurdles you will have to face in choosing theatre as your major. However, before you engage in screaming matches and decide to run away from home and climb on a bus to Manhattan, we implore you to *listen* to your family's objections and make every effort to see things from their point of view.

Though not always the case, these objections often are raised out of love and concern. Especially for parents who don't know much about theatre (and perhaps even more so with those who do), they hear the words "theatre major" and worry that their child will starve for the rest of his or her life.

The first thing to do is sit down with your family and ask them to tell you in detail why they are opposed to your studying theatre in college. Before you get defensive, *listen* to them. Do they make any good points? Is there something you hadn't considered before? Take a day or two and deliberate over everything they said before issuing your response. Don't let pride be an issue here. Assuming that their concerns are from a loving place, treat their feelings sensitively.

Then, if you're still determined, do your research and try to address their concerns one by one. When presented in the right tone, many parents can be receptive to mature logic. Hopefully, they will see how much this means to you and support your decision. If not, it is unfortunate, but not insurmountable.

There is a fine line between being respectful of your family's desires for you and not living the life that you were meant to live. If your family is not comfortable paying for you to pursue theatre in college, remember there are other ways. Try every scholarship and work–study opportunity possible. You can almost always—with the right amount of resourcefulness—make it work.

Don't forget the art of compromise. If your dad sees your potential for a future in politics because you were the star of the debate team, and the thought has some appeal to you, a minor in communications or political science is always something to consider.

4. The Importance of Being Realistic

Those are some of the basic considerations for people contemplating whether a theatre major is a good fit. Again, for anyone who is interested in one of the many careers in the theatre, getting a bachelor's degree in theatre is a viable option. However, let us issue the following caveat to the serious performer who knows no option in life but to be a star.

Notes

This Means You, Elphie

Stop us if you've heard this one: Pursuing a career as an actor can be, for many people, totally, absolutely, wholly unpleasant at times. You know all those horror stories that go in one ear and out the other? About waiting tables and unemployment checks and audition lines that wrap around several blocks?

The thing is, they're not just stories that happen to everyone *but* you. To decide to be a working actor is on some level *irrational*. There is no stability, which we know, we know . . . you don't care about, because you *live* for spontaneity. You care about the way your heart races when you hear Cheyenne Jackson sing "Don't Walk Away." You care about what it would be like to star opposite William H. Macy in "Speed the Plow." You care about the thrill that you get when you're up there, in front of a live crowd, holding the audience in the palm of your hand, bringing joy and entertainment to the masses!

But still, it's kind of irrational. And truth be told, you may not get to make money at it consistently.

We know, we know. You're different! But there is a saying you'll hear time and again from people who have been actors their entire lives: "If you can do *anything* else with your life and be happy, do it."

We'll say it again. Going to college and getting a performance degree because you've decided to try to make your living as an actor will be viewed by many as a silly thing to do. Got it?

Keeping It Real

So, legitimately assess your talents and level of desire. Is theatre a hobby? Something you enjoy doing after class but aren't sure if you really want to commit to? Or is this your unmistakable passion in life?

If you're still reading and *know* that playing make-believe is silly—but you know what? It's your life and you'll be silly if you want to—then that's *fantastic*. Because as *Dead Poets' Society* puts it, "Medicine, law, business, engineering . . . these are noble pursuits and necessary to sustain life. But poetry, beauty, romance, love . . . these are what we stay alive for."

As hard as a life in the theatre can be, there is something unmistakably magical about it.

You have a realistic understanding of the risks involved, and you are committed to going for it. Getting a degree in theatre is an excellent initial step in pursuing a life in professional theatre, and if a life on the stage (or near it) is absolutely a part of who you are, then don't let the previous paragraphs or what anyone says deter you—you'll encounter a lot of bitter, jaded people along the way, rest assured.

Last Tip!

Just take some advice from Thoreau—"Go with confidence in the direction of your dreams. Live the life you've imagined."—and read on. This book was written especially for you.

 **RECAP**

Step 1: *My Decision*

Questions to Consider:

1. Is a theatre degree right for me?
   - How serious am I about pursuing a career in theatre?
   - Why do I want this degree? Do I have good reasons for choosing this major?
   - Do I have enough experience with theatre to base a college decision on it?
   - What are my expectations about getting a theatre degree? Are they realistic?

2. How will a theatre degree affect my life after college?
   - What careers interest me? What sorts of degrees do people in those careers hold?
   - Could a theatre degree prevent me from doing something else I might be interested in?
   - Will I be able to make a living with a theatre degree?
   - How do theatre professionals make money?

3. What are the drawbacks to getting a theatre degree? Have I honestly considered my parents' opinions?
   - Am I doing everything in my power to weigh this decision carefully and thoroughly?
   - Am I giving my family the opportunity to express their thoughts on the matter? Am I hearing them out? Am I getting defensive?
   - Have I rationally addressed their concerns?

4. Do I know what I'm getting myself into?
   - Is there anything other than theatre I could do with my life and be happy?
   - Do I have a good sense of my own talent and desire?
   - Am I willing to make serious sacrifices for theatre? Do I have realistic expectations of what my life will be like?

Step 2

My Location

All right, you've taken the first big step and decided that you're ready to declare yourself a theatre major. (How'd the fam take the news?) Now the big question is: Where should you go?

Geographic Concerns

Geography is the most important issue to begin the process of elimination. It can knock out a huge chunk of options, and in some cases, results in instantly eliminating 49 states.

Some of you may not care at all. You would go wherever you find the best fit, be it in Florida, New York City, or Wyoming. Most people, however, have some idea of where they'd like to be on the map, and you must evaluate how important location is to you.

For example, the University of Michigan may be the perfect school for you. But if you dismiss it just because you don't know much about the state of Michigan or it doesn't sound like a cool place, you could miss out on your dream school.

If, however, you are from Texas, *know* you want to be within driving distance of your family, and can't *stand* cold weather, cementing your home area as a "must" on your list is perfectly reasonable. You'll likely be happier in Texas, Oklahoma, or Mississippi than in Michigan.

Make sense? Let's have a look. There are a number of factors to consider when assessing which region would be best for you.

Now Playing ▶ Things to Consider

In State versus Out of State

Generally speaking, in-state public schools are markedly cheaper than out-of-state schools or private schools. As you consider your financial resources and scholarship eligibility, determine if "in state" is a must.

Some parents can only pay for school if students stay in state. If that is the case and you don't want to take out loans or can't get scholarships, then needless to say, you can eliminate the other 49 states from your search.

Also examine whether your family has any in-state or out-of-state connections. For example, perhaps your mother works for a branch of a university or your dad's alma mater is where you've always wanted to go—there could be substantial financial aid available if so.

Distance from Family and Friends

How far do you want or are willing to be from your family? This is a huge issue for most high school students. Some want to go to college with their friends and be near their families. Others want to get far away as possible and establish a new identity for themselves. There are pros and cons for both.

Getting as far away as possible may seem like a good idea, but when you need to visit home, who's going to pay for the plane ticket? What if you miss your dog more than you anticipated? What if something happens to a family member?

Conversely, you may think you want to keep everything the same as it was in high school. You love your family and these are your best friends, after all. But how will you know what's out there in the world unless you try it? What about getting outside your comfort zone and trying a new location while freeing yourself to make new friends?

This is a personal decision that should be *carefully* considered. If unsure, a happy medium might be a distance that is still drivable but one where you are still able to gain some independence.

Another point to consider: With the proliferation of instant Internet communication tools like Skype and Facebook, families and friends can feel better connected even over long distances.

Climate

What kind of weather do you prefer? There are some people whose mood is drastically influenced by the weather. Yes, deciding you have to study theatre in Hawaii because it looks incredible is unwise. But choosing to go to one of the many outstanding schools in Florida or North Carolina because you hate winter and love the beach is definitely something worth adding to the list. On the other hand, if you can't stand being in brutal heat, maybe New England or the Northwest is where you should begin. This is an issue that should be a "must have" only if it is exactly that for you. Most people can usually reach a compromise.

I Want to Go to College in New York City. Period.

(or LA or Chicago or . . .) because of the opportunities. The truth is, going to college in the city where you want to establish yourself and your career is not for everyone. The temptation to "get there ASAP" is a significant one. Let's examine the pros and cons, using New York as an example.

On one hand, New York City provides endless performance and cultural opportunities. It's the biggest city in America, with plenty of chances to see and study theatre all day, every day. There are opportunities for connections, you would be able to get accustomed to the city, *and* maybe audition for and land a Broadway show your freshman year.

The truth is, however, New York is a tough city and results in a dynamically different "college experience" than you would get in many other regions. Rather than a community-based campus, one is swept into a dizzying sea of subways and taxis. Students have to worry about classes while walking three blocks to do laundry, pay for their metrocard, and juggle a social life. A number of students give up on New York and decide they don't like it because they're trying to acclimate themselves to the obscenely intense lifestyle while taking a full load of classes—and that's a lot to ask of yourself.

There's plenty to be said for attending one of the fabulous theatre schools in New York, but in most cases, it's best not to decide on this as a "must have" until you've given a fair look at schools in other parts of the country.

Use these factors to help decide if you're open to looking anywhere or if it's best for you to look within a specific region.

Notes

 **RECAP**

STEP 2: *My Location*

Questions to Consider:

1. Do I have to go in state?

   - Do I already know at this point that out of state is not an option for me? (Determining this will be covered in more detail later in the book if you're not sure yet.)

2. How far do I want to be from family and friends?

   - What is my ideal distance from my home?

   - How important is it to me that I go to college with my friends from high school?

   - Are there familial commitments that require me to be within a certain distance?

   - How will I get home when I need to? Can I afford that?

3. How does climate factor into my choice?

   - Does my happiness depend largely on the weather?

   - What are my needs versus preferences regarding climate and environment?

   - Is there an area of the country I've always felt a connection with or want to be close to (mountains, beach, big city, and so on)?

4. Do I need to go to New York, LA, or Chicago, or are there equally good opportunities elsewhere?

   - Have I visited the city previously for an extended period of time? How comfortable am I there?

   - Am I sure I'm good at big-city life?

Step 3

My Training

Now that you've thought about where you want to be, the next step in the process of elimination is deciding which style of training is right for you. Do you want the versatility of a liberal arts education or the rigor of a conservatory's approach?

1. Your Options

What is the difference between "liberal arts" and "conservatory"? These are words you will hear often as you attempt to select your training program. Here are the cut-and-dry definitions:

Conservatory: A school of advanced studies, usually specializing in one of the fine arts.

Liberal Arts School: A school with training in all the academic disciplines, such as languages, literature, history, philosophy, mathematics, and science, that provides information of general cultural concern.

Conservatory Style: A program at a liberal arts school with training that is nearly as focused as at a conservatory.

The difference between these three options is the percentage of your total credit hours spent within your major. As a general rule:

Conservatory: ¾–all credits in major

Conservatory style: ½–¾ credits in major

Liberal arts style: ½ or fewer credits in major

As you can see, if you go to a conservatory, you're almost completely immersed in theatre. If you go to a liberal arts school with a conservatory-style program, most of your hours are still in theatre. And if you opt for a traditional liberal arts approach, your hours will be about half and half.

2. Conservatory Training

This is probably the best option for you if:

1. You feel 99% certain that there is nothing else in this entire world that could make you happy but performing. Nothing else piques your interest in terms of professional pursuits.

2. You can afford it.

3. You can't get enough theatre. You are driven; want to be the absolute best; and have the self-discipline, maturity, and commitment to immerse yourself in that world for four years without burning out.

Sound like you? Most acting students would love to go to a conservatory. And yet most don't. There are a number of reasons many students ultimately *choose* not to attend a conservatory.

There is a sentiment shared among some casting directors that conservatory training is necessary in today's exceedingly competitive environment. Even if that's not true, there's no question that training at one of the nation's top conservatories will get you ready for the real world.

 Things to Consider

Your Odds of Getting In
Conservatory programs generally only accept polished applicants. Most students coming out of high school don't have the experience—regardless of raw talent—to be accepted.

Narrowness of Study
It is said time and again that interesting people make interesting actors. The largest downside to the conservatory approach is the lack of time you'll spend learning about things other than theatre.

We are not talking about having to sit through calculus. Rather, instead of taking seven ballet classes in a day, it might be beneficial to spend one of those hours in a world religion, American history, sociology, or human sexuality class.

When you attend a conservatory, you are eating, sleeping, and breathing theatre for four years. It goes from being a fun after-school activity to your entire life overnight. But if you can handle it, given the amount of competition and the amount of training your peers will often have in all areas of theatre, and if you are truly serious about doing this as a career, keeping conservatories on your list of options is an excellent idea.

You Will Still Take Other Classes
"Conservatory" does not mean that you won't take any general education classes. You will still have certain core requirements to meet, even at a conservatory. You will, however, spend significantly less time in these classes than at a liberal arts school.

Notes

3. Conservatory-Style Approach

This is an interesting option, as you are still attending a liberal arts school, but the training is nearly as intense as it would be at a conservatory. This is probably the best option for you if:

1. You're relatively certain you want to be a performer.

2. Conservatory training is out of your price range.

3. You want to have at least *some* life outside the theatre. Whether you want to take a class on the human genome or go to a college football game, these options are more accessible at a liberal arts school.

4. You have a great deal of raw talent but not a ton of experience yet.

4. Traditional Liberal Arts Style

This is probably best for you if:

1. You want to have theatre as a major but are still examining other options for after college.

2. You have many interests outside of theatre.

3. You are eager for a true "college experience," be it joining a fraternity or sorority, attending classes with people outside your major, involving yourself in non-theatre activities, and so on.

Which is right for you? If you're fairly certain about wanting a conservatory or if you're definitely learning toward a liberal arts environment, you will be able to focus your list on that kind of school.

 **RECAP**

STEP 3: *My Training*

Questions to Consider

1. How much time do I want to spend in theatre classes?

   - Do I have other interests I'd like to explore while in college?

   - How certain am I that theatre is The Only Thing I Want To Do?

2. What types of programs can I afford? What types of programs can I get into?

   - Have I taken stock of my resources? Can I afford a conservatory?

   - Do I have the drive and experience to get into a conservatory?

   - Do I have the drive and focus to successfully complete a conservatory degree?

   - Have I honestly appraised my strengths and weaknesses as a theatre artist?

3. How important is a "college experience"?

   - Are there any extracurricular activities I've always looked forward to when thinking of college (such as playing or watching sports, joining a fraternity or sorority, singing in an a capella group, running for student government, and so on)?

Step 4

My Degree

Now that you've thought about your location and type of training preferences, it's time to consider what degree path you'd like to take. Do you want a bachelor of arts (BA), or would a bachelor of fine arts (BFA) be a better fit?

1. Types of Degrees for Theatre Majors

Your ultimate decision on this may not need to be made prior to registering, but it can be helpful to evaluate now, as the degrees offered by a school can heavily influence your decision of where to go.

The BA and BFA are the degrees you'll hear referenced most frequently. One of the most common questions is, "What's the difference?" Here are the definitions:

A **Bachelor of Arts** (BA) degree is awarded for an undergraduate course or program in either the liberal arts, the sciences, or both. Bachelor of arts degree programs are generally four years.

A **Bachelor of Fine Arts** (BFA) degree is the standard undergraduate degree for students seeking a professional education in the visual or performing arts and is generally four years.

Well, those sound the same, right? What's the difference? The word "fine."

The degrees differ in that the majority of the course load in the BFA consists of roughly two-thirds or more hours in the major discipline. The BA is usually around half of the credit hours in the major.

What does this mean?

The **BFA in theatre**, simply put, is a more theatre-focused, intense version of a **BA in theatre.** They are equally valid degree options for the theatre major.

These are in some ways analogous to the last section: "conservatory" versus "liberal arts." How much time do you want to spend studying theatre in college? By this logic, a descending list of the ratio of time spent in theatre classes might look something like this:

BFA from a conservatory
BFA from a conservatory-style liberal arts school
BFA from a liberal arts school
BA from a conservatory-style liberal arts school
BA from a liberal arts school

This is not a ranking of the prestige of degrees. It's simply an explanation that a BFA from a conservatory might result in 17 of 20 hours per week in a given semester being theatre classes, whereas a BA from a liberal arts school might consist of 10 hours per week in theatre classes each semester.

2. Choosing the Right Degree for You

Schools will engage in rigorous debates on the merits of both the BA and the BFA. Many excellent theatre schools only offer a BA. Others insist that you *must* get a BFA if you're serious. Let's take a minute to look at which degree might be right for you.

The BA

The bachelor of arts is an excellent option for your theatre degree. It is more versatile than the BFA in that you are exposed to more classes outside of your major. Many schools don't offer a BFA because they believe so strongly in this degree and, again, the idea that "interesting people make interesting actors."

The theory goes that if you're only learning about acting, you may be lacking in the life experiences to make your acting worth watching. By exposing yourself to other areas of study, you are enriching yourself personally, gaining new perspectives, and cultivating your general knowledge.

For this reason, a BA can be the right choice if you are sure that you want to be a theatre professional. It is almost certainly the right choice, though, if you are unsure. A BA will make the transition to another major (or career) easier should you decide to change. It is, in a sense, a less binding commitment.

The BFA

Most schools require auditions, essays, and lots of ongoing evaluation for their BFA program. This is because of the gravity of the commitment to one's primary discipline that accompanies the BFA degree. It is often described as "intense" and "focused" because you'll be spending most of your day in the theatre building taking classes and then heating up dinner before attending rehearsal at night.

There are high expectations for students on a BFA path, often including requirements for production hours, internships, auditions, and so on. If you are fairly certain that theatre is for you, and you know you're quite good at it, this gives you the opportunity to train, train, train. It can put you in excellent shape for competing at the professional level.

The disadvantage to the BFA is that it is harder to shift gears if you decide you're not in love with theatre. You miss out on a number of potentially interesting classes, you risk burning out, and you have a more limited breadth of knowledge when it comes to other skills and other fields should theatre not ultimately work out after college.

In many colleges, every theatre major starts as a BA and can elevate this status to BFA after a year or two of proven dedication and growth. This is a nice system, as it gives both you and the faculty the opportunity to assess whether a BFA is the best choice.

The BM and others

Another degree possibility is a **bachelor of music (BM)**. This is perhaps a good choice if you're from a classical singing background and equally interested in doing opera as well as musical theatre. It's also worth considering if you enjoy performing but are just as interested in conducting, playing an instrument, music directing, or composing someday.

The **artium baccalaureatus (AB) degree** is the same as a bachelor's in arts (BA). In the past, the AB was used to designate classical studies, but currently the BA and AB are indistinguishable.

The **bachelor of science degree (BS)** takes a more focused approach to a subject than a BA and usually includes a balance of liberal arts, technological knowledge, math and computer-oriented skills, and practical skills needed for a particular discipline within the field. In the context of theater, a BS typically indicates a greater emphasis on the technical and practical aspects of theatre.

Planning Ahead

Here's why this should be a consideration now. If you are 100% certain that you want to do theatre, want all the training you can get, and the thought of too many general education classes makes you sick, you might want to make sure you're looking at schools that do in fact offer a BFA.

Just to remind you: There is a very solid argument to be made (and often is) by professors that the BA is the best degree for everyone. There is also the school of thought that with the competition out there these days, you're doing yourself a disservice by getting anything short of a BFA. You must decide for yourself how you feel about this. Examine your own personality, level of talent, desire, preferences, and priorities.

3. In-Between Options

Just like anything else, degree types aren't black and white.

 Other Possibilities to Consider

The Double Major

If you elect to pursue a double major, this means you're going for two degrees simultaneously. For example, you're really interested in doing missionary work in South America so you want to major in Spanish, but you also love theatre and want it to be your career. This is a fine aspiration, but make sure you're aware of the hours that will be required. Some theatre programs discourage double majors, as they don't want their students to split their focus. It's doable, but know that it is a heavy workload—and you'll want to plan on being in school for more than four years. In a BFA program, double-majors are usually not allowed, since your theatre classes will consume the majority of your credit hours and take priority in your schedule.

Another potential double-major option is trying to earn two different theatre degrees (for example, musical theatre performance and costume design). Again, some students *do* this, but you will need to evaluate these possibilities school by school and carefully weigh whether you can take that much theatre at once.

The Theatre Minor

In case you're not sure, a "minor" is simply a secondary specialized area you want to work on while you pursue your major.

A theatre minor is not an option at all schools, so you'll want to do your research. This could be a good choice if you're interested in teaching high school theatre. Your primary path would be education, but a theatre minor could supplement that. Or if you're interested in doing advertising for a living but eager to head up your community theatre, this might be the way to go.

 **RECAP**

STEP 4: *My Degree*

Questions to Consider

1. How much time do I want to spend studying theatre?
   - Do I want to think of nothing but theatre for four years?
   - How many waking moments do I want to spend training?
   - Would greater breadth of knowledge and exposure to new ideas help me as an artist?

2. How much flexibility do I want in my degree?
   - Will I someday want to do something other than theatre? Do I want a degree that could help me in other careers?

3. Should I get a combination degree?
   - Have I thought about the time and energy required of a double major?
   - Have I examined other options (joint major, minor, and so on)?

Notes

Step 5

My Emphasis

You have some idea of whether you'd like to shoot for a BA or a BFA. Now let's look at the emphasis or "specialization" options within your degree. If you opt for a BFA in theatre, do you want to go for the acting or the musical theatre track? If you're going to get a BFA in production arts, do you want to focus on design or tech? How can you customize your degree?

1. Options for Emphasis

Whether you're seeking a BA or a BFA, there may be options for an "emphasis" in your degree. That means what your degree is in *specifically.* At some schools, you can get a BA in theatre arts, and that's your only option. Others, though, have opportunities for BAs or BFAs in musical theatre, playwriting, dance, costume design, and so on.

The Language of Your Degree

Here are a couple of examples of how your diploma might read:

Bachelor of Arts in Acting
   or
Bachelor of Fine Arts in Scenic Design

Don't get too hung up on the words on your diploma. What's important are the course offerings that *lead* to those words. Every college has a different way of describing the emphases and specializations within their degrees. While this is a good step to consider, it's best not to eliminate too many schools based solely on this criterion.

For example, for performers, oftentimes your diploma will read "BA/BFA in performance," as opposed to "BA/BFA in acting" or "BA/BFA in musical theatre." Performance is an all-encompassing term, but the "acting" track involves different credit hours than the "musical theatre" track. Although "performance" at such a school would go on both the straight actor and the musical theatre actor's diploma, the classes they have taken are different.

Carnegie Mellon, for instance—one of the undisputed power-houses of both straight acting and musical theatre training—only offers performers a degree in "drama." But again, you can choose your course offerings in a track best suited to your pursuits.

Schools with Specialized Degrees

A "BA in theatre" is common to most schools. This is absolutely fine and especially serviceable if your theatrical pursuits are somewhat general at this stage.

If, however, you are aware that you definitely want to be a stage manager or a dramaturge or a musical theatre performer, an excellent *clue* as to whether a school excels in an area is (sometimes but not always!) if it offers a specialty in that area.

Let us explain that concept further. You know you want to study stage management. How do you know if a school has good training for stage managers?

If a school goes so far as to *offer* a BFA in stage management specifically, it is often a safe bet that this is a school that prides itself on its training in stage management. Even if you want a BA and not a BFA, you will still be able to take a variety of high-caliber courses in stage management. Make sense?

Do keep in mind, though, that there are plenty of schools that do not offer degrees in stage management per se but still have wonderful training opportunities for stage management within the theatre degree.

If you want to be a legitimate triple-threat performer, looking for a school with a BA/BFA in musical theatre (or "performance" with a musical theatre track) is not a bad idea. This lets you know that you are attending a school with a degree path designed for musical theatre actors versus going to a school with a BA in theatre that also does some musicals and has voice and dance teachers.

2. "Acting" versus "Musical Theatre"

"Should I get a BA/BFA in acting or musical theatre?" is a question we hear a lot.

First off, be realistic with yourself. If you have no talent in musical theatre performing and no interest in it, then stick with straight theatre. Take movement classes and voice lessons (all part of straight acting), but there's no need to be spending your time in Tap III and advanced music theory when you could be attending a Meisner elective.

But if you like musicals a great deal, what better time to work on your skills than in college? You are increasing your opportunities of getting work exponentially if you can act and sing. You are increasing them even *more* if you can act, sing, and dance. College is an excellent opportunity to accentuate the positive and *improve* on the things you wish you were better at.

The decision about your emphasis gives you the opportunity to decide where you'd like to spend the majority of your study. The list for potential emphases is endless. There are BFAs in everything from dance to arena concert technician work. Think about whether you have a niche in the theatre world you'd especially like to pursue. Then keep an eye out for schools that offer a BA or BFA track for your special interest (but don't eliminate schools because of their lack of a BFA in puppetry!).

 **RECAP**

STEP 5: *My Emphasis*

Questions to Consider

1. What aspect of theatre am I most interested in?

   How certain am I of my interest in a particular field? Is a general theatre degree better for me?

2. What do I need training in? What do I want to improve on?

   Am I pushing myself to succeed or pushing myself into something I don't want?

Step 6

My Opportunities

OK, so you've decided on your major. Now, what theatrical opportunities matter most to you within this major?

1. Performance Prospects within School

Since you are pursuing a degree in the performing arts, it's a good idea to check out how much you will actually get to perform at your school. Some programs have restrictions on who is able to audition for certain productions, whether or not freshmen are able to audition, and how many student-run productions are available.

Now Playing **Things to Consider**

Mainstage Productions

Mainstage productions are the students' chance to showcase their talents to their college community, fellow peers, and faculty as well as to the public. The number of mainstage productions a program offers differs from school to school, just as the number of musicals versus straight plays varies depending on the programs, strengths, and student body. Many programs also restrict freshmen from auditioning for their mainstage productions.

It is also important to investigate how many students are estimated to be involved in a mainstage production per year.

Are BFAs and BAs treated equally in terms of auditioning? If you are a theatre major, can you audition for a musical? Is it likely that you will be involved with one or more mainstage productions each year?

Examine the mainstage seasons over the past several years. Did the season include musicals and plays? Have a mix of contemporary and traditional pieces? Push the envelope? Do shows that interest you?

Student-Run Organizations

If mainstage opportunities are limited, it may be important to find a program that offers a plethora of student-driven productions. Student-driven organizations range from improvisation troupes, a capella groups, Shakespeare societies, theatre for young audience organizations, original works troupes, and much more. Also, if your chosen school has a film/TV department, many of the film majors seek performing arts majors for their films.

Workshops and Clinics

Workshops and clinics help complement and enrich a student's experience in a performing arts program. Often, theatre and musical theatre programs bring in visiting artists who offer master classes and workshops. These guest artists can include Broadway stars, prominent alumni, casting directors, and local distinguished directors. These workshops can be vocal clinics, movement workshops, helpful question-and-answer sessions, and much more. If these are of interest to you, check out what guest artists have visited your desired program in the past and who they are anticipating having for the upcoming year. Getting to hobnob with master class guests such as Jason Robert Brown or a casting director like Dave Clemmons can be thrilling and enormously beneficial for students.

Summer Stock/EMC Program

One of the things we *strongly* encourage you to inquire about when looking at schools is their involvement in assisting students in pursuing summer work. "Summer stock" is the name given to theatrical productions that are performed by a "stock company," or a group of core resident actors, during the summer. Summer stock experience is *invaluable* during your time in college, as it gives you a taste of the real world. You can

Notes

end up performing 10 shows in one summer while working around the clock doing costumes and lighting, *or* you might do one long run of a show with Broadway veterans. Both experiences are key in shaping you as a performer. It doesn't pay much (usually just enough to make peanut butter and jelly for the week), but the personal and professional relationships you forge with these people often stay with you throughout your life, *and* stock enables you to get professional credits on your resume before you finish your degree.

Professional theatres tend to hire college students from large "cattle call"-type auditions (less pejoratively known as "unifieds"), in which all the producers show up and watch hundreds of college students audition at once. Among the most popular of these auditions are SETC, NETC, MWTA, SWTFA, and Strawhats.

Different schools place different emphasis on summer stock. Some say, "Do it if you want," and others *actively* promote it. Many colleges help to prepare you for these by offering screening workshops and classes to get your material ready. Again, this sort of thing implies that the professors care about your work outside the department. A school that leaves it all to you may put you at a disadvantage.

If a school has a connection to a specific regional theatre, it may be easier for you to land summer employment that way. Because of a school's relationship with a theatre (perhaps a faculty member regularly performs or directs there), it may typically cast students in productions.

2. Internships and Mentors

While pursuing your theatrical education, many colleges and universities offer assistance in finding an internship or mentor to help further establish your connections in the theatre community. These opportunities facilitate career exploration and help gather industry acquaintances.

Now Playing ▶ **Things to Consider**

Internships

An internship is a wonderful opportunity for a performance major to transfer what he or she has learned in the classroom and theatre to a more professional setting. Beginning to establish network connections during your time at college is invaluable to your success later in your career. Find out what local theatres, casting agencies, or other theatre-related internships are available for credit or no credit. Also, many schools offer internships in areas other than their main campus. If you have a desire to study a semester somewhere other than the school's primary location, find out what internships are offered through the school in other settings.

Mentor Programs

Many schools offer a mentor program that links current students (or recent grads) to professionals who have had proven success in the performing arts. These professionals are often prominent directors in the surrounding areas of the school, working actors, casting directors, or other major players in the theatrical world. Mentors guide young performers by helping them navigate career development plans and set realistic career goals, introducing them to experts in the field, and mainly being a person to turn to for any and all performing arts–related questions. These relationships can be fostered anywhere from one year to the entire four years, and hopefully beyond that.

3. A Showcase

Showcase presentations are used to assist students in their senior year transition into the professional theatrical world. This is where you'll have the opportunity to show your stuff to agents and casting directors. Several years ago, only a few top theatre schools had showcases. Now, many agents say they feel like they go to one every night (during "showcase season" between February and May). More and more schools are having New York and LA showcases and, indeed, many students get their agents and book work from being seen through this venue. Many BFA programs offer a showcase, but others prefer the "bring the biz people to the school throughout the year" approach. This means that rather than a formal showcase at the end of the year, casting directors and agents are brought to the school periodically and seniors are given the chance to "audition." Some BA programs offer a showcase as well. A number of programs require their seniors to audition to be accepted to perform at their showcase while others are guaranteed the opportunity. Is a showcase essential? No. There are plenty of great theatre programs that don't opt for a showcase. Nevertheless, getting your face and name out there can be a huge leg up to prepare you for beginning your career. Also, although a school may not have a showcase right now, that does not mean that by the time you are a senior one won't be in the works in either LA or NYC.

Now Playing ▶ Things to Consider

Who Attends the Showcase

Industry professionals including top agents (legit, film/TV, print, commercial), casting directors, managers, producers, directors, and playwrights often attend the top showcases throughout the nation. Find out who typically attends the showcase at your desired school, how they promote each year's showcase, and if the attendance is typically high or low each year.

Location of the Showcase

Showcases are typically held on their own campus or in New York City, LA, or Chicago. If you are committed to a theatre or musical theatre career in one of these cities, a showcase might be essential for you. If you have a desire to pursue film and TV, finding a program that offers a showcase in LA might be your best option. Musical theatre performers might specifically need a program that offers a showcase in New York City.

Success of the Showcase

Showcase success stories differ dramatically from school to school. Depending on the program, showcase presentations can result in an audition or representation from an agency or auditions for Broadway productions, national tours, and summer stock. Auditions for theme parks, industrials, and film/TV projects are also common. Check the outcome of the most recent graduated class. Did these students receive a callback? Did anyone sign with an agent? Are they working in their desired field? Talk to the students themselves when possible. You'll probably get more candid responses.

Last Tip!

By securing work at an "Equity" theatre during summer stock employment or throughout the school year, you can begin your journey to become a member of Actors' Equity Association (AEA), the union that represents actors and stage managers in the theatre. Students may enroll in the EMC program, which allows actors still in training to credit their theatrical work at an AEA theatre toward their eventual membership in AEA. Candidates must complete 50 creditable weeks of work at any theatre that participates in the program in order to join and become a full AEA member.

Now Playing ▶ **RECAP**

STEP 6: My Opportunities

Questions to Consider

1. What are the performance opportunities within the program?

    - How many mainstage productions are produced each year? Can freshmen audition?

    - Are there student-run productions? What types?

    - Does the school provide unique workshops or clinics?

    - Do I have an interest in doing summer stock? An interest in the EMC program?

2. Are there internship and mentor programs offered?

    - What companies and professionals participate in these programs?

    - What year am I allowed to participate?

3. Will I get a showcase my senior year?

    - Who attends the showcase?

    - Are they successful?

    - Where are the showcases performed?

Notes

Step 7

My Surroundings

Now that you know what opportunities you'd like from your program, what do you need in a campus and surrounding area in order to be happy?

1. Campus Life and Size

When you think of a college campus, you might picture one that you can see from your favorite movie: a campus filled with over-flowing frat houses, packed dorms, and a quad scattered with an array of students—all on college grounds that provide every-thing you could possibly need. Or you may picture yourself in a big city where your campus is literally the entire metropolitan area. How large of a campus do you want? Would you prefer a college big enough that you rarely see the same person twice? Or an intimate setting where you feel particularly connected with the entire community?

 Things to Consider

Campus Life

Deciding on what you need in a campus goes beyond what you want in a theatre or musical theatre program. When you leave your acting class for the day, you want to make sure you are happy with the rest of your college experience. If walking around a city and exploring all it has to offer is appealing, a New York City or Chicago college might be best. If these seem a bit daunting but you still imagine yourself in an urban setting, somewhere like Emerson College in Boston could be a good fit. Emerson borders the Boston Commons (a sort of large garden in the middle of downtown Boston) with its campus but is set in a significantly smaller city than New York or Los Angeles. Or do you want a more typical college experience with a classic campus? Would you rather fall asleep to the sound of honking taxis or the partying sorority next door? If activities such as shopping, going to concerts, and visiting museums excite you, it may be wise to look for a college in or near a major city. If having to drive is not up your alley, attending school in a city eliminates that factor with public transportation. Also, if an internship is in your future, an urban area may present many more opportunities. On the downside, cities can be unpleasant (and sometimes scary) places. Your late-night options may become limited due to safety concerns. Also on the downside (or upside, depending on how you look at it), there are more distractions in a city as opposed to a secluded campus.

Many colleges with drama programs are located in urban areas for a simple reason: the professional theatres. From fringe companies to major touring shows (and everything in between), cities tend to have an abundance of theatrical performances and opportunities. Colleges closer to these opportunities can encourage their students to watch, learn from, and work with professional actors.

If you are a nature person and enjoy outdoor recreational activities, considering a rural campus is a good idea. Also, rural campuses tend to have a stronger sense of community and a less frenetic pace. Just make sure a less populated setting has enough amenities to fit your basic needs. If you're not bringing a car, how will you get around? Where's the nearest airport? How far away is the mall? Are there opportunities in the surrounding community for internships?

Deciding on what makes you happy as a person, along with your theatrical needs, will inform your decision greatly.

Campus Size

Ultimately, how many people would you like to be surrounded with for four (or possibly more) years? 60,000 or 1,000? When it comes to choosing a school, one size certainly doesn't fit all.

Colleges that have a rural campus can be limiting when it comes to meeting people outside of your college community. Programs that are based in urban settings allow for students to be surrounded by not only their classmates but everyone who happens to live and work in that city as well. Large schools may have larger class sizes, though, and the sheer number of people can be overwhelming.

Current Students/Campus Visit

The only real way to make an educated decision on what school is right for you is to check out the campus. Yes, visits to campuses can be costly for you and your family (traveling, lodging, and so on), but in the long run it is worth it.

Besides being able to check out the actual campus, you get the opportunity to check out what campus life is like. While you walk around, scan the bulletin boards to see what student productions are holding auditions. Maybe there is a cool fundraiser happening that you could totally picture yourself being a part of in the future. Check out the dorms. Maybe there is a residence hall that offers a "quiet" floor that you could definitely see yourself living there. How about the cafeteria? Since you just decided you are a vegan, make sure they offer something that you can happily eat.

There is no better way to truly get the inside scoop unless you chat with current students. If possible, arrange to have an overnight visit with a student—one in the musical theatre or theatre department would obviously be ideal. Students will be able to honestly share what gripes they have with the school and what they love and adore about their college. Friend the students on Facebook and follow up with them after your visit. Even if you can't afford to visit a school, you probably have a friend of a friend or a distant relative that you know at the particular school. Friend them to get the juicy gossip and insight.

While you are there, make sure to do the following:

- Meet and chat with at least a couple of professors in the acting department. Be prepared with some substantial questions that you truly want answers for.

- Get business cards and email addresses of any faculty you meet with. Follow up when you return home to thank them for their time.

- Grab those financial aid forms.

- Sit in on an acting class if the school allows. What better way to see if this is an environment that you can see yourself in?

- Participate in a group information session. Listening to other potential students' questions can eliminate some lingering questions you may also have.

2. Outside Interests

Having a passion for the performing arts is fantastic, but when looking at a school, it's important to consider your interests outside of theatre as well. Are you an avid chess player? Find a school that has a chess team. Do you find yourself dividing your time between the sports field and the theatre? Make sure to find a school that allows you to have time for both. Do your parents want you to continue to pursue your interest in mathematics? Investigate the opportunity for either being able to get a minor in an outside interest or at least the availability to take classes outside your major.

 Things to Consider

Extracurricular Activities

Being able to pursue all areas that interest you can help inform you as a performer. On the negative side, spreading yourself too thin can weaken your abilities inside the classroom and theatre. Decide what things in your life you simply can't live without. If being on a sports team is a huge part of who you are, don't deny yourself that experience in college. Find a school that encourages you to join the lacrosse team but also works with your schedule to allow you to participate in mainstage productions. You can perhaps balance the two by going the BA route and only auditioning for shows in the off-season. Once you evaluate what you need in order to be a well-rounded and happy individual, eliminate the programs that don't offer options to facilitate your needs and outside interests.

Off-Campus Interests

It may be impossible to find a school that offers everything you are committed to and excited to have in a college experience. If that's the case, it's important to look at what is offered in the community, town, or city that your school is located in. If you regularly attend church on Sunday, make sure to find a school that either has a strong religious background or is set in a community where a church is easily accessible. If you enjoy bike riding but the school doesn't have a cycling club, investigate if there is one in the surrounding towns. If rock climbing or surfing is a large part of what defines you, there's no shame in focusing your search in an area in the mountains or near a beach.

3. Regional Theatres

Many schools have strong ties with the surrounding regional theatres in their community. These regional theatres are often a student's first chance to perform professionally. Also, some schools have strict restrictions on whether you are allowed to perform off-campus throughout the school year. If building your resume with outside theatre credentials during school is important to you, find a program that has a connection with a certain theatre. Perhaps even more important, going to a school in an area with thriving theatre (especially places you may not immediately think of, such as Cincinnati, Houston, Seattle, or San Diego) gives you the opportunity to *see* compelling and challenging theatre year-round and at a deeply discounted student price. This can be one of your greatest learning opportunities.

 Things to Consider

Performing Off-Campus

It can be difficult to balance performing in a show on campus with all of your schoolwork, much less performing off-campus and dealing with rehearsal commitments and time restraints. However, many students successfully conquer both. Schools often have strong ties to surrounding theatres, and students can have a leg up when it comes to auditioning. Colleges are sometimes willing to cooperate with outside theatre rehearsals and performance schedules as long as you are given the OK by the department. If getting a chance to delve into the professional world while still studying is of interest to you, make sure to explore what opportunities are available through the community. This aspect warrants looking into your prospective schools' individual policies. Many universities (like Pace in New York City) *encourage* outside auditioning. Others do not allow it under any circumstances during your time as a BFA student. Most require the department auditions come first, and *if* you're not cast (or if it's an exceptionally good opportunity), permission may be granted.

 **RECAP**

STEP 7: *My Surroundings*

Questions to Consider

1. What do I need in my campus in order to be happy?

   - Do I want a small or large campus?

   - Do I want a campus that is in an urban or rural environment?

   - How many people will I be content being surrounded with? Would I be overwhelmed with a city full of unfamiliar faces?

2. Can I pursue interests other than theatre?

   - What extracurricular activities help make me who I am?

   - Are there opportunities for me to be involved with sports, clubs, or organizations that are separate from my major?

   - What does the surrounding town or city offer? Can I be involved heavily in my community?

3. Are there regional theatres connected to the school?

   - Do I have a desire to perform outside of my chosen school? Does the school allow me to audition for surrounding theatres?

   - Am I ready to audition and perform professionally?

Notes

Step 8

My Money

*You've figured out what you need
and want in your program.
Now, what can you afford?*

1. Financial Factors

Pursuing a theatre or musical theatre degree is certainly not cheap. Deciding on what you and/or your family are capable of spending is unique to each student. While it is certainly possible to apply for loans, you must remember that when you graduate, you will be responsible for paying off these loans. It is imperative to investigate what types of loans and grants are available at each school or in your community.

Being realistic with yourself may be difficult when it comes to money, but it is essential when applying to school. In addition to the amount of money it costs each year to attend school, there are also many fees associated with simply applying. Talk with your parents and create a realistic budget. Keep track of all fees associated with applications and travel and audition expenses.

Many families treat college loans as a necessity or a foregone conclusion. If you have scraped together every penny possible, applied for every scholarship, and *still* need a few extra dollars to get to your dream school, then by all means take out college loans. That's what they're there for. There is truly no need, however, to view college loans as the default option. In countless instances, going to a less expensive school (where perhaps you get more in scholarships) and taking out fewer loans can be much more sensible than taking out hundreds of thousands of dollars to go to a school that you feel you *have* to attend. We know many students who went to less expensive universities with a decent or good program who work consistently and are much happier than the (insert prestigious but inordinately expensive school here) graduates who have hundreds of dollars in loans to pay every month. It might be in your best interest to forsake the "perfect" school you can't quite afford and go to a college with a great department that will give you a full ride. You can take the money you would have used for tuition and spend it on other things that will add to your quality of life.

2. Scholarships

If you decide to apply for scholarships, it is crucial to start the process early. You must have an organized system to find, apply, and win scholarship money. A good place to start is right at your high school. Schedule an appointment with the counseling office and ask if they can help navigate what scholarship opportunities are available for you. Often, the counselors are aware of scholarships that are being offered in your community, town, or state.

The vast majority of scholarships are offered directly from colleges. The scholarships are granted to students based on eligibility in certain areas. These areas include merit, ethnicity, financial need, intended major, and many more. Research what scholarship opportunities are available at your top schools.

However, there are many scholarships that are offered specifically for the performing arts that aren't in connection with a college. For example, an amazing scholarship program called Young Arts (www.youngarts.org) offers scholarships to seniors and recent graduates who demonstrate excellence in the arts. This program not only offers master classes and the chance to hobnob with some of the world's most renowned artists but also affords you the opportunity to win awards ranging from $5,000 to $10,000, with over $500,000 annually given in total awards. By simply registering for this scholarship prospect, you qualify for their scholarship list service and are granted access to over $3 million in scholarship opportunities to universities and colleges. Not so shabby! This is just one example—there are many performing arts scholarships to be researched.

Notes

If you're reading this early in high school, *keep your grades up!* Study hard for standardized tests. If you do well, there are often *full-ride* academic scholarships. Needless to say, if you score a 34 on your ACT, have a 4.0, and have taken several AP classes, this can lower your stress considerably when it comes to finances.

Make a list of all potential scholarships. Once you have determined what is available, you must create a winning application. Work with a high school counselor or trusted adult to help better the odds. While a scholarship application may seem simple enough (how hard can writing a page be, really?), these scholarship judges read hundreds, even thousands, of applications, so yours must stand out. Along with creating a compelling application, remember to be neat and organized and always follow their guidelines.

3. Work Programs/Job Availability

The Federal Work Study program provides students with funds that are earned through part-time employment at the school. As of right now, there are 3,400 colleges/universities that participate in the program. The financial aid department within your school determines financial need. Work programs are a fantastic way for students to earn income while pursuing their education. Work programs are built around a student's schedule and allow for flexibility that outside jobs may not permit. Research what on-campus jobs are typically offered at your desired school. Want to play librarian and be responsible for putting away all the plays in the library? Work part-time hours at the gym in between workouts? There are numerous options. Do your research.

Depending on where you want to apply, there are often countless job opportunities located on or near campus. If you know going into college that you will need to have a part-time job, it is important to find a school that is able to offer potential job opportunities. If you decide on a city, there are countless restaurants, shops, and stores that happily hire college students. If you are in an area that is not heavily populated with these opportunities, perhaps there are nearby families in need of babysitting or handyman jobs. A good way to investigate potential work prospects is to ask students who attend the school. If you go for an on-campus interview, try to connect with students and see what they do to earn some income.

Last Tip!

It is important to not jeopardize your schoolwork with job commitments, but it is also important to have a well-rounded college experience. Make personal time for yourself outside of the performing arts world. Stash away some cash so you can have a meal off campus once in a while or catch a movie on a Saturday night. Remember, it's important to be a "human" as well as a polished theatre professional.

 **RECAP**

STEP 8: *My Money*

Questions to Consider

1. What can I afford?
   - What are my financial limitations?
   - What is my budget?

2. What scholarships are available to me?
   - What can my high school counselor recommend?
   - Am I eligible for a scholarship through my desired college?
   - Who can help me make a winning scholarship application?

3. What work opportunities are available at my desired school?
   - Does my dream school offer a work program?
   - Are their jobs available in the local community or town?

Step 9

My Audition

So you have an idea of where you want to go to college. Now what should you prepare to get into this dream school?

1. Audition Requirements

Once you've narrowed down the list of colleges you are interested in, it is important to investigate what each school requires in an audition. Are you going for a BFA in acting? You'll need to find some quality monologues. Going for musical theatre? You'll not only need monologues but some appropriate songs as well.

Now Playing **Things to Consider**

Choosing Material

This could very well be one of the most daunting tasks of the college audition process. What do the auditors want to see? What material suits your personality and style? Where do you find the right pieces? Choosing material appropriate for you is an entirely unique process; however, there are certain things to keep in mind:

1. DO choose contrasting material that has clear differences in characters, moods, intentions, beats, and emotional content.

2. DO read the entire play your monologue is from.

3. DO avoid pieces that require a dialect.

4. DO choose pieces that are in the present. Storytelling monologues are not a good choice.

5. DO time your audition to make sure you aren't going over the allotted time (no compromises—the auditors have to sit through *tons* of these). Become well acquainted with quality and brevity.

6. DON'T perform a piece from a movie or TV show.

7. DON'T choose a monologue from a book of monologues written "just for your audition!" and not from full plays.

8. DON'T choose a piece that is extremely overdone. There are numerous lists available online, and many schools post on their sites which pieces they would prefer you don't do.

9. DON'T perform material that is meant to shock the auditor (excessive use of curse words or overly dramatic material).

10. DON'T choose monologues and songs that are not appropriate to your age range.

When choosing material, you need to really do your homework. Choosing a monologue the week before will definitely show in your audition. Performing a piece you are not connected to but was the "only one you could find" will be a problem as well. You need to *love* your material.

However, pieces become outrageously overdone because a lot of people tend to *love* the *same* material. This is where the "doing your homework" part comes in. Schools tend to like well-researched songs and monologues. Choosing a moderately known but beautiful Golden Age number such as "There But for You Go I" instead of the obvious "Oh What a Beautiful Mornin'" gives you instant credibility. Just because you should actively avoid doing the classically overdone "Tuna Fish Monologue" from Christopher Durang's *Laughing Wild*, doesn't mean you can't find a piece similar to it. Read plays from authors who write in a similar style to Durang's or read some of his lesser-known works. You are bound to find monologues that not only excite you but also excite the auditors for not having to hear the same piece over and over again. A key phrase here is "read plays"! Many students complain that they "can't find anything," but they haven't put in the time to look through scripts.

Notes

Paying Attention to the School's Guidelines

Each school has different requirements for auditions. Auditors are not pleased when a student does not follow their guidelines. Make sure you pay close attention to what is being asked of you and adhere to the rules. If a school requires you to perform a contemporary monologue, put that Viola ring speech you've been working on away. If there is a strict time limit, make sure your pieces comfortably fit in the time constraints—it is never fun to be cut off. Some schools also require that you perform a piece from a selection of their choosing—make sure to do so! If you are unclear as to what is expected of you, call admissions and double check. Better safe than sorry.

Headshots and Resumes

It's important to make your headshot and resume look as professional as possible. Headshots are your chance to let the auditors in on who you are. Avoid school photos and blurry printouts from your computer. Although financial restraints may not allow for professionals headshots to be taken, you can certainly make the most of what you've got. Headshots should be in color as opposed to black and white, be 8x10 inches, and be a solid representation of what you look like. This is not the time for glamour shots or your senior photo. Keep this in mind: one of the key jobs of a headshot is to remind the auditor of who you are: if they look at the photo and look at you, will they know it's the same person? If the answer is yes, you're on the right track. If it's no, then this photo may not work as a headshot.

Resumes can be tricky when you are first starting out. If you have a lot of experience, fantastic! If not, don't worry. Colleges are sympathetic to the fact that many aspiring performers have a limited resume. Things that should be included are:

- Name, height, weight, hair and eye color
- Email address and phone number
- Theatrical experience
- Training (include teachers' names)
- Awards/honors
- Special skills

Colleges are using the resume to see what *kind* of things you've done. The resume is another way for the auditors to get to know you to see if you are the kind of student they believe will fit with their program. They're not judging how many roles you've had or whether your school offered advanced acting classes but rather trying to figure out where you are in your training.

To put your headshot and resume together, place the resume on top of the headshot and staple in all four corners. Both picture and resume should be 8 × 10 inches.

2. The Big Day

Finally, the big day has arrived! It's time to showcase all of your hard work. It's time to focus, relax, and, most important, have fun! There are a couple things to remember when the big day rolls around.

 Things to Consider

Calming Nerves

For the lucky few who don't get nervous for auditions, congratulations! For the rest of us, the audition room can be one of the scariest places on earth. For college auditions, the obvious answer for calming nerves is being as prepared as possible. Knowing your monologues and songs inside and out will be a huge relief when the nervous energy starts to flow. If you are still not totally comfortable with a piece, it will show. Make sure you practice, practice, practice before showing up for any college audition. And practice in front of someone! Get feedback from directors, teachers, and local college professors. Doing it under your breath in the mirror the day before doesn't count as practice.

It is also important to have some alone time before an audition. Escape from any family and friends and have a moment to yourself. Do your favorite warm-up exercises and take some deep breaths.

The Environment

Your audition begins the moment you enter the door. Not the audition room door, but rather the actual building where your audition is being held. It is extremely important to present your best possible self the moment you arrive. Be friendly with the monitor and make the most of the time you are waiting. If you have any last-minute questions, don't hesitate to ask the monitor. Often, schools have currently enrolled students around to help and answer questions. By all means, ask any lingering questions you may have.

Be professional but also carry a positive and happy attitude. Be considerate and supportive of the fellow auditionees. Be on time and ready to go when called.

When you are in the actual audition room, be as open and as friendly as possible. Remember, while the auditors are clearly looking for talent, they also want to choose a student they potentially want to be with for the next four years. If they ask you questions, answer them honestly. If they ask if you have any questions, be to the point and clear, but don't ask them for feedback on your audition, or "Am I gonna get in?" This is a chance for you to perform in front of an "audience" for five minutes, so have fun!

Audition Attire

You want to make the best first impression possible. You need to be well groomed and polished. With that said, you want to be as comfortable as possible. You don't want your outfit to hinder your performance. Dress as you would if you were going to a professional interview. Beat-up sneakers are probably not the best option. However, if you have never worn heels before, this is not the best time to practice in them. If you have a ton of movement in your monologue, don't wear a skirt. Wear an outfit that is a representation of you and your style.

For musical theatre majors, there will most likely be a vocal and a movement or dance portion. Have your music properly marked and laid out nicely in a binder. Be sure to be polite and pleasant with your accompanist! Give him or her the tempo you would like for your song and be sure to thank him or her after you sing. Some students wear an outfit that they can easily transition from their monologue/song portion into the dance portion. Others students pack an entirely different comfortable movement outfit. Be conscious of what shoes you should pack for both portions.

Last Tip!

Although this may be obvious, it's vital to remember that the auditors want you to do well. Truly. Try to remember that when you walk in the room. The people behind the desk are there for you, and they want you to amaze them with your talent.

 **RECAP**

STEP 9: *My Audition*

Questions to Consider

1. What are the audition requirements for each school?

   - Have I chosen audition material that suits my age, personality, and style?

   - Have I followed all of the school's audition guidelines?

   - Is my headshot and resume ready to go?

2. Am I ready for the Big Day?

   - What helps me to calm my nerves? What can I do to be better prepared?

   - How can I present my best possible self?

   - Am I dressed appropriately? Do I feel comfortable in my attire?

Notes

Step 10

My Homework

Looks like most of the work is done, right? Wrong! The best way to stay on track is to give yourself some easy homework to keep you focused and organized.

1. College Calendar Checklist

It's easy to get lost in a sea of applications, audition dates, and deadlines. Keep yourself on track by following this month-to-month outline of what you should be doing each step of the way.

Summer Before Senior Year

☐ Tour the schools you have decided are of interest to you. Make sure to set up an appointment to meet with someone on the theatre faculty while you are visiting. Chat with current students about their experiences.

☐ Look up audition dates and schedule as soon as possible. Many schools begin accepting audition requests as early as August 1.

☐ Finalize your list of colleges. Be sure your list includes "safe" schools, as well as "reach" and "realistic" schools. Organize all materials (information packets, financial aid forms, and so on) from schools in their own separate file.

☐ If you took AP exams in May, you will receive your AP grade reports in July.

☐ Be sure to register early for the fall SAT test.

Notes

❏ Begin researching playwrights and plays that are of interest to you. See as many shows/musicals as you can. Start to get a good idea of what type of material you may want to do for your auditions.

September

❏ Auditions for Early Decision candidates typically take place in November. Be sure to schedule your audition date this month if planning to apply Early Decision or Early Action. Scheduling an audition date during this month even for regular admission is also wise to ensure you get the day and time you want.

❏ Get started on your applications right away if you plan to apply through an Early Decision or Early Action program. Deadlines for early applications tend to fall in October or November.

❏ Get working on those college essays! Write strong essays that focus on personal experiences. Make sure to have someone proofread and edit.

❏ Update your resume—your list of accomplishments, involvements, and work experiences—with your senior year activities. Don't be afraid to brag. This is the time to showcase all that makes you shine.

❏ It's time to start narrowing down your audition material. Check out school websites to make sure you are finding appropriate material. Talk with your drama teacher or an audition coach about scheduling some coaching sessions.

October

❏ Now is the time to ask your teachers, guidance counselors, employers, or any other qualified adults for some letters of recommendation. Give them plenty of time to meet your deadlines.

❏ Take the SAT test. Be sure your scores are sent to each of your choice colleges.

❏ If you are applying Early Decision or Early Action, be sure to get all forms in as soon as possible.

❏ Begin preparing audition pieces.

Notes

November

- ☐ Auditions for Early Decision and Early Action candidates take place between now and February.
- ☐ Submit Early Decision and Early Action applications on time.
- ☐ Download your FAFSA forms for financial aid. Get to work on them!
- ☐ Follow up with your teachers to ensure that letters of recommendation are sent on time to meet your deadlines.
- ☐ Submit applications as early as possible for colleges with rolling deadlines (admission decisions are made as applications are received).
- ☐ Meet with a trusted advisor, coach, or teacher to show your audition pieces. Ask for feedback. Be confident in the choices you are making, but be open to feedback and insight.

December

- ☐ Try to wrap up college applications before winter break. Make copies of each application before you send it for your records.
- ☐ Spend your break connecting with students who attend your desired program. Ask the questions that are still lingering for you.
- ☐ Write thank-you notes to everyone who provided you with a recommendation letter.

January

- ☐ Take a big breath! Early Decision and Early Application responses arrive this month.
- ☐ If you are waitlisted, don't worry. Now is your chance to express to the school how much you truly want to attend. Send a follow-up letter to explain that this school remains your number-one choice.
- ☐ Many colleges include your first-semester grades as part of your application folder, called the mid-year grade report. Have a counselor send your grades to colleges that require them.
- ☐ Auditions continue in January. Continue to work on your audition material.

February

- ❏ Contact your colleges and confirm that all necessary application materials have been received.
- ❏ February 1 is the application deadline for many colleges.
- ❏ Don't get senioritis! Colleges want to see strong second-semester grades.
- ❏ Auditions typically continue in February. Keep working on your material.

March

- ❏ Admissions decisions begin to arrive this month. When you open your letters, be sure to read everything. There may be some things that need immediate action on your part.
- ❏ Auditions typically continue in March.

April

- ❏ Most admissions decisions and financial aid award letters arrive this month.
- ❏ Now you need to make a final decision. Discuss everything with your parents. Once you have decided on your school, send the enrollment form and deposit check to the school you select before May 1 (the enrollment deadline for most schools).
- ❏ Notify each of the schools to which you were accepted that you will not be attending (in writing) so that your spot can be freed up for another student.
- ❏ On the waiting list? Contact the admissions office, let them know of your continued interest in the college, and update them on your spring semester grades and activities.

May

- ❏ AP exams are administered.
- ❏ Study hard for final exams. Most admission offers are contingent on your final grades.
- ❏ Thank your counselors, teachers, coaches, and anyone else who wrote you recommendations or otherwise helped with your college applications.
- ❏ Thank your coaches and teachers who helped prepare you for the auditions.
- ❏ Treat yourself to a big ice cream cone.

2. College Checklist

Don't drive yourself nuts remembering deadlines. Keep track of all the important dates with this easy-to-follow chart.

	College 1	College 2	College 3	College 4	College 5
Application Deadline					
Campus Visit					
Financial Aid Forms Sent					
Requested Grade Reports Sent					
Audition Materials Selected					
SAT Test Date					
SAT Scores Sent					
AP Scores Sent					
Request Recommendations					
Recommendations Sent					
Thank-You Notes for Recommendations Sent					
Draft Essays					
Essays Proofread by an Adult					
Audition Date Requested					
Audition Date					
Alumni/Current Student Interview					
Application Sent					
Received Letter from Admissions					
Deadline Date to Accept Admission and Give Deposit					
Deposit Placed					
Accept Financial Package					
Notify the Other Schools that You Are Not Attending Their Program					

3. Some More Homework

NACAC Performing and Visual Arts College Fair

Although there is a great deal of information on the Internet about every theater program under the sun, sometimes it's helpful to talk to a real person. The National Association for College Admission Counseling (NACAC) Performing and Visual Arts College Fair gives you just that opportunity.

Performing and Visual Arts (PVA) Fairs take place in the fall in major cities across the country. These free fairs give students and their parents the chance to speak face to face with representatives from a wide variety of theatre programs. Unlike general admissions representatives at traditional college fairs, representatives at a PVA Fair are familiar with their school's theatre programs and admissions requirements and will be able to give you a fuller picture of the arts at their school.

Before attending a fair you should check online to see which schools will be represented. If you haven't already, investigate the schools that appeal to you and make a list of which booths you would like to visit. Develop a set of questions you would like answered by a real person. Going in with a plan ensures that you get the most from your experience, and it will also keep you from getting overwhelmed if the fair gets hectic.

This is a great opportunity to win over reluctant parents, and we encourage you to bring them along. Theatre admissions representatives tend to have a great deal of experience pitching a theatre degree to practical-minded guardians. If anyone can convince dad that your dreams deserve pursuing, it's the folks at these fairs.

More information and schedules are available from their website: www.nacacnet.org

National Association of Schools of Theatre

One way to assess a theatre school's legitimacy is by its accreditation. When a school says it is "accredited," it means that it measures up to an established set of standards. Accreditation is basically a stamp of approval.

The National Association of Schools of Theatre (NAST) is one group that accredits theatre programs across the US. Not all legitimate theatre schools are members of NAST, but many are. If you encounter a school you've never heard of, NAST accreditation tells you that someone has recognized it as a worthy theatre school, and it's probably worth investigating.

In addition to accreditation, NAST offers a range of theatre- and school-related services for individuals and institutions. There is information for potential students and parents available through their website: nast.arts-accredit.org/index.jsp

4. Summer Prep Programs

You've done your research. You've followed the college calendar checklist. Still itching for something more to feel better equipped for the college audition process? Maybe a summer college preparatory program for theatre or musical theatre is for you. Here are *some* (of the *many*) to check out.

American Conservatory Theatre, San Francisco, California

http://www.act-sf.org

A.C.T. was the first American theater to win a Tony Award for the quality of its training program as well as its performances. A.C.T. was also the first independent theater in the nation to win academic accreditation and the authority to grant a master of fine arts degree in acting. Because A.C.T. is accredited, you can earn undergraduate academic credit upon satisfactory completion of their Summer Training Congress (STC) program.

Boston University, Boston, Massachusetts

http://www.bu.edu/cfa/theatre/sti/

The Boston University Summer Theatre Institute is a five-week program for serious and mature high school students. It is designed for those who wish to test their interests and abilities in a professional training environment. In this program, students develop confidence and technique, acquire insight and expertise, and learn to meet intellectual and artistic challenges. College credit is also available.

CAP 21 Conservatory, New York City, New York

http://www.cap21.org/summer_program.html

This five-week intensive program trains pre–college-age students in the field of musical theatre performance. Equal importance is placed on acting, singing, and dancing.

Carnegie Mellon Pre-College, Pittsburgh, Pennsylvania

www.cmu.edu/enrollment/pre-college/drama

> The Pre-College Drama Program gives students the chance to participate in a professional training program with three options: acting, music theatre, and design/technical production. The program focuses on the exploration of a conservatory training program with emphasis on creativity, craft, and discipline.

Emerson College Summer Arts Academy, Boston, Massachusetts

http://www.emerson.edu/academics/
professional-studies/high-school-student-programs/
pre-college-studio-programs

> Acting Studio offers high school sophomores, juniors, and seniors an opportunity to train in an intensive pre-college acting program. Students selected for Acting Studio participate in rigorous acting, voice, and movement classes to become equipped for the stage. They polish their performance skills by participating in master classes, evening rehearsals, and Friday evening showcases. During the five-week program, Acting Studio students refine audition pieces and perform selections consisting of monologues or scenes in a final showcase performance for peers and parents.
>
> Musical Theatre Studio offers high school sophomores, juniors, and seniors an opportunity to train in an intensive pre-college musical theatre program. Applicants who are chosen for the program attend challenging singing, acting, and dance classes to learn the art of performing live musical theater. Students polish their performance skills by participating in master classes, evening rehearsals, and Friday evening showcases. During the five-week program, Musical Theatre Studio students refine audition pieces and perform musical scenes consisting of songs and dances in a final showcase performance for peers and parents.

MPulse, University of Michigan, Ann Arbor, Michigan

http://www.music.umich.edu/special_programs/youth/
mpulse/mustheater.htm

The Musical Theatre Workshop is an exciting program that gives students the opportunity to work on the Ann Arbor campus with faculty members in the renowned University of Michigan Department of Musical Theatre. The Musical Theatre Workshop enrolls approximately 40 students and is designed for those who are considering BFA degree programs in college. Extra sessions are devoted to the application and audition process for university programs. The workshop is open to high school juniors, although applications from sophomores of exceptional ability and experience are considered. Admission decisions are based on a student's application (including training and experience), recommendations, transcript, and audition. Applicants must have at least a B average in a rigorous college-prep program in order to have their audition reviewed or be invited to campus to audition.

Northwestern University Cherub Program, Chicago, Illinois

http://www.northwestern.edu/nhsi/theatre_arts/
index.html

As a theatre arts student, you will receive wide-ranging and intensive instruction in the techniques, aesthetics, and literature of the theatre. Core classes provide the foundation for your theatre arts curriculum and include:

- Acting
- Voice/movement
- Performance theory
- Text analysis
- Production crew

Both core and elective classes give you tremendous opportunity for individual instruction, with a teacher–student ratio of approximately 1:4. To complement your course of study, there are guest lectures and field trips to professional productions in Chicago. Nearly every minute of every day is filled with challenging curricular activities.

This two-week Musical Theatre Extension program will begin after the five-week Theatre Arts program has concluded and will focus on musical theatre training. The structure of the Musical Theatre Extension mirrors the existing musical theatre certificate program at Northwestern University. Students must conclude the rigorous five-week theatre arts training before beginning their specialized training in musical theatre. As a musical theatre cherub, you will continue the work of the prerequisite theatre arts program. You will receive additional instruction and direction in the core classes of acting and voice/movement with a focus and concentration on musical theatre. Included in your study will be classes in musical theatre acting, dance (jazz, tap, and musical theatre styles), musical theatre history, and voice classes."

NYU/Tisch School of the Arts, New York City, New York

http://specialprograms.tisch.nyu.edu/object/hsnyc.html

Students earn six college credits after successfully completing intense training in drama, dramatic writing, film, or photography. Courses are paired with visits to museums, screenings, concerts, and theatrical productions, as well as meetings with established and emerging artists. In addition to completing coursework, in past summers, students have seen productions of *The Color Purple, Mary Poppins, The History Boys, Wedding Singer, Sweeney Todd*, and *In The Heights*. Students have also visited the Metropolitan Museum of Art, the Guggenheim Museum, and the American Museum of the Moving Image; attended outdoor music concerts in Central Park; and explored some of New York's rich cultural and artistic history with trips to Ellis Island and Lincoln Center.

Oklahoma City University, Oklahoma City, Oklahoma

http://www.okcu.edu/music/academy/hsmtp.aspx

This intensive program is for students who are serious about pursuing a career in musical theater performance. Mornings are spent in the classroom with a demanding pre-college curriculum of dance, music theory, and acting. Afternoons feature master classes in audition preparation, vocal health, musical theater history, monologue preparation, and voice master classes with Bass School of Music faculty and special guests. Evenings are reserved for rehearsals for a fully staged musical. On Saturday mornings,

Notes

students get the chance to select their schedule with "Saturday Electives," featuring classes such as make-up lab, Pilates, yoga, tap, stage combat, and performance career preparation.

University of California, Los Angeles, California

http://www.universityofcalifornia.edu/academics/humanities.html

In the arts and humanities, scholars, artists, and students explore the range of creative expression and thought, past and present, in languages and literature, the visual arts, music, film, dramatic art, philosophy, and the classics. Faculty and students in the arts and humanities include scholars, critics, and historians of culture and the arts, as well as creative writers, composers, painters, and sculptors.

The study and appreciation of music, art, literature, and cultural traditions contribute to the well-being of society and serve as the basis for informed reflection upon the ethics and values that determine our humanity.

University of Southern California, Los Angeles, California

http://summer.usc.edu/4week/

This rigorous, conservatory-style training course is designed for students with a serious interest in acting. The emphasis is on process. The core practice classes are in movement, voice, and acting. Contemporary theatre text will be used in scene study. Students will also study theory/history and text analysis.

This rigorous, conservatory-style training course is designed for students with a serious interest in musical theatre. The emphasis is on process. The core practice classes are movement, voice, acting, and "acting the song." Students will also study theory/history and text analysis.

5. Other Summer Prep Programs

My College Audition, New York City, Boston, and New Jersey

www.mycollegeaudition.com

Besides the one-on-one coaching provided at My College Audition throughout the school year, during the summer a series of BOOT-CAMPS are run for the aspiring high school performer. BOOTCAMPS are typically held for one weekend and provide students with monologue selection and preparation, song selection and preparation, dance preparation and resume/headshot preparation. At the end of a BOOTCAMP, students are required to perform in a mock audition in front of a panel of professionals. Students leave with prepared materials for all of their college auditions and also written feedback to help continue their growth.

The coaches at My College Audition are young, working professionals in all areas of the performing arts including theatre, television, film and commercial/print. All of the coaches are graduates of prestigious theatre or musical theatre programs and pride themselves on being in touch with all current college audition trends.

For a full list of upcoming BOOTCAMPS, check out: www.mycollegeaudition.com

The Open Jar Institute, New York City

http://www.openjarproductions.com/

NYC Summer Camp

Founded in 2003, The Open Jar Institute is New York City's most challenging and Broadway-integrated actor-training program in Musical Theater. Select students work one-on-one with Broadway's best professionals (directors, choreographers, agents, casting directors and performers) in a small classroom setting designed to challenge and inspire artists to 'jump out of the open jar'—leaving behind all limitations!

Under direction of Director/Choreographer Jeff Whiting, who's work includes numerous Broadway and national tours (*Hair*, *Hairspray*, *The Scottsboro Boys*, *Young Frankenstein*, *Jersey Boys*, *The Producers*, *Wicked*, and *Walt Disney Entertainment*) the Institute connects students with Tony Award-winning actors, challenging

Notes

courses in technique taught by New York's best coaches, and valuable insight into shaping a successful career in acting.

During the daytime of this one-week institute in NYC, students participate in technique workshops in acting, singing, dancing, as well as audition techniques. After dinner, students see a hit Broadway show, tour backstage, and meet members of the cast. The week culminates in the chance to be seen and work with a New York casting director and agent.

- **Junior session:** Students entering 7th, 8th, or 9th grade.
- **High School Session:** Students entering 10th, 11th, or 12th grade.
- **College session:** College Students and Young Professionals

Admission to the institute is by audition only. Visit the website for audition information: www.openjarproductions.com

Part 2

The Surveys

Introduction

Choosing a college is an intimidating process, and we work with hundreds of students each year who feel overwhelmed by the decision. The lack of a comprehensive resource for students specifically interested in comparing theatre schools inspired us to begin a series of in-depth "profiles" of schools' programs.

First, allow us to tell you about a remarkable resource: www.schoolsfortheatre.com. This fantastic website allows you to search for colleges based on various criteria. You can compare and contrast degree options and search by region. The website has served as an invaluable tool for students seeking to pursue a theatre major, and we thoroughly endorse schoolsfortheatre.com as a "must have" in your college search.

This is the survey's first edition, and thus, only some schools are listed in the following pages. These are not *the* "best" schools for theatre in the country, and they are not ranked. But they are certainly *among* the best, and we assure you that you can receive a quality education in theatre at any one of these institutions. They have made a name for themselves, and that's why they're listed here.

We chose these schools after extensive research, as well as interviewing casting directors and spending time at auditions finding out which schools make consistently good showings. These are programs that we feel we can personally vouch for.

The surveys were collected during the 2010–2011 academic year.

Admittedly, this first edition leans toward institutions that offer musical theatre as well as acting degrees, but please check out our updated website and blog for more information on which facets of theatre are considered schools' strengths, as well as for additional information on more "straight theatre" schools. Also, there are some schools that have listed profiles more for their straight acting programs vs. musical theatre programs or vice versa. For more information about a department—including other contributors' input—visit our website (www.mycollegeaudition.com).

We have also attempted to include a healthy sampling of staples, up-and-comers, schools with unconventional approaches, and schools you may not know at all.

Just because a college isn't in this book does not make its department in any way less credible. We hope to add additional top-caliber schools in future editions.

Abilene Christian University

Abilene, Texas

www.acu.edu

Contributor: **Adam Hester, Chair, Department of Theatre**

Give Me the Facts

Population of College:
5,000

Conservatory or Liberal Arts:
Liberal arts

Degrees Offered:
* BFA in theatre with tracks in musical theatre, acting, directing, technical/design, theatre education

Population of Department(s):
Capped at 50 in Department of Theatre

Theatre Scholarships Available:
Four for incoming freshmen: $1,000–1,500; more than 20 theatre scholarships available for upperclassmen

Popular/Unique/Specialized Classes Offered:
Capstone class is Arts and Culture: A Christian Aesthetic, Dance Auditioning, Stanislavsky/Method Acting, Beginning Acting/Beginning Directing Combined Lab

Is an audition required to declare theatre as a major? For BFA?
We only offer the BFA. We accept up to 12 freshmen each year based on audition/interview.

How many students audition versus how many get accepted each year?
Approximately 75 audition for 12 slots

Do you make cuts after freshman year and subsequent semesters?
Freshman year is a probationary year, although it is more of an exception to cut a student at the end of the freshman year. Cuts in later semesters are made with regard to GPA and barrier requirements.

Can students minor in theatre/musical theatre?
Yes

Give Me the Scoop

Would I get a showcase at the end of senior year?
Yes. Students in the acting track and the musical theatre track are required to participate in showcase. Agents have signed numerous students based on the showcase.

Will I be able to audition/perform as a freshman?

All theatre students are required to audition. Freshmen are often cast in main-stage roles.

What ways can I be involved with the department aside from performing?

Theatre students take a practicum course each semester with instruction in technical aspects to receive well-rounded knowledge of theatre. Freshmen acting/musical theatre track students are in a majors-only acting class with scenes directed by junior/senior directing students. The theatre has a chapter of Alpha Psi Omega.

Say I get a BA rather than a BFA. Will I actually get to perform?

We only offer the BFA.

I love to sing, but I don't consider myself a dancer. Can I still seek a degree in musical theatre at your school?

A dance audition will be held at the initial audition for the program. If the department does not think you can compete in musical theatre but can in the acting track, you will be placed in the acting track but can still audition for musicals.

I want to get a BFA in acting, but I also love to sing. Can BFA/BA acting students take voice lessons with top voice faculty?

Acting track students are required to take two semesters of private voice. Students in the musical theatre track take private voice every semester.

Do you discourage or encourage students to audition for theatre outside of the department during the academic year?

Students must petition to audition for anything outside the department during the academic year.

Does your school regularly work in conjunction with any regional theatres?

No

What do students typically do during the summers? Do you actively promote participation in summer theatre auditions?

Students are encouraged and coached to attend unified auditions including SETC, NETC, Strawhats, and Midwest auditions. ACU theatre students have had enormous success in unified auditions securing summer stock work.

How many musicals versus straight plays do you do in a season?

Two to three musicals, two to three straight shows, and two Shakespeare during Shakespeare Festival (including summer)

What are some of your alumni up to? Do you have an active alumni network?

We have an active alumni network working both through the university's alumni connections and through the department's. In the Theatre Department's weekly newsletter, alumni are regularly highlighted as well as spotlighted on our main web page at www.acu.edu/theatre. Alumni are working professionally on Broadway, off-Broadway, national tours, in MFA programs, regional theatres, teaching, and on cruise ships.

Give Me the Technical Info

What is the portfolio/interview process for a technical theatre student?
Prospective students interested in design/technical track will present their portfolio during their interview time and are considered part of the 12 who will be accepted in the incoming freshman class.

What do you expect to see on a technical theatre resume?
The resume should reflect the various experiences the student has had in technical theatre, including design. These might include running the light or sound consoles, working in properties, costume construction, set construction, hanging a light plot, and so on. If a student has designed sets, lights, or costumes for a production, his or her design renderings or plots should be included in the portfolio, accompanied by pictures of the production showing his or her work.

I'm interested in lighting, sound design, and stage management. What major should I go for? Can I minor?
BFA in theatre with design/technical track; the minor does not have a specific focus but rather a general menu of classes that a student may choose.

Give Me Some Insight

What do you look for in a potential student?
In addition to the expected answers of a strong audition package or impressive portfolio, we are looking for students with depth who are interested in exploring how their gifts in theatre might impact the culture in positive ways. We hunt for a "teachable quality"—a student who is hungry to learn all the aspects of theatre and seems devoid of ego. During the interview, we will want to get a peek into his or her plans for the future. Not only do we want to observe the strong drive that it will take to persevere in the industry but also a heart for how he or she might bring a greater sense of humanity to those around him or her.

What are some of the auditors' pet peeves?
Students who don't listen or take direction during a cold reading. Using overdone material or material that is currently on Broadway. A student who is inarticulate in the interview.

After I audition, is there a good way to follow up?
Touch base by sending an email. We like staying in the loop with a prospective student's theatre career by receiving updates, such as what play he or she is currently working on.

What's one of the best auditions you have ever seen?

I remember a girl who entered with great confidence yet appeared to have such a generous spirit. Of course she was extremely well prepared; she nailed her song and monologues, but it was something more. That special something was about bringing this fascinating essence of who she was and breathing life into the characters she offered up. Her interview was more of that kind of generosity of spirit. She was articulate, funny, and insightful; she seemed really comfortable in who she was, what she wanted, and, in a way, it felt as if she had come to offer *us* a gift.

If there were one thing you never wanted to see in an audition again, what would it be?

A prospective student who talks negatively in an excessive way about previous theatre mentors.

What's the best advice you can give me regarding auditioning for your school?

* Prepare well.
* Try to move the focus off of yourself so you can embrace the opportunity.
* Bring an eager and adventurous spirit to the audition.
* Listen and engage during the interview.
* Enjoy this time to meet new people.

Give Me the Lowdown

Because the ACU Theatre is interested in exploring the connection between faith and art, students are encouraged to imagine how they fit into that conversation. What kinds of questions and associations regarding the spiritual life of the artist do they wrestle with? How does an artist of faith connect with the culture? In addition to receiving a well-grounded training in theatre, the ACU Theatre will explore spiritual values that will prepare students for their life in the arts.

Our mission statement is to provide quality training and opportunity for the disciplined theatre artist in a nurturing environment that models Christian values. We strive to enflesh that. We believe that the ACU Theatre should not only be a place where a student is challenged intellectually and receives excellent preparation, transforming their skillset, but the theatre should also be a place where there are mentors and examples of deeply spiritual artists who can guide in inner formation. Although we have high standards that involve discipline and commitment, we function as a community that seeks to care for and encourage one another.

Ball State University

Muncie, Indiana

www.cms.bsu.edu

Contributor: Andrea Sadler, Recruitment Coordinator, Department of Theatre and Dance

Give Me the Facts

Population of College:
20,000

Conservatory or Liberal Arts:
Liberal arts

Degrees Offered:
* BFA in musical theatre, acting
* BA/BS in dance, design and technology, theatre education, theatrical studies, production

Population of Department(s):
400

Theatre Scholarships Available:
Presidential Scholarships in the Arts (1/2 tuition)

Popular/Unique/Specialized Classes That You Offer:
Voice and movement for acting, Pilates for all students, special topics for all areas

Is an audition required to declare theatre as a major? For BFA?
An audition is required for all performance options; all other areas of study are encouraged to interview for scholarships but not required for entrance into nonperformance programs.

How many students audition versus how many get accepted each year?
We see over 600 a year, and the BFA programs accept 16 in acting (see about 120), 16 in musical theatre (see about 200), and 20 in dance (see about 80). No cap on other programs—rest of numbers from these areas.

Do you make cuts after freshman year and subsequent semesters?
No

Can I minor in theatre/musical theatre?
Minor in theatre only, but not available until junior year

Give Me the Scoop

Would I get a showcase at the end of senior year?
An audition is held with casting directors and talent agents from New York, Chicago, and LA. If cast, you are in the showcase. Open to BFA students only.

Will I be able to audition/perform as a freshman?
Not as a first-semester freshman. Auditions are open to freshmen in the second semester.

What ways can I be involved with the department aside from performing?
Reflex (comedy club), Alpha Psi Omega (service organization), BSU Backstage (tech organization), Prism Project (show with and for autistic children), Student Dance Association (dance organization). Class credit given for work in box office, scene shop, costume shop, main office, and other locations.

Say I get a BA rather than a BFA. Will I actually get to perform?
The BA programs are open to audition.

I love to sing, but I don't consider myself a dancer. Can I still seek a degree in musical theatre at your school?
Acting, singing, and dancing are all held in equal parts. Dancing is a large portion of our program.

I want to get a BFA in acting, but I also love to sing. Can BFA/BA acting students take voice lessons with top voice faculty?
Voice will have to be done privately.

Do you discourage or encourage students to audition for theatre outside of the department during the academic year?
Occasionally. Your commitment is to your education, and if outside shows conflict, then we strongly discourage.

Does your school regularly work in conjunction with any regional theatres?
Yes

What do students typically do during the summers? Do you actively promote participation in summer theatre auditions?
Summer theatre work and intensives

How many musicals versus straight plays do you do in a season?
Two musicals each year, two large-scale straight plays each year, several smaller shows that vary in style—16 each year in all.

What are some of your alumni up to? Do you have an active alumni network?

We have an active network. Alums are in film, national tours, grad school, Disney, and active in New York, Chicago, and LA, among other locations.

Give Me the Technical Info

What is the portfolio/interview process for a technical theatre student?

Simple and relaxed. More of a conversation. Examples of work are not required but appreciated.

What do you expect to see on a technical theatre resume?

Motivation, dabble in all areas, ability to learn new systems.

I'm interested in lighting, sound design, and stage management. What major should I go for? Can I minor?

Minor in design and technology is offered, usually matched with theatre education majors. Light and sound are under design and technology, while stage management is under a production major. Design tech and production are two majors that go well together and are done in four years.

Give Me Some Insight

What do you look for in a potential student?

Kindness, motivation, grades and test scores, well rounded, eager

What are some of the auditors' pet peeves?

Not reading the entire play before a monologue is performed, cut music correctly, overacting, dialect use, rudeness

After I audition, is there a good way to follow up?

Via email or a thank-you card

What's one of the best auditions you have ever seen?

The more the student can just talk to us, the better. Be natural.

If there were one thing you never wanted to see in an audition again, what would it be?

Performing self-written songs or monologues or items that are not from published plays or musicals

What's the best advice you can give me regarding auditioning for your school?

Relax; be yourself; don't overthink it; and be prepared to take adjustments and be talked to, not talked at.

Barnard College, Columbia University

New York, New York

www.barnard.edu

Contributor: **W. B. Worthen, Alice Brady Pels Professor in the Arts**

Give Me the Facts

Population of College
2,300

Conservatory or Liberal Arts:
Liberal arts. Barnard College is a selective liberal arts college for women. The college partners with Columbia University, and the department offers major programs for Columbia College (CC) and the School of General Studies (GS) at Columbia. Both CC and GS are coeducational.

Degrees Offered:
* BA

Population of Department(s):
80 majors. Barnard College Theatre Department houses the undergraduate major program for Columbia College and the Columbia University School of General Studies; Theatre majors (Barnard students) and drama and theatre arts majors (at CC and GS) all follow the same set of requirements and comprise one group of "majors." While Barnard College admits women, CC and GS are coeducational; the undergraduate theatre program has both male and female majors.

Degree Requirements (hours):
A minimum of 10 classes, 3–4 hours each

Theatre Scholarships Available:
No

Most Common Academic/Need-Based/Miscellaneous Scholarships:
For first-year students who are U.S. citizens/permanent residents: Admissions is need-blind, financial aid is need-based, and college guarantees to meet 100% of need. For transfer students, admissions is need-aware and financial aid is need-based. For international citizens, admissions is need-aware, with a limited amount of full-need scholarships.

Popular/Unique/Specialized Classes That You Offer:
The department offers a wide range of classes in global theatre studies and provides the opportunity for all majors to undertake a thesis in any area of the major: acting, directing, design, playwriting, solo performance, or formal research. A range of approaches to acting (realism, Suzuki, Viewpoints, improvisation) are offered at various levels, courses in all design disciplines (scenic,

costume, lighting, sound); students take playwriting with several produced playwrights and also devise new theatre work in the performance workshop course. Recent topics for research courses included Nazism in Performance, Traditional Indian Theatre, and Shakespeare, Theory, and Performance.

Is an audition required to declare theatre as a major?
No

How many students audition versus how many get accepted each year?
All Barnard College, Columbia College, and General Studies undergraduates declare a major in the second year of full-time study; we accept all students who declare the major. Auditions required for acting classes and stage productions. Senior theses are vetted by the faculty, but qualified students generally receive first or second choice.

Do you make cuts after freshman year and subsequent semesters?
No

Can I minor in theatre/musical theatre?
No

Give Me the Scoop

Would I get a showcase at the end of senior year?
No, the department does not have a showcase. We do offer a workshop course in auditioning for professional work and MFA studies.

Are showcases successful?
(Not applicable)

Will I be able to audition/perform as a freshman?
Yes. We have a special class restricted to first-year students, though first-year students may be placed in other classes as well. First-year students are also able to audition for the production season and are frequently cast.

If there is a graduate program, will I get the same performance opportunities as an undergraduate?
The Columbia University MFA programs are, on occasion, available to undergraduates for course work, and so provide potential opportunities for undergraduates. The Theatre Department casts from undergraduates who audition, so there is no competition from graduate students.

What ways can I be involved with the department aside from performing?
The department has extensive crew and technical theatre assignments, as well as work-study involvement in departmental and publicity operations.

Say I get a BA rather than a BFA. Will I actually get to perform?
We offer only the BA; auditions are open to all students.

I love to sing, but I don't consider myself a dancer. Can I still seek a degree in musical theatre at your school?

No. The Dance Department, however, does offer a range of courses open to Barnard and Columbia undergraduates.

I want to get a BFA in acting, but I also love to sing. Can BFA/BA acting students take voice lessons with top voice faculty?

The department typically offers two courses—Acting the Song and Acting the Musical Scene—focusing on singing and acting; these courses are open to all by audition and are taught by established professionals in the New York City theatre. Voice lessons are also available on campus through the Music Department.

Can acting students audition for musicals? Can musical theatre students audition for straight plays?

The department produces plays with music every two or three years, and the audition process for those plays is the same as for all productions. Barnard and Columbia undergraduate theatre clubs, however, produce a wide range of musicals on campus, and many theatre majors participate in them.

Do you discourage or encourage students to audition for theatre outside of the department during the academic year?

We do not discourage it; many of our majors also perform in Columbia University/Barnard College's extensive network of undergraduate theatre groups as well as auditioning for professional productions in New York.

Does your school regularly work in conjunction with any regional theatres?

Many of our students do internships in theatres in New York during the academic year as well as the summer.

What do students typically do during the summers? Do you actively promote participation in summer theatre auditions?

Many students audition for summer programs. We have one or two programs for which we have financial support in specific fields (playwriting).

How many musicals versus straight plays do you do in a season?

The season is typically four productions, one of which may be a musical every two or three years. One production is directed by directing students as the senior thesis; the other three are professionally/faculty directed.

I also like to play sports. Do you encourage musical theatre/acting students to pursue other interests?

(Not applicable)

What are some of your alumni up to? Do you have an active alumni network?

Many alumni are working in New York City theatre; several have pursued graduate degrees in English, theatre, or performance studies at top PhD programs; others have pursued careers unrelated to theatre.

Give Me the Technical Info

What is the portfolio/interview process for a technical theatre student?
Meet with the production manager; all interested students will be provided with work in technical theatre, which is required of all majors.

What do you expect to see on a technical theatre resume?
We do not expect a resume from incoming students. Students who have previous experience will be given technical assignments commensurate with their abilities.

I'm interested in lighting, sound design, and stage management. What major should I go for? Can I minor?
The theatre major enables specialization in any area of design, as well as in directing, acting, playwriting, theatre studies, and solo performance.

Does your school specialize in any division of technical theatre?
No

Give Me Some Insight

The department does not require auditions for admission. Auditions for classes and productions generally take place over two nights at the beginning of the semester; class assignments and callbacks follow the following day and students are placed in class and/or cast very quickly. Information on auditions is available on the department website at www.barnard.edu/theatre.

Give Me the Lowdown

The Barnard College major in theatre

The Columbia College major in drama and theatre arts

Situated at the intersection of the arts and the humanities, and in a world theatrical capital, drama and theatre studies at Barnard and Columbia is committed to the interaction of creation and critique in the shaping of articulate performance: to the distinctive practices of reading, writing, and research and their capacity to illuminate and ignite the conceptual work of performance; to drama as the exploration and instigation of consequential action; to acting as a means of claiming and clarifying embodied meaning; to design as a practice for shaping meaning in material, space, and time; to directing as an inquiry into the form and tempo of the theatre's world-making; and to playwriting as the struggle to invent new performance languages to impel, enrich, and interrogate that world and ours.

The Barnard College theatre major/Columbia College major in drama and theatre arts builds on its liberal arts setting by imagining an integrative approach to performance, drama, and theatre studies. Taking advantage of a wide variety of studio coursework, of the Department's production season in the Minor Latham Playhouse, as well as of a rich panoply of drama and theatre studies courses, students' creative work develops in dialogue with critical inquiry into the literature, history, culture, and theory of western and non-western performance, typically combining coursework in theatre and drama with study in other fields, such as anthropology, architecture, art history, classics, dance, film, languages, literature, music, and philosophy. Students work with accomplished artists, directors, designers, actors, and playwrights whose work enlivens and enriches the contemporary American theatre; they also study the critical, historical, and theoretical lineaments of drama, theatre, and performance with celebrated teachers and internationally recognized research scholars. The coursework in the major also engages productively with Barnard's "nine ways of knowing" and with Columbia's Core Curriculum, by considering how critical questions and traditions are animated by the forms, genres, and practices of dramatic theatre and by conceiving the mutual responsiveness of critical and artistic work to those questions. Making, thinking about, and writing about art are an essential part of any undergraduate education: For this reason, the courses offered in the Barnard Theatre Department and casting for its theatrical production are open to majors and nonmajors alike.

In a small program, students receive individual attention and ample performance and production opportunities. All students develop a vocabulary for conceptualizing performance in common courses in the history, literature, and theory of various world performance traditions. They also engage in the range of disciplines sustaining modern theatre—acting, design, directing, dramaturgy, and playwriting—before taking up culminating work on a senior thesis. An original creative project, the thesis can take several forms: a significant research essay; a new play; or acting, dramaturging, directing, or designing as part of the department's annual showcase of thesis productions. Theatre is a site of cultural innovation, transmission, and contestation, involving a variety of verbal, visual, spatial, musical, and gestural languages. Barnard/Columbia theatre majors understand the power of performance as an act of articulation—in speech, through movement and embodiment, as the manipulation of space, and in the construction of an expressive event. Theatre majors are well placed to pursue advanced professional training in the arts, as well as undertaking the kind of humanistic education that provides a solid platform for success in a wide range of endeavors. In recent years, students have gone on to do graduate work in acting, dramaturgy, playwriting, arts management, and theatre studies in prestigious MFA and PhD programs as well as professional careers.

The Barnard College Theatre Department collaborates closely with two graduate programs housed at Columbia University. If you are interested in MFA or PhD studies in drama, theatre, and performance studies at Columbia, please see the Columbia University Doctoral Program Subcommittee on Theatre and the Theatre Division of the Columbia University School of the Arts.

Boston University, School of Theatre

Boston, Massachusetts

www.bu.edu

Contributor: **Paolo S. Difabio, Assistant Director, School of Theatre**

Give Me the Facts

Population of College:

There are approximately 270 students (BFA and MFA combined) in the School of Theatre (performance and design/production majors)

Conservatory or Liberal Arts:

New conservatory (see additional notes at end)

Degrees Offered:

* BFA in acting, design, production, theatre arts, stage management
* MFA in design, directing, production, theatre education

Population of Department(s):

Approximately 170 students in BFA performance (acting and theatre arts); approximately 80 students in BFA design, production, stage management; approximately 30 MFA students

Theatre Scholarships Available:

Performance awards of approximately $5,000–$7,500 offered annually to 10–15 incoming freshmen in all BFA programs (based on artistic review and financial need). For most MFA programs, tuition is either partially or fully funded.

Is an audition required to declare theatre as a major? For BFA?

For application to the BFA and MFA programs, either an audition (performance) or portfolio review (design/production) is required.

How many students audition versus how many get accepted each year?

We get an average of about 800 BFA applicants each year and are looking for a total freshman class of 60 students (40 performance, 20 design/production).

Do you make cuts after freshman year and subsequent semesters?

No

Can I minor in theatre/musical theatre?

Non-CFA students can minor in theatre (it is a 28-credit course/credit sequence with no audition required). There is no minor or major in musical theatre.

Give Me the Scoop

Would I get a showcase at the end of senior year?

Yes, in New York City as part of our InCite Arts Festival (www.bu.edu/cfa/incite).

Will I be able to audition/perform as a freshman?

No. Because of the rigorous academic workload in our Freshmen Performance Core (a seven-course sequence of classes), the average academic workload for our freshmen is about 35–45 hours. We rehearse Tuesday–Friday nights (7 p.m.–11 p.m.) and on Saturdays (10 a.m.–6 p.m.), so when students are eligible for casting (starting in the fourth semester), the average work week is about 75–85 hours. For this reason (in addition to other curricular reasons), students are not eligible for casting in the first three semesters.

If there is a graduate program, will I get the same performance opportunities as an undergraduate?

The MFA programs are very, very small (we only have about five to six graduate students in directing and theatre education combined in any given semester); this limited population does not hold great impact on our casting. Additionally, the school has a "guaranteed casting policy," meaning that all undergraduates eligible for casting will be cast, even if the school must add shows to its season to meet the needs of a given casting pool.

What ways can I be involved with the department aside from performing?

The school does offer work-study positions in its office for students who are eligible and awarded such grants as part of their financial aid package.

Say I get a BA rather than a BFA. Will I actually get to perform?

We do not offer a BA program. However, if a student were a theatre minor, then he or she could audition and be considered for casting as part of the School of Theatre production season. However, unlike the BFA majors, theatre minors are not "guaranteed" casting.

I want to get a BFA in acting, but I also love to sing. Can BFA/BA acting students take voice lessons with top voice faculty?

We do offer a four-semester progression of courses in "Singing for the Actor" and "Musical Theatre Performance." We feel strongly that since the approach to performance in songs is the same as it is for monologues and scenes, students must still ask fundamental questions of character, intent, obstacle, and, most important, action.

Do you discourage or encourage students to audition for theatre outside of the department during the academic year?

If a student wishes to pursue an opportunity with a professional company or film outside of his or her schoolwork, he or she must receive faculty approval for time away from classes. This is not done to be difficult or prevent a student from pursuing a valuable opportunity; instead the faculty wants to ascertain if the opportunity is worth the time missed outside of studio classes. We feel strongly that our students' first commitment is to their college training and experience, and if an opportunity will take too much time away from classes, a student should consider a "leave of absence" in order to commit the necessary time to the "outside project." Students taking a leave of absence will be automatically granted return to the program within the first two years from the time they left BU. Returning after two years may require re-auditioning and re-application to the program.

Does your school regularly work in conjunction with any regional theatres?

The School of Theatre has a long tradition of embracing the value of the professional theatre's participation in the education of our students. We have now arrived at a landmark number of professional theatre ventures that embrace the possibilities of building strong bridges between the study and practice of the theatre arts. For more information (including a complete list of our Professional Theatre Initiative affiliates), please visit www.bu.edu/cfa/theatre/professional.

What do students typically do during the summers? Do you actively promote participation in summer theatre auditions?

Summer months can span from internships or apprenticeships with one of our Professional Theatre Initiative (PTI) affiliates throughout the country, to working with our Boston University Summer Theatre Institute (BUSTI) for high school students, to taking liberal arts elective courses toward their BFA degree requirements either in Boston or back home, to just taking a summer away from theatre to recharge (in mind, body, spirit, and sometimes wallet).

How many musicals versus straight plays do you do in a season?

Our season, which is broken down into four quarters—Fall is Q1 and Q2, Spring is Q3 and Q4—is dictated by our directors (faculty, guest artists, graduate students, and advanced undergraduates in the theatre arts program who have studied directing). If no one is proposing a musical, we will not force one upon the season. Generally, we do about one to two each year, but a number of our productions are plays with music in them (hardly musicals). Because of the guaranteed casting policy and the number of PTI casting opportunities that we include, our season of casting at the BU School of Theatre can do anywhere from 25–40 shows each year.

What are some of your alumni up to? Do you have an active alumni network?

We have a very active, professional, and connected alumni network. We are firm believers in the fact that going to BU is more than just a four-year experience. We could run down a list of famous alumni whose names are highly recognizable, but that's not our style. We believe that any alumni actively pursuing artistic opportunities are "working" alumni. And we are also just as proud of those alumni who go on to pursue careers outside of theatre as well.

Give Me the Technical Info

What is the portfolio/interview process for a technical theatre student?
Prior to the portfolio review, each applicant must submit an electronic portfolio, including a resume and a photograph of the applicant. Applicants may upload 28 images, in addition to their resume and photograph, to the school's portfolio submission website. JPEG format is preferred for all work.

Applicants should edit their portfolios so that they can discuss each entry and move through the entire collection within 10 minutes. Faculty discussion of the work will likely extend the interview by an additional 10 minutes. Applicants should include a variety of materials. Often, a preliminary quick study says the most about an artist's intention and native talent. Applicants should expect the interview to be friendly and informative. For an in-person interview, the applicant should provide a hardcopy portfolio containing the same or different images from the online portfolio. The applicant retains the portfolio at the conclusion of the interview.

Design and production portfolios should demonstrate the broadest range of theatrical and artistic expression. Anything that suggests the applicant's ability to communicate using the tools of the visual artist can be included, such as actual theatre renderings, related painting or graphics, working drawings, ground plans, lighting plots, props, masks, photography, and photographs of sculpture, murals, or other nontransportable works.

Stage management portfolios may contain prompt books, programs, director's notes, and examples of creative writing. The interview provides the primary basis for evaluating applicants to the stage management program. Applicants should come prepared to discuss their activities in the theatre.

I'm interested in lighting, sound design, and stage management. What major should I go for? Can I minor?
All incoming BFA design/production students will begin in a Freshmen Design Core where a core sequence of courses introduces them to the curriculums of all our design/production BFA majors. It is not until the end of the freshman year that students will declare their BFA major focus and begin more advanced study in that specific design/production field. All students can minor in a liberal arts discipline outside of the College of Fine Arts.

Give Me Some Insight

What do you look for in a potential student?
Cognitive understanding of the text and material; an emotional awareness of the character, the scene, and circumstances; a physical availability necessary to fully engaging the story telling. We are also looking for students who demonstrate a strong generosity of spirit and a willingness to take directions, make choices, and be unafraid of risks.

What are some of the auditors' pet peeves?

Students who aren't willing to engage in a conversation about themselves

After I audition, is there a good way to follow up?

Students are always welcome to email the faculty for whom they auditioned and follow up with any questions about the program.

What's one of the best auditions you have ever seen?

The ones where students picked materials to their strengths, made bold choices, and presented an artistic generosity both in their work and their willingness to work made us want to spend more and more time with them in the audition.

If there were one thing you never wanted to see in an audition again, what would it be?

Someone who doesn't care

What's the best advice you can give me regarding auditioning for your school?

Be yourself, be daring, take risks, choose work that demonstrates your strengths, be willing to fail, and always remain open to the idea of possibilities.

Give Me the Lowdown

The School of Theatre is an energetic place that vales the notion of "the new conservatory." From inside that idea, several core School of Theatre values emerge:

We believe in the artistic possibilities of collaboration that involve faculty, students, alumni, and guest artists in potent explorations of the art form that encourage working together as the best means of achieving artistic growth.

We believe that artists must be provided with a rigorous curriculum that allows mastery of their skill in their particular area of interest.

We believe that every member of our community is a part of the artistic home that we create together. In that home, we nurture an appreciation of challenge, a conviction for the value of everyone's potential, and a belief in the need for intellectual growth as a core part of developing artistic growth.

We believe that the School can serve the profession by interacting with it and providing a laboratory for the development of new work or new approaches to existing work. Like our colleagues in the sciences, the role of the arts in a university that prizes its excellence as a research institution is no less able to be on the forefront of exploring new possibilities for theatre.

Brigham Young University

Provo, Utah

www.byu.edu

Contributor: **Tim Threllfall, Associate Professor, Theatre and Media Arts**

Give Me the Facts

Population of College:
34,000

Conservatory or Liberal Arts:
Conservatory-style preprofessional in a liberal arts setting

Degrees Offered:
* BFA in music dance theatre (MDT), acting
* BA in theatre studies, theatre education

Population of Department(s):
Approximately 400; there are 65 majors in the BFA music dance theatre program and 40 in the BFA acting program

Theatre Scholarships Available:
Half tuition. Very limited due to the extremely low cost of tuition for members of the Church of Jesus Christ of Latter-day Saints, which owns and operates the university.

Popular/Unique/Specialized Classes That You Offer:
MDT is a truly interdisciplinary program with many courses team-taught by three faculty members, one each from music, dance, and theatre. Accredited by NAST, NASM, and NASD.

Is an audition required to declare theatre as a major? For BFA?
MDT auditions via a prescreen audition are due in November, followed by an invitation-only live audition the first weekend of January in Provo. The initial video (DVD) auditions are open to any interested individual.
BFA acting auditions are open only to those already accepted to the university. A minimum of two auditions is required for admission to the BFA acting program.

Admission to the MDT program does not include acceptance to the university. Admission to Brigham Young University is highly competitive and involves a process separate from the MDT program audition. Admission guidelines are readily available at the BYU website.

How many students audition versus how many get accepted each year?
MDT admits approximately 16 students each year. The number of those auditioning varies year to year.

Do you make cuts after freshman year and subsequent semesters?

No. We are committed to the success of each student we accept into the program.

Can I minor in theatre/musical theatre?

No. A minor is not offered.

Give Me the Scoop

Would I get a showcase at the end of senior year?

Yes. BYU graduating BFA seniors travel to both LA and New York for a showcase each April. The 2011 showcase will be the 10th annual Senior Showcase. The showcase is by audition and open to both BFA performance program majors. Generally, 12–18 students attend the Senior Showcase each year.

Will I be able to audition/perform as a freshman?

Freshmen are required to play "as cast" in the mainstage musical(s) during their freshman year. All MDT students must perform in the ensemble of a production once while in the program.

MDT students also have the opportunity to audition for a very select show choir that produces a professional caliber Broadway musical revue each year and tours both nationally and internationally. The BYU Young Ambassadors have traveled extensively throughout the world during their annual month-long tours.

What ways can I be involved with the department aside from performing?

The BYU Theatre and Media Arts Department has an extensive film program. BFA performance majors are encouraged to work in the numerous student films produced on campus. In addition, the LDS Church operates a fully functioning film studio minutes from the BYU campus. The Utah film market is very active, with recent films such as *127 Hours* shot in the state, and film properties such as *Napoleon Dynamite,* which began as a BYU student film, provide additional opportunities.

As of January 2011, nearly half of the entire BYU student body was also employed by BYU. With fewer graduate programs than most universities of its size, BYU has more work-study and research opportunities for undergraduates than many similar institutions.

An unprecedented 77% of all BYU students speak a second language due to LDS Church missionary service. Opportunities for cultural exchanges and study abroad at BYU are exceptional.

Say I get a BA rather than a BFA. Will I actually get to perform?

Most all BYU campus productions are open to anyone who auditions.

I love to sing, but I don't consider myself a dancer. Can I still seek a degree in musical theatre at your school?

The MDT degree is granted one-third from music, one-third from dance, and one-third from theatre. Equal emphasis is given to all three disciplines. However, exceptional talent in two of the three areas will qualify an applicant for the program. There are also 7.5 elective hours that allow MDT students to focus on an area of particular interest or special need. However, the program truly is interdisciplinary.

I want to get a BFA in acting, but I also love to sing. Can BFA/BA acting students take voice lessons with top voice faculty?

Yes. BFA acting and BFA music dance theatre students take many classes together, and BFA acting students are required to take private vocal instruction.

Do you discourage or encourage students to audition for theatre outside of the department during the academic year?

About 75% of all MDT students work in at least one summer stock company during their time in the program. There is also a requirement within the MDT program to work in one show outside the university prior to graduation.

Does your school regularly work in conjunction with any regional theatres?

The BYU Music Dance Theatre program works with Tuacahn Center for the Arts in St. George, Utah. Tuacahn is a LORT-contracted theatre with an annual budget of about $7 million per year and is housed in a $23 million state-of-the-art outdoor amphitheatre.

What do students typically do during the summers? Do you actively promote participation in summer theatre auditions?

BYU has unofficial connections with at least three professional theatre companies. While no roles in these companies are guaranteed to BYU students, traditionally many BYU students and alumni work regularly with these professional venues. At least one is a LORT theatre that offers a six-month season and AEA EMC points. Many BYU students have joined Actors' Equity from work with this organization.

How many musicals versus straight plays do you do in a season?

MDT produces one mainstage musical in a 1,400-seat venue every other year. In the opposite years, two musicals are presented: one in a 500-seat proscenium and one "new" musical in a flexible black box. BYU is a member of the National Alliance for Music Theatre (NAMT) and attends the NAMT conference each year in New York, looking for new musicals to mount. BYU recently produced the made-for-television new musical *Berlin,* which garnered an Emmy and a CINE Golden Eagle Award. The show was broadcast on the satellite network owned by the LDS Church and was available to over 50 million homes worldwide.

BYU theatre and media arts generally have a season of about nine stage productions during the academic year. One large musical every other year and two smaller musicals every other year are also part of the programming.

What are some of your alumni up to? Do you have an active alumni network?
BYU carefully tracks its alumni and their work. The BYU MDT website offers a document with the names of the numerous Broadway, national tours, regional theatres, films, television shows, and other entertainment projects our alumni are involved with. The list is too extensive for this format. Google BYU MDT and the first reference will take you directly to the website. Then look under the heading "alumni."

Give Me the Technical Info

What is the portfolio/interview process for a technical theatre student?
We interview technical theatre students on campus in Provo and at regional high school theatre conferences, as well as ACTF regional gatherings.

I'm interested in lighting, sound design, and stage management. What major should I go for? Can I minor?
The theatre studies major with an emphasis in specific technical areas

Does your school specialize in any division of technical theatre?
Costume design

Give Me Some Insight

What do you look for in a potential student?
A commitment to personal excellence as a performer, a learner, and an individual

What are some of the auditors' pet peeves?
A lack of preparation. The MDT website is particular and specific in regard to the taped audition presentation. Auditions that follow the format are always at a distinct advantage.

After I audition, is there a good way to follow up?
November 15 is the last date for submission of an audition DVD. Students selected for the live audition in January are notified before the end of the fall term. Those invited to the live audition usually number about 30. Slightly more than one-half of those invited to the live audition will be admitted to the program for the following fall. Notification of acceptance into the program generally is completed within three weeks of the live audition. Very little follow-up on the part of student applicants is necessary.

What's one of the best auditions you have ever seen?

We are always looking for auditions that reveal the personality and soul of the performer. Each person is individual and unique. That individuality revealed in the work, whether while dancing, singing, or acting, is the "edge" we look for.

If there were one thing you never wanted to see in an audition again, what would it be?

Any material, no matter how "overdone" is still engaging if it is spectacularly performed. Finding something fresh is always advisable, but if you do an old standard wonderfully and it is your best work, don't hesitate to use it. Stay within your age range and type. It is difficult to adjudicate the work of 19 year old if he or she has chosen to play a 70 year old with an accent.

What's the best advice you can give me regarding auditioning for your school?

BYU operates under a dual mandate to educate students both in their field of study as well as spiritually. This unique blend of the sacred and secular is what makes BYU unique. Many find this duality of purpose exactly what they are seeking. For others not interested in a spiritual education, BYU would not be the right choice.

BYU is owned and operated by the Church of Jesus Christ of Latter-day Saints. All who attend the university are required to take religion courses and adhere to a very strong "Honor Code." This code includes complete abstinence from alcohol and tobacco, as well as sexual activity outside the bonds of legal marriage. Dress and grooming standards that include modest clothing, hair above the ears and collar for men, no facial hair for men beyond a moustache, no excessive hair colors or styles, and no tattoos is also enforced.

Brown University

Providence, RI

www.brown.edu

Contributor: **Lowry Marshall, Professor of Theatre**

Give Me the Facts

Population of College:
Approximately 5,900 undergraduates from 50 states and 90 countries

Conservatory or Liberal Arts:
Liberal arts

Degrees Offered:
* AB in theatre arts and performance studies with various tracks and focuses including performance studies, acting/directing, playwriting, all design areas, and technical theatre
* MFA in acting, directing, playwriting
* PhD in performance studies

Population of Department(s):
Approximately 20 undergrad senior majors each year but 200 or more additional students who are deeply involved in classes and productions.

Degree Requirements (hours):
For an AB in theatre arts and performance studies, 10 courses are needed; five are specifically required and the others chosen according to the area of focus.

Theatre Scholarships Available:
Contact financial aid

Most Common Academic/Need-Based/Miscellaneous Scholarships:
Contact financial aid

Popular/Unique/Specialized Classes That You Offer:
Too many to list, but among them: Acting Outside the Box, Directors and Designers Collaboration, Solo Performance (senior capstone project), Stage Movement, Voice for the Actor, Acting for Camera, The Creative Ensemble (part of our summer Apprentice Company training in coordination with the Brown/Trinity Playwrights Repertory Theatre), Writing for the Musical Theatre, and Songwriting for the Theatre. We offer many unique academic offerings in a wide variety of research areas, a well-developed dance program with specialties in modern and African dance forms, and an excellent persuasive communications course.

Is an audition required to declare theatre as a major? For BFA?

No. We don't offer the BFA degree. The only requirement for a theatre major is acceptance at Brown along with a desire and commitment to study theatre.

How many students audition versus how many get accepted each year?

We don't require auditions for anything other than cocurricular productions and our summer Apprentice Company. Acceptance at Brown is highly competitive.

Do you make cuts after freshman year and subsequent semesters?

Absolutely not. Any Brown student is eligible to take any theatre course and to audition for any production, no matter what his or her major or year of graduation.

Can I minor in theatre/musical theatre?

We don't have minors. You may take as many theatre courses as you choose without declaring a major, or you may double-concentrate in theatre and another area, as many students do.

Give Me the Scoop

Would I get a showcase at the end of senior year?

Not in the traditional sense of "showcase." Our most talented students often choose to create a full-length, entirely original solo show as a capstone project. Many of these have gone on to tour and to be produced in major cities in the United States and abroad. A very large proportion of our students go on to graduate studies in major American graduate programs.

Are showcases successful?

See above

Will I be able to audition/perform as a freshman?

You will be treated no differently than any senior theatre major.

If there is a graduate program, will I get the same performance opportunities as an undergraduate?

Yes. Our graduate program is housed in our downtown Trinity Repertory campus. This choice was made in order to ensure that undergraduates remain in control of undergraduate performance spaces and play all roles in undergraduate productions. We pride ourselves on having the most active undergraduate program in the country, with between 75 and 90 separate productions on campus each year. There is *always* something to audition for at Brown.

What ways can I be involved with the department aside from performing?

Above all, Brown Theatre is student-centered, so opportunities to work in student and student/faculty organizations abound. Students choose our seasons and produce our shows. We have several amazing all-student-run theatre groups on campus that produce many shows each year. One of them has its own well-equipped black box theatre. Our faculty-directed season (called "Sock and Buskin") is chosen by a board made up of both students and faculty, with students in the majority. It's been around for well over a hundred years, making it the oldest college producing organization of its kind in America. There are work-study opportunities, design opportunities, and many opportunities for playwrights to have their own new plays and musicals produced, in some cases with professional directors attached.

Say I get a BA rather than a BFA. Will I actually get to perform?
Every Brown student is eligible to audition for every role on campus.

I love to sing, but I don't consider myself a dancer. Can I still seek a degree in musical theatre at your school?
We don't offer a degree in musical theatre per se, but actors who sing are frequently cast in musical theatre productions. Even though there is no degree in musical theatre, Brown has turned out an enormous number of successful musical theatre performers and writers. A few years back, alum John Lloyd Young won the Tony Award for Best Actor in a Musical for his creation of the role of Frankie Valli in *Jersey Boys* on Broadway. And numerous Brown actors have appeared in Broadway musicals, including *Bloody, Bloody Andrew Jackson*, *Spring Awakening*, *Avenue Q*, and so on.

I want to get a BFA in acting, but I also love to sing. Can BFA/BA acting students take voice lessons with top voice faculty?
All Brown students are eligible to study with leading voice faculty in our applied music program, which is part of the Music Department.

Can acting students audition for musicals? Can musical theatre students audition for straight plays?
Yes and yes.

Do you discourage or encourage students to audition for theatre outside of the department during the academic year?
We neither encourage nor discourage working away from campus, but we do ask our students to recognize that when they choose to spend time away from Brown, their experience at Brown will, of necessity, be impacted. It is a matter of personal choice. In recent memory, several high-profile professional performers have made Brown their home, managing to continue their careers as they pursue their studies in Brown classrooms and studios.

Does your school regularly work in conjunction with any regional theatres?
We share our MFA programs with Tony Award–winning Trinity Repertory Theatre, and our undergraduates benefit in a great many way—through access to workshops and new play productions and through engagement with our MFA faculty, who frequently offer their support for campus productions.

What do students typically do during the summers? Do you actively promote participation in summer theatre auditions?

Many students travel abroad or work in professional summer theatres. Some apprentice at prestigious summer festivals like Williamstown or the Hangar, and some find theatre-related internships. Brown offers its own terrific summer Apprentice Company (http://brown.edu/Facilities/Theatre/btprep/). We encourage students to be involved in our summer companies, but we also facilitate their attendance at auditions for other companies.

How many musicals versus straight plays do you do in a season?

We normally do one professionally written musical on our main stage every other year. In alternate years, we produce one faculty-directed original student musical and develop at least one other original musical for production on student stages.

I also like to play sports. Do you encourage musical theatre/acting students to pursue other interests?

Each student must make that choice for him- or herself. Varsity sports can impact performance opportunities due to season conflicts, but many theatre majors have been involved in sports throughout their years at Brown. One was even captain of the men's baseball team.

What are some of your alumni up to? Do you have an active alumni network?

There are Brown alums everywhere in the business, and they are a generous and welcoming lot with active organizations in major theatrical and film/television centers. Kate Burton, John Krasinski, Laura Linney, Masi Oka, and JoBeth Williams are just a few of our television and film notables. Kate Burton, Scott Shepherd (GATZ), and John Lloyd Young light up New York stages. There were three Brown alums in the New York productions of *Bloody, Bloody Andrew Jackson*. Playwrights Adam Bock, Stephen Karam, Peter Nachtrieb, and many others are at the vanguard of new American playwrights. Musical theatre writers like Duncan Shiek and David Yazbek follow in the footsteps of earlier Brown greats such as Burt Shevelove and Alfred Uhry. Todd Haynes, Simon Kinberg, and Tom Rothman are film industry notables. Brown/Trinity grads are at the helms of major American regional theatres, including Peter Dubois at Boston's Huntington and Kevin Moriarty at the Dallas Theatre Centre.

Give Me the Technical Info

What is the portfolio/interview process for a technical theatre student?

As in all areas of specialty, the technical/design student must be accepted at Brown, after which he or she will meet with advisors and begin to work out a plan. There is so much theatre going on all over campus that talented technical and design students are always in demand.

What do you expect to see on a technical theatre resume?

Everything and nothing. Some of our very best designers have found their passion here at Brown under the tutelage of our exceptional design/tech staff.

I'm interested in lighting, sound design, and stage management. What major should I go for? Can I minor?

You can major in theatre arts and choose to focus in one or more of these areas. We don't have a minor, but you can double-concentrate or simply take the courses you're interested in.

Does your school specialize in any division of technical theatre?

We have excellent instruction and mentoring in scenic design, costume design, lighting design, sound design, and stage management, along with many, many production opportunities to practice your chosen craft.

Give Me Some Insight

What do you look for in a potential student?

Passion, enthusiasm, sense of humor, brilliance, common sense, kindness, and a sincere interest in other people and ideas, plus the ability to create and sustain a life outside of the theatre. "You have a life, and theatre is a part of it."

Give Me the Lowdown

Brown faculty and staff believe deeply in the value of a liberal arts approach to the study of theatre. Our students are "the happiest in the country" for a very good reason: Brown is a place of limitless opportunity where every curiosity can be satisfied. Theatre students are invariably treated with respect. They have a major say in virtually everything that shapes our programs. We offer a wonderful education in theatre history and performance studies, as well as excellent instruction in the various arts and crafts of the theatre.

Many of our graduates have gone on to found important theatre companies in New York and elsewhere. Our alumni return to campus with great regularity to share their expertise with our current students. Successful alums and other theatre and film people send their children to Brown because of the individualized attention every student receives, and these parents are generous in offering their time for workshops and master classes.

We have a highly successful summer theatre company that develops three new plays each year, written by Brown alums and other unaffiliated playwrights, who bring their talents and expertise to campus to share with our apprentices and precollege TheatreBridge students. In the 2009–2010 season, new plays that were originally developed in the summer at Brown were named the #1 and #2 most frequently produced plays in American professional theatres by *American Theatre* magazine. (They were *Boom* by Peter Nachtrieb and *Speech & Debate* by Stephen Karam.)

Theatre is "the whole university in one course," and we at Brown believe that work in the theatre—with its expansive exploration of communication and motivational skills, text and verse analysis, design and writing skills, physical and verbal agility, and historical and literary contexts—prepares our students to be successful at many other professions as well. Brown alums have successfully chosen medicine, law, teaching, science, and diplomacy, and most will attest that the years they spent studying the theatre arts are what sets them apart from others in their chosen field. Most of all, of course, we encourage our students to grow into self-sufficient, self-confident, entrepreneurial artists, who are prepared to create their own work when jobs may be scarce and find their own joy in a life of creative fulfillment.

California State University, Fullerton

Fullerton, California

www.fullerton.edu

Contributor: **Jim Taulli, Associate Dean, College of the Arts**

Give Me the Facts

Population of College:
36,000

Conservatory or Liberal Arts:
Both

Degrees Offered:
* BFA in musical theatre, acting
* BA in general theatre studies, specialized theatre studies, playwriting, design and technical production, directing
* MFA in acting, directing, design

Population of Department(s):
Approximately 600 majors

Theatre Scholarships Available:
We have no scholarships for incoming students but do have many for continuing students that have specific criteria.

Is an audition required to declare theatre as a major? For BFA?
Yes

How many students audition versus how many get accepted each year?
About 150

Do you make cuts after freshman year and subsequent semesters?
Not after the freshman year, but we do in the middle and at the end of the sophomore year.

Can I minor in theatre/musical theatre?
No

Give Me the Scoop

Would I get a showcase at the end of senior year?
Yes, both BFA programs do showcases at the end of the senior year—musical theatre in New York and acting in LA.

Are showcases successful?
Yes

Will I be able to audition/perform as a freshman?
Not in the first semester but all semesters after that.

If there is a graduate program, will I get the same performance opportunities as an undergraduate?
Absolutely

What ways can I be involved with the department aside from performing?
There are crew assignments, clubs, play readings, one acts, and so on.

Say I get a BA rather than a BFA. Will I actually get to perform?
All majors in the department are permitted to audition for the season of plays. However, preference is given to those students in the BFA and MFA programs. That said, many of our BA students are cast each semester.

I love to sing, but I don't consider myself a dancer. Can I still seek a degree in musical theatre at your school?
No. CSUF is a triple-threat program. Our training puts equal emphasis on singing, dancing, and acting.

I want to get a BFA in acting, but I also love to sing. Can BFA/BA acting students take voice lessons with top voice faculty?
No, only musical theatre students receive private voice lessons. This is because of the cost of the lessons. However, the musical theatre area can recommend private teachers that students can hire.

Do you discourage or encourage students to audition for theatre outside of the department during the academic year?
If the student is in either of the professional training programs, the student must request permission from the acting/directing faculty before he or she auditions for anything outside of the department.

Does your school regularly work in conjunction with any regional theatres?
Yes

What do students typically do during the summers? Do you actively promote participation in summer theatre auditions?
We have several companies (including cruise lines) that audition our students on our campus.

How many musicals versus straight plays do you do in a season?
Two musicals and six plays in our main season; two musicals and six plays in our off-campus venue

What are some of your alumni up to? Do you have an active alumni network?
Yes, theatre students are working in all capacities of theatre. Last year we had five students on Broadway and eight students in national and international tours. Our students are seen in television and film on a regular basis.

Give Me the Technical Info

What is the portfolio/interview process for a technical theatre student?
Each semester, both graduates and undergrads present their work to the design faculty for review.

What do you expect to see on a technical theatre resume?
No resume is expected at the undergraduate level.

I'm interested in lighting, sound design, and stage management. What major should I go for? Can I minor?
Mostly our students specialize in two design/tech fields. There are no minors in the theatre program.

Give Me Some Insight

What do you look for in a potential student?
Talent, drive, passion, and a relentless work ethic

What are some of the auditors' pet peeves?
Students being unprepared. Also, students who have been miscoached.

After I audition, is there a good way to follow up?
All students are notified of the outcome within a week of the audition, but a pleasant email is always OK.

If there were one thing you never wanted to see in an audition again, what would it be?
Indicative, over-the-top, look-at-me choices.

What's the best advice you can give me regarding auditioning for your school?
A good audition is akin to an opening night performance. Material that is well chosen that shows both vocal ability and solid acting choices with a relaxed joy of performing.

Give Me the Lowdown

Please visit www.fullerton.edu/arts/theatredance/index.htm.

Carnegie Mellon University, School of Drama

Pittsburgh, PA

www.cmu.edu

Contributor: **Alison Popivchak, Administrative Associate, School of Drama**

Give Me the Facts

Population of College:
300 Drama School undergrad and grad students

Conservatory or Liberal Arts:
Conservatory

Degrees Offered:
- BFA in drama with options in acting/music theatre, design, directing, dramaturgy, production technology, management
- MFA in costume production, design, directing, dramatic writing, production technology, management

Population of Department(s):
All numbers are approximate (undergrads):
26 acting/MT students, 12–16 design students, 12–16 production technology and management students, 5–10 dramaturgy students, 5 directing students

Degree Requirements (hours):
See curriculums at www.drama.cmu.edu.

Theatre Scholarships Available:
Very few

Popular/Unique/Specialized Classes That You Offer:
We have many unique and popular classes. See curriculums at www.drama.cmu.edu.

Is an audition required to declare theatre as a major? For BFA?
Yes

How many students audition versus how many get accepted each year?
We audition approximately between 1,200–1,300 students for the acting/MT option. We accept approximately 26 students.

Do you make cuts after freshman year and subsequent semesters?
No

Can I minor in theatre/musical theatre?
No

Give Me the Scoop

Would I get a showcase at the end of senior year?
Yes. All actors/MTs travel to New York City and LA for our showcase presentation. The majority of graduating students find representation with an agent or manager or both.

Will I be able to audition/perform as a freshman?
Our freshmen and sophomores are "performing" in all classes. They have end-of-semester projects, which are shared with faculty and students. All students in all years are welcome to perform in "Playground" and "dance light." As a conservatory acting-training program, we do not have our students formally perform before an outside audience until their junior year. All students are encouraged to perform during the summer breaks.

If there is a graduate program, will I get the same performance opportunities as an undergraduate?
We have no graduate acting program.

What ways can I be involved with the department aside from performing?
All freshmen and sophomores are required to participate in production crew for two to three weeks each semester. This is a "run crew" that works on lights, costumes, and so on. Many of our students are in the work–study program. Some students join fraternities and sororities. As a major university, there are numerous university organizations that our students may participate in.

Say I get a BA rather than a BFA. Will I actually get to perform?
Students in the School of Drama only receive a BFA and will perform—a lot. You will be cast formally in at least one major production each semester in your junior and senior years.

I love to sing, but I don't consider myself a dancer. Can I still seek a degree in musical theatre at your school?
We do not give a degree in music theatre, despite the fact that we have a very strong music theatre option. All students in our school receive a BFA in drama.

  We have two options under the umbrella of "acting": acting and music theatre. The students in the acting option are required to take two years of dance: a year of ballet and a year of jazz.

I want to get a BFA in acting, but I also love to sing. Can BFA/BA acting students take voice lessons with top voice faculty?
Yes, absolutely. The students in the acting option have the opportunity to take two years of singing class with a teacher who teaches singing in the MT option. Acting students may also study singing privately with a member of the MT faculty. Actors can take music skills classes, which are offered to the music theatre students, with the permission of the MT faculty.

Do you discourage or encourage students to audition for theatre outside of the department during the academic year?

We discourage freshmen, sophomores, and juniors from audition for outside work during the academic year. Seniors are allowed to accept outside work during the school year with permission of the acting/MT faculty.

Does your school work regularly in conjunction with any regional theatres?

Yes

What do students typically do during the summers? Do you actively promote participation in summer theatre auditions?

Yes. We encourage students to peruse acting work during the summer. We often have theatre companies, whose work we admire, come in to audition our students during the school year.

How many musicals versus straight plays do you do in a season?

This depends on the particular class and season, but usually one major main-stage musical and at least one or two musicals in the studio theatre. Cabarets are performed several times each semester (perhaps four cabarets in a year) and other musical events are held as well.

What are some of your alumni up to? Do you have an active alumni network?

We have very well-known actors and music theatre actors who continue to make their mark in the professions. As the oldest conservatory training program within a university in the United States, the School of Drama has had the privilege of training the next generation of innovators and leaders in the theatre, film, television, and diverse performing arts industries for nearly one hundred years.

Give Me the Technical Info

What is the portfolio/interview process for a technical theatre student?

Applicants to the School of Drama Production Technology and Management Option should already have practical experience in theatre, as well as some background in mathematics and physics, organization and management, or both. Applicants must demonstrate basic proficiency in project planning and execution by submitting a portfolio for review. See www.drama.cmu .edu/148.

Portfolio Review Guidelines:

Provide 15 examples of work including:

* Evidence of your thought process for technical or management solutions
* Drafting, drawing, or CAD
* Paperwork developed for schedules, reports, budgets, estimates, and so on

* Photos of work, both finished and in process (not all samples have to pertain directly to theatre)
* Include a resume and/or curriculum vitae

The portfolio review will also include a short interview, where the faculty will get a sense of your drive, aptitude for production technology and management, and potential to learn and develop in this rigorous program.

Provide two letters of recommendation from sources capable of describing your work and evaluating your professional promise.

I'm interested in lighting, sound design, and stage management. What major should I go for? Can I minor?
School of Drama Design and Production Technology and Management students take classes together for the first three semesters. After three semesters, students then choose to focus on particular design areas, such as lighting and sound design, or focus on production or management areas. A minor is possible for design or production technology and management.

Give Me Some Insight

What do you look for in a potential student?
* Well-prepared audition pieces
* An actor who will be open to our training and has warmth, spontaneity, humor, and is flexible
* An actor who can find a physical and emotional connection to the material he or she is working on
* Individuality, personal charm, and creativity
* An actor who is kind and generous and enjoys the process of collaboration with other actors, directors, designers, and production students
* An actor who has sensitivity about the world around him or her and is interested in making positive changes through his or her work

What are some of the auditors' pet peeves?
Not being well prepared with their monologue or bringing a negative attitude into the room (however, this is very rare)

After I audition, is there a good way to follow up?
Check with the admissions office and make sure all your forms and transcripts are properly submitted.

What's the best advice you can give me regarding auditioning for your school?
Be well prepared. Use the audition experience to learn more about yourself. Be yourself and trust yourself and your inner resources. Have fun.

DePaul University

Chicago, Illinois

www.depaul.edu

Contributor: **Melissa Tropp, Admissions Assistant, The Theatre School**

Give Me the Facts

Population of College:
Approximately 25,000 over two campuses

Conservatory or Liberal Arts:
Conservatory

Degrees Offered:
* BFA in acting, costume design, costume technology, dramaturgy/ criticism, lighting design, playwriting, scenic design, sound design, stage management, theatre arts, theatre management, theatre technology
* MFA in acting, directing, arts leadership

Population of Department(s):
340 students: 50% performance, 25% theatre studies, 25% design and tech

Theatre Scholarships Available:
Entering first-year BFA and MFA students are automatically considered for talent scholarships. Returning students become eligible for merit awards each year.

Popular/Unique/Specialized Classes that You Offer:
Each major's curriculum is highly specialized and uniquely tailored as a professional training program for that major. It is more structured than flexible, but there are some electives that change from year to year.

Is an audition required to declare theatre as a major? For BFA?
The BFA and MFA acting programs require an in-person audition for consideration. All other majors require an interview or portfolio review.

How many students audition versus how many get accepted each year?
This varies quite a bit between the 15 majors we offer. Overall, we have about a 15% admission rate.

Do you make cuts after freshman year and subsequent semesters?
All majors have an invitation-to-return policy where students are evaluated by their faculty and invited to return the next year.

The BFA acting program is divided into two phases: the probationary phase (first year) and production phase (second, third, and fourth years). First-year acting students must receive an invitation to return into the production phase of the program. The first year of the acting program has a capacity of 42 students. At the end of the first year, all of the first-year students who wish to remain in the program (we typically lose a handful of students voluntarily) are evaluated, and 26 of them receive an invitation to return into the production phase. Students not invited to return that are in otherwise good academic standing can transfer into another college at DePaul University. A transfer into another Theatre School BFA major may also be possible through consultation with an advisor.

There is no further mandatory reduction after the first year, and no other majors have any form of cut or attrition.

Can I minor in theatre/musical theatre?

There is a theatre studies minor available to DePaul students in other colleges. This includes classwork only and no production work. There is no musical theatre major or minor.

Give Me the Scoop

Would I get a showcase at the end of senior year?

All graduating BFA and MFA actors participate in the Graduate Showcase. Our showcase happens in New York City, Chicago, and LA, and is presented to industry professionals in all three of those major markets, along with a networking reception afterward. Other majors are invited to participate in any or all of the showcases in those cities. Many students receive meetings with agents or callbacks to audition for local work while they are still in the showcase city.

Will I be able to audition/perform as a freshman?

First-year BFA acting students act in class every day, but not in productions. Instead, those students get to work in other aspects of a production (crew, makeup, PR/publicity, and so on). Starting in the first quarter of second year, BFA acting majors have guaranteed casting each quarter.

If there is a graduate program, will I get the same performance opportunities as an undergraduate?

Yes, all BFA and MFA acting majors receive equal and guaranteed performance opportunities.

What ways can I be involved with the department aside from performing?

Involvement in any aspect of production is limited to full-time theatre majors. Students can work part-time in the scene shop, administrative or admissions theatre offices, or as assistants to faculty members.

Say I get a BA rather than a BFA. Will I actually get to perform?

We do not offer a BA program.

I want to get a BFA in acting, but I also love to sing. Can BFA/BA acting students take voice lessons with top voice faculty?

BFA students can take private voice lessons from faculty or seek opportunities at DePaul's School of Music.

Do you discourage or encourage students to audition for theatre outside of the department during the academic year?

Acting majors are not allowed to audition outside of school during the year. Honestly, they don't have time anyway; they are all already in rehearsals or in production in our own season.

Does your school regularly work in conjunction with any regional theatres?

While we have informal relationships with dozens of the theatres in the Chicago theatre community, there is no one theatre with which we have an established formal connection.

What do students typically do during the summers? Do you actively promote participation in summer theatre auditions?

There is no typical way to spend your summer: some students stay in Chicago to audition, some go home and work summer jobs, some look for study abroad or internship opportunities. We consider summer to be students' own time and do not pressure them to participate in theatre if they would like a break.

How many musicals versus straight plays do you do in a season?

We do about 40 productions each year, and many of these will have elements of music and dance. We produce a full mainstage musical every other year.

What are some of your alumni up to? Do you have an active alumni network?

We issue a monthly publication on our website called Theatre School News. This is generally 20–25 pages of what our alumni are working on, along with what major they were and when they graduated: http://theatreschool.depaul.edu/theatre_school_news.php.

Give Me the Technical Info

What is the portfolio/interview process for a technical theatre student?

Applicant must apply and provide all supplemental materials as well as schedule an interview slot though our website. For more information, students should refer to the "how to apply" checklist for their major of choice on our website.

What do you expect to see on a technical theatre resume?

This would vary between all the design and tech majors we offer. We're just hoping to see enough experience to demonstrate a basic understanding of the kind of work associated with the program.

I'm interested in lighting, sound design, and stage management. What major should I go for? Can I minor?

You should go for our lighting design, sound design, or stage management majors. We offer seven different specific majors in the design and technical areas of theatre, so it's a good idea to look at them all carefully and select the one you really want. We offer a minor in theatre studies that includes a few classes in design for nonmajors, but there is no production work attached.

Give Me Some Insight

What do you look for in a potential student?

Quite simply, we are looking for fit. Students who are creative, open, and eager to work generally do very well.

After I audition, is there a good way to follow up?

There's not really any need to follow up, unless we are still missing some of your application materials. You should always feel welcome to contact us if you have any questions, however.

What's the best advice you can give me regarding auditioning for your school?

Breathe. We want you to do well, so take the time you need to get the job done. Keep communication open—if something does not make sense, please ask. And most important: Have fun. Our audition process is set up to give you a chance to work and play. You should try to get to know us just as much as we're trying to get to know you.

Give Me the Lowdown

Acclaimed as "a legendary training ground" (*Chicago Tribune*), The Theatre School was founded as the Goodman School of Drama in 1925 and joined DePaul University in 1978. A fully accredited school within a major urban university, The Theatre School is the Midwest's oldest theatre conservatory and is renowned as one of the top professional theatre training programs in the United States.

Undergraduate Program

The current enrollment numbers approximately 330 students from around the United States and several other countries. The faculty–student ratio of 1:6 allows for the continuous interaction and supervision essential for professional theatre training. A majority of the faculty and staff maintain their connections and professional work in all aspects of Chicago's renowned and thriving theatre industry. This distinguished professional faculty emphasizes not only the theory but also the practice of theatre.

As part of this intensive "learning by doing" philosophy, The Theatre School presents more than 40 productions each season in a variety of venues. These include The Theatre School Showcase, a four-play series of contemporary and classic plays, and Chicago Playworks for Families and Young Audiences, a three-play children's theatre series, presented at the historic Merle Reskin Theatre (formerly the Blackstone), a Broadway-style 1,325-seat house located in Chicago's downtown theatre district.

The Theatre School's undergraduate program is a highly specialized conservatory offering 12 bachelors of fine arts (BFA) programs in all aspects of the theatre. Each of our 12 BFA majors is a four-year professional training program designed to provide our students with not only the skills but also the experience necessary to prepare them for their career.

Individual attention: We have strict capacities for each of our programs, which are designed to provide each student with personalized instruction and ample production opportunities for practical experience.

Highly structured: Each of our 12 majors has a four-year progression-based curriculum, with each quarter building on the previous quarter and each year building on the previous year. Responsibilities and expectations of our students increase each year both in the classroom and in production.

Learning by doing: Learning does not stop in the classroom. Each year The Theatre School produces more than 40 productions of varying shapes and sizes to give our students ample opportunity to synthesize what they are learning in the classroom. Outside of the director of each of these productions, who is a member of the faculty, a guest artist, or a graduate directing student, every other person involved in the production is a student doing what he or she is here to study. Students in some majors are also placed in professional internships as a bridge to their chosen career field.

Working professionals: Our students learn from people who know what it is like to work in business—because they do. The Theatre School has 28 full-time, tenure-track faculty who are all accomplished theatre professionals and continue their professional work while teaching our students. We also employ more than 50 adjunct, or part-time, faculty who are hired right out of the Chicago theatre community for their individual expertise. Being a professional training program, it is important to us that our faculty has a finger on the pulse of what is happening in the profession and bring that into the classroom.

Elon University

Elon, North Carolina

www.elon.edu

Contributors: **Fredrick Rubeck, Department Chair, Performing Arts**
Kimberly Rippy, Program Assistant and Auditions Coordinator

Give Me the Facts

Population of College:
5,000 undergraduates

Conservatory or Liberal Arts:
Blend of conservatory-style training within a liberal arts-based institution

Degrees Offered:
* BFA in acting, dance, music theatre
* BA in theatrical design and production, theatre studies

Population of Department(s):
Total of 240 majors among all five different degree programs

Theatre Scholarships Available:
Talent-based scholarships of varying amounts available in all areas. Work–study also available.

Popular/Unique/Specialized Classes That You Offer:
We offer a broad range of styles and skills classes. Our senior seminar is a year-long course specifically designed to aid in the transition from college to the business. We have travel courses in New York City, LA, and Italy. The university also specializes in broad study courses in many different locations.

Is an audition required to declare theatre as a major? For BFA?
The BFA degrees require an audition. The design and production program requires an interview/portfolio showing. The BA in theatre studies is an open-enrollment program.

How many students audition versus how many get accepted each year?
We audition/interview approximately 700 prospective students each year. We accept 16 into each BFA program each year.

Do you make cuts after freshman year and subsequent semesters?
We do *not* have a cut system.

Can I minor in theatre/musical theatre?
We offer minors in theatre arts and in dance. There is no minor in music theatre.

Give Me the Scoop

Would I get a showcase at the end of senior year?
We bring a wide array and number of industry professionals to our campus rather than traveling to the city for this function.

Will I be able to audition/perform as a freshman?
Yes, all majors are required to audition for the productions. Casting is open. A few special productions are specifically intended for first-year students.

What ways can I be involved with the department aside from performing?
We have student organizations in performing arts, student directed/choreographed works, a student-led improv group, work–study positions in all areas, and open crew assignments on every production.

Say I get a BA rather than a BFA. Will I actually get to perform?
This depends on the quality of your audition for each show and how well suited you are for the production. It also depends a lot on your own personal drive and determination to succeed. You will be competing with approximately 140 BFA majors who are intensely training for the profession.

I love to sing, but I don't consider myself a dancer. Can I still seek a degree in musical theatre at your school?
We evaluate students on a combination of singing, acting, and dance. We expect students will have high scores in at least two of the areas and show potential and willingness to work in all three areas. The music theatre degree requires courses in all three areas.

I want to get a BFA in acting, but I also love to sing. Can BFA/BA acting students take voice lessons with top voice faculty?
Yes.

Do you discourage or encourage students to audition for theatre outside of the department during the academic year?
We allow this so long as they have first met all department obligations and as long as the production would not necessitate their missing classes, rehearsals, or performances. The department must come first.

Does your school regularly work in conjunction with any regional theatres?
We do not currently have a formal relationship with a regional theatre, but our alumni regularly work in the regional markets all over the country.

What do students typically do during the summers? Do you actively promote participation in summer theatre auditions?
We *actively* promote the practice of working professionally in the summers. We coach/assist with audition preparation. Each year, over 50% of our majors work professionally in the summer.

How many musicals versus straight plays do you do in a season?

The department produces three comedy/dramas, two major musicals, and one studio musical each year. We produce three dance concerts annually. We also mount two music theatre revues and a wide variety of student-produced works, including plays, musicals, and dance concerts.

What are some of your alumni up to? Do you have an active alumni network?

We have a very active alumni network on both coasts and a growing group of alumni in Chicago. Thanks to the Internet, all of these groups interact and provide support for one another quite easily. We have alumni on Broadway, off-Broadway, in New York City dance companies, in regional theatre and dance companies, on national tours, on cruise lines, in film, in series television, and in the commercial markets, both national and regional.

Give Me the Technical Info

What is the portfolio/interview process for a technical theatre student?

Students bring in examples of their work (this can be in a variety of forms—digital, paper, web, and so on). Faculty will view and discuss the work with the candidate but also discuss their goals for college and beyond.

What do you expect to see on a technical theatre resume?

We simply want to see a record/listing of the relevant work the student has done up to that date. This might include non-theatre work that demonstrates skills related to design and production.

I'm interested in lighting, sound design, and stage management. What major should I go for? Can I minor?

We offer a degree in theatrical design and production. Students select a focus by selecting electives in their desired area. Or a student can keep a broad focus by taking a variety of classes. We encourage students to explore various areas to gain a fuller understanding and sensitivity.

Give Me Some Insight

What do you look for in a potential student?

Drive, passion, potential, and flexibility/willingness. We also seek good, nice people who will get along well with each other and be positive energies within the department.

What are some of the auditors' pet peeves?

There are none. We just want to see great work, no matter what kind of material. But please do follow directions.

After I audition, is there a good way to follow up?

One can certainly write or email simple thank-you messages. Please do not ask for feedback; we audition too many people to provide that service. Otherwise, wait patiently for the stated decision date and only contact us if you have not heard by that time.

What's one of the best auditions you have ever seen?

Each person is so different that I would not want anyone to presume there is one "perfect" way to audition. Be yourself, prepare well, do material you love, and follow the instructions. This is a "mini performance" you love to perform, right? Love the audition.

What's the best advice you can give me regarding auditioning for your school?

Follow instructions and ask questions that you need to ask, but don't overdo it. Choose material you love, do it very well (get good coaching). Be flexible. Be honest. Be nice to everyone you encounter in the audition process. Be nice to yourself. Remember that we really, genuinely want you to succeed and be one of the people we choose. We sincerely desire that with each audition.

Give Me the Lowdown

We offer a unique blend of conservatory-style training in a liberal arts environment. We train you in the art and business of "show business." Our faculty are experienced, working professionals who bring a wealth of real-world expertise to the classroom. Our productions are top-notch professional shows with fully realized production elements.

Emerson College

Boston, Massachusetts

www.emerson.edu

Contributor: **Eric Weiss, Performing Arts Admissions Coordinator**

Give Me the Facts

Population of College:
3,400 undergrads, 800 grads

Conservatory or Liberal Arts:
A hybrid; "the nation's premiere institution in higher education devoted to communication and the arts in a liberal arts context."

Degrees Offered:
- BFA in acting, musical theatre, design/technology, stage and production management
- BA in theatre studies, theatre education (both available with concentration in acting)
- MA in theatre education

Population of Department(s):
Approximately 500 undergrads and 75 grads

Theatre Scholarships Available:
Emerson Stage Awards are given to students accepted to Performing Arts and are determined by artistic merit. For students entering the college in 2010, the amount of the Emerson Stage Awards were $14,000 annually.

Popular/Unique/Specialized Classes That You Offer:
Stage Combat, Playing the Self, The Art of Comedy, Solo Performance, Makeup Effects for Film and Television, Directing the Musical, Playwriting for and with Youth, Drama as Education, Action Theatre, Theatre for Young Audiences, Design Research, Theatre into Film, Ensemble, Design Essentials, African-American Theatre and Culture, Autocad, Topics in Design Presentation, Principles of Dramaturgy, Stage Management III, and Musical Theatre Styles I & II

Is an audition required to declare theatre as a major? For BFA?
An audition is required for applications to any performance major, BFA or BA. BA theatre studies and BA theatre education (without the acting concentration) require an additional essay.

How many students audition versus how many get accepted each year?
* BFA acting: approximately 450 auditions, approximately 23 freshmen
* BFA musical theatre: approximately 750 auditions, approximately 23 freshmen
* BA theatre studies and education (combined): approximately 375 auditions, approximately 30 freshmen

Do you make cuts after freshman year and subsequent semesters?
We have a re-audition process at the end of sophomore year for students in the BFA acting and musical theatre programs. We don't favor the word "cut" because students that do not continue in the BFA performance programs are directed into the BA theatre studies acting program.

Can I minor in theatre/musical theatre?
No, but you can minor in dance, performance studies, or music appreciation.

Give Me the Scoop

Would I get a showcase at the end of senior year?
We offer showcases for BFA acting and BFA musical theatre, and a portfolio showcase for BFA design/technology. Other majors offer differing types of professional development.

Will I be able to audition/perform as a freshman?
Freshmen do not perform in mainstage (Emerson Stage) productions but are allowed to participate in incredibly productive student organizations, student films, classroom projects for directing classes, and so on.

If there is a graduate program, will I get the same performance opportunities as an undergraduate?
Although our graduate students participate in Emerson Stage and can audition for productions, the graduate program is an MA in theatre education—not a performance-training program—so there is typically not competition between graduates and undergraduates.

What ways can I be involved with the department aside from performing?
Students do the bulk of the practical work for Emerson Stage productions—performing, designing, stage managing, technical work, run crews, dramaturgy, and so on. Outside of Emerson Stage, there is an extremely active student life with many opportunities to explore your interests—Musical Theatre Society, Shakespeare Society, various comedy troupes, the Evvy's, directing projects connected to classes, students films, and so on.

Say I get a BA rather than a BFA. Will I actually get to perform?
Yes, casting for Emerson Stage shows is blind to major within performing arts.

I love to sing, but I don't consider myself a dancer. Can I still seek a degree in musical theatre at your school?

Yes, we'll train you.

I want to get a BFA in acting, but I also love to sing. Can BFA/BA acting students take voice lessons with top voice faculty?

Yes, private voice is required for musical theatre majors and available to the entire college regardless of major with the same restrictions of adding any elective class—instructor has the space in his or her schedule, it fits in the student's schedule, and so on.

Do you discourage or encourage students to audition for theatre outside of the department during the academic year?

In coordination with their faculty advisors, students are encouraged to be productive on and off campus but to be responsible with their time so as not to hinder their studies.

Does your school regularly work in conjunction with any regional theatres?

ArtsEmerson, although it is not a regional theatre. It is not uncommon for regional theatres to contact us with opportunities for our students.

What do students typically do during the summers? Do you actively promote participation in summer theatre auditions?

We encourage and prepare our students to be productive during the summer, whether it is working in the theatre or seeking internships or other opportunities.

How many musicals versus straight plays do you do in a season?

Emerson Stage typically produces two musicals, one Theatre for Young Audiences piece, one evening of student-choreographed dance, one original student-written work culled from a playwriting competition, and three straight plays that round out the yearly eight-production season. Some of our more established student organizations also produce eight productions a season. There is a lot of variety.

What are some of your alumni up to? Do you have an active alumni network?

Our alumni are working in every aspect of film, television, and theatre from Hollywood to Broadway and everything in between. They are teachers, designers, directors, producers, technicians, actors, solo performers, performance artists, playwrights, stage managers, and on and on and on. They work in our industry; they find and forge the connections between our industry and others. They go on to graduate school. They start their own companies. They create their own work. They are active, productive, and engaged.

Give Me the Technical Info

What is the portfolio/interview process for a technical theatre student?
Students wishing to major in design technology or stage and production management will interview with faculty who will discuss their portfolio and resume with them.

What do you expect to see on a technical theatre resume?
We expect to see evidence of experience in theatre and an interest in art.

I'm interested in lighting, sound design, and stage management. What major should I go for? Can I minor?
We do not offer minors in theatre. We offer a lighting concentration within design technology and courses in sound design. We offer a degree in stage and production management.

Give Me Some Insight

What do you look for in a potential student?
Passion, creativity, potential, self-motivation, strong work ethic, an interest in collaboration, and a willingness to learn

What are some of the auditors' pet peeves?
Lack of preparation

After I audition, is there a good way to follow up?
Although we don't give feedback on auditions or interviews outside of an admission response, we are always open to questions; email is preferred.

What's one of the best auditions you have ever seen?
We've seen so many, it is hard to say, but there is no replacing honesty, simplicity, and connection. It is always a joy to watch an actor make a discovery.

If there were one thing you never wanted to see in an audition again, what would it be?
Attitude problems

What's the best advice you can give me regarding auditioning for your school?
Be yourself. Allow us to see who you are through the choice and execution of your material. Breathe.

Give Me the Lowdown

Emerson College is a unique place. It resides comfortably between a liberal arts college and a conservatory. Students here find the connections between their academic classes and the intense focus of their major, joining ideas and professions in creative ways. Our Performing Arts students build their lives in the theatre and use the arts as an orienting principle for viewing everything that they do.

It is an incredibly exciting and productive environment. Between Emerson Stage, ArtsEmerson, and dozens of highly organized student groups, there is an overabundance of opportunity to see and do and create. And all of this is framed in a world-class city with a blooming theatre community.

Our campus boasts five mainstage theatres: the brand new Paramount Center housing the Paramount Theatre and the Paramount Black Box, the 10-year-old Tufte Performance and Production Center housing the Semel and Greene theatres, and the completely restored Majestic Theatre. But these spaces are not the strength of the school—the strength of the school is the people. From our industry professional faculty and staff to our passionate students, our training and community foster the growth of professional, industry-leading artists.

Florida State University

Tallahassee, Florida

www.fsu.edu

Contributor: **Kate Gelabert, Head, BFA Music Theatre**

Give Me the Facts

Population of College:
31,005 undergraduates

Conservatory or Liberal Arts:
Liberal arts

Degrees Offered:
School of Theatre:
* BFA in music theatre (BM in music theatre, College of Music joint program), acting
* BA in theatre
* MFA in directing, acting (Asolo Conservatory, Sarasota, Florida)
* MA and PhD in theatre

School of Dance:
* BFA
* MFA
* MA in Studio and Dance-Related Studies, American Dance Studies

Population of Department(s):
Music Theatre Program currently has 33 students, both BFA and BM

Theatre Scholarships Available:
Yes, approximately 22 various scholarships. Amount varies from year to year.

Is an audition required to declare theatre as a major? For BFA?
For the BA, no. For the BFA, yes.

How many students audition versus how many get accepted each year?
The 2010 MT auditions saw 205 students (168 BFA, 37 BM), with an acceptance of 19 BFA and 4 BM.

Do you make cuts after freshman year and subsequent semesters?
We do not have a cut system. However, students may be dismissed for academic reasons or not making adequate progress as demonstrated in their yearly juries.

Can I minor in theatre/musical theatre?
No

Give Me the Scoop

Would I get a showcase at the end of senior year?
Yes, if you are in good standing

Are showcases successful?
Very

Will I be able to audition/perform as a freshman?
Yes

If there is a graduate program, will I get the same performance opportunities as an undergraduate?
We do not have an MT graduate program.

What ways can I be involved with the department aside from performing?
BFA students must take tech classes, so they will be working on the other side of performance as well. We have work–study opportunities as well as campus organizations.

Say I get a BA rather than a BFA. Will I actually get to perform?
Possibly

I love to sing, but I don't consider myself a dancer. Can I still seek a degree in musical theatre at your school?
Our ideal is the triple-threat potential, but we look at the potential in two of the three areas as well.

I want to get a BFA in acting, but I also love to sing. Can BFA/BA acting students take voice lessons with top voice faculty?
Acting students have had the opportunity to study with MT voice faculty. It isn't always a sure thing depending on the number of majors the voice faculty must accommodate. However, there are voice graduate students well qualified to teach.

Do you discourage or encourage students to audition for theatre outside of the department during the academic year?
Students must request our approval in order to audition and perform in outside activities. This is purely for the protection of the students. Most of us know the community well enough that we can assess the quality of the past work and decide if the experience would be beneficial or not.

Does your school regularly work in conjunction with any regional theatres?
We have the MFA Acting Conservatory in Sarasota that works with the Asolo Theatre.

What do students typically do during the summers? Do you actively promote participation in summer theatre auditions?
We strongly encourage students to attend regional auditions for summer employment after their freshman year. A great majority does work professionally.

How many musicals versus straight plays do you do in a season?
We do two musicals, one fundraiser concert version of a show, and various cabarets and recitals.

What are some of your alumni up to? Do you have an active alumni network?
Our alumni network is extremely strong, especially in New York City. At our annual New York City and LA showcases, we all get together and there are alums from 20 years ago hanging out with recent grads. Our grads are working all over the country, on Broadway, off-Broadway, regional theatre, television, and films. We had our first Tony Award nominee this year: Montego Glover, star of *Memphis*, nominated for best actress.

Give Me Some Insight

What do you look for in a potential student?
An honest audition . . . one that tells us something about the person as well as something about his or her current level of talent. We want to know the student is trainable and that by the end of four years, we feel comfortable sending him or her out.

What are some of the auditors' pet peeves?
Unfortunate habits displayed by students due to bad coaching.

After I audition, is there a good way to follow up?
We let students know at the very end of our audition process by letter or phone call. Some students have written thank-you notes after their audition.

What's the best advice you can give me regarding auditioning for your school?
Be honest and be yourself. Choose material that suits you. Sing songs that you love singing and are comfortable with. Don't go for the big-money note if you can't nail it. Treat your songs like a monologue. Choose a monologue you can relate to and is as age appropriate as possible. Don't do a classical piece just to impress . . . make sure you understand the language and style. Dance honestly . . . don't "cheese" it up. If you are limited in your dance training, do the very best you can and try to enjoy the experience.

Give Me the Lowdown

The BFA in music theatre at Florida State University is a prestigious and competitive degree that began in 1981 and has evolved into one of the top training programs in the nation. Run jointly with the College of Music and with the cooperation of the School of Dance, it is designed to provide comprehensive training in singing, dancing, and acting, thoroughly preparing students to work professionally upon graduation. During the four-year program, students receive a liberal studies education as well as concentrated training in performance (private voice lessons, acting, movement, and dance), theory and sightsinging, music and theatre history, repertory, and technical theatre. In addition to the specialized coursework, students have a variety of performance opportunities that include the musical productions as well as straight plays, films, operas, vocal ensembles, recitals, and dance concerts. Upon graduation, the Music Theatre Senior Showcase in New York City is an opportunity for graduating seniors to perform for an invited audience of agents, casting directors, master teachers, and alumni. Graduates have signed with agents, gained employment, and made important connections in the business as a result of this experience. The FSU New York City alumni network is over 20 years strong and ever embracing of the newly graduated seniors. Montego Glover (BFA 1996) is the current star of the Broadway hit musical, *Memphis*, and was a Tony Award nominee for best actress for 2010. Kevin Covert (BFA 1992) is also in the show but will be leaving in January to begin rehearsals for the revival of *How to Succeed in Business Without Really Trying*, starring Daniel Radcliffe. Jessica Patty (BFA 2001) will be leaving the Broadway show, *The Addams Family*, to begin work on a brand new Broadway-bound show. Those are just a few of our alum working in the New York City area. There are many more, all over the nation, working in all aspects of the industry.

Fordham University

New York, New York

www.fordham.edu

Contributor: Eva Patton, Theatre Program Manager

Give Me the Facts

Population of College:
The Lincoln Center Campus, where the theatre program is located, has 1,739 students enrolled.

Conservatory or Liberal Arts:
Liberal arts (BA)

Degrees Offered:
- BA with concentrations in performance, design and production, playwriting, and directing

Population of Department(s):
118 majors

Theatre Scholarships Available:
Theatre scholarships are pending; at least one full-ride talent scholarship should be in place by fall 2011/spring 2012.

Popular/Unique/Specialized Classes That You Offer:
All freshmen theatre majors—performers, directors, playwrights, and designers—begin with Collaboration, a year-long course where they create work together. This creates the foundation for the four years of working together as a company and valuing each other as theatre artists.

Is an audition required to declare theatre as a major? For BFA?
Yes. We have a BA preprofessional program.

How many students audition versus how many get accepted each year?
Approximately 650 students audition and interview for approximately 20–25 performance spots, 1–2 directing spots, 1–2 playwriting spots, and 8–12 design and production and stage management spots.

Do you make cuts after freshman year and subsequent semesters?
No

Can I minor in theatre/musical theatre?
We have a theatre minor. No audition required.

Give Me the Scoop

Would I get a showcase at the end of senior year?
Yes. They are very well attended by industry professionals and New York City theatres.

Will I be able to audition/perform as a freshman?
Yes

If there is a graduate program, will I get the same performance opportunities as an undergraduate?
We are an undergraduate program, but we have an MFA in playwriting program beginning in 2011–2012, in association with the off-Broadway theatre Primary Stages. Undergraduate actors will get to perform in both BA and MFA playwriting students' work.

What ways can I be involved with the department aside from performing?
Fordham has excellent relationships with the New York City professional theatre world. All Fordham theatre faculty are working professionals, and we introduce our students to the professional world through internships and by inviting guest artists to Fordham, as well as guest directors and designers, and so on. There are amazing opportunities in and outside of school. Also, every student has a lab contract working in an area of the theatre—costume shop, box office, electrics. It's part of our goal in making sure everyone is getting a well-rounded education. Even if a student is a performance major and wants to design costumes, we encourage that. We believe in experiential learning, and we produce 20 studio and four mainstage shows every year, so there are numerous opportunities in many areas.

Say I get a BA rather than a BFA. Will I actually get to perform?
Yes. Four mainstage shows and 20 studios.

I want to get a BFA in acting, but I also love to sing. Can BFA/BA acting students take voice lessons with top voice faculty?
We have a musical theatre course taught by Alison Fraser, two-time Tony Award nominee, and the class is open to all performance students.

Do you discourage or encourage students to audition for theatre outside of the department during the academic year?
We discourage it, but we don't strictly forbid it. We encourage students to focus on school. So many outside professionals from New York City are *here* that to go outside almost doesn't make sense. With that said, a few students in the past have taken a term off to do a play or a movie and came back.

Does your school regularly work in conjunction with any regional theatres?
We've coproduced with several off-Broadway theatres, including The Public and Primary Stages, and we will continue to do this in the future. Also, we've

workshopped original plays for several theatres such as 13P and Clubbed Thumb.

What do students typically do during the summers? Do you actively promote participation in summer theatre auditions?
Many students work at summer theatres, some do internships in New York City, some produce in the New York Fringe Festival (this past year, Fordham students won best director and best actor), and some study abroad (Fordham offers several programs).

How many musicals versus straight plays do you do in a season?
Even though we're not a musical theatre program, we do a musical every few years, and a lot of our plays have music in them.

What are some of your alumni up to? Do you have an active alumni network?
We have an amazing alumni network. The Fordham Alumni Theatre Company was founded four years ago, and every summer, we produce a piece produced, directed, acted, and written by Fordham theatre alumni.
Please see www.fordham.edu/academics/programs_at_fordham_/theatre_department/alumni for an extensive list of all that our alumni are doing.

Give Me the Technical Info

What is the portfolio/interview process for a technical theatre student?
A portfolio with representations of your work (this may include design work, art work, sketches, slides, photos, and so on)

What do you expect to see on a technical theatre resume?
The resume is not as important to us as the work and the potential for growth.

I'm interested in lighting, sound design, and stage management. What major should I go for? Can I minor?
Design and production. You can work in some of these areas and take some classes as a theatre minor.

Give Me Some Insight

What do you look for in a potential student?
Imagination, intellectual curiosity, the ability to deeply question, a collaborative and generous spirit, professionalism, and someone who takes great joy in the work and process, someone with immense innate talent with great potential for growth who we think has the potential to become a working actor. And yes, we can get a real sense of that in just three minutes.

What are some of the auditors' pet peeves?
Not reading the website carefully and coming in unprepared, going over the monologue time limit, and lack of familiarity with our program and school (lack of research).

After I audition, is there a good way to follow up?
A follow-up isn't necessary, but if students want to write a thank-you note or send a thank-you email to faculty who auditioned them, that's always a kind gesture.

What's one of the best auditions you have ever seen?
Oddly enough, when a student was so nervous he couldn't remember his piece. A faculty member gave him some adjustments, and he was able to take the direction and turn on a dime—again, and again, and again with just a single line of text. He exhibited great joy in the process and transformed before our very eyes. He was playful, fearless (by taking a risk with each new direction), and in those moments we saw that he had the talent—very raw talent—but a great imagination and physical instrument. We accepted him.

If there were one thing you never wanted to see in an audition again, what would it be?
Neil LaBute monologues (the faculty is unanimous on this after this year)

What's the best advice you can give me regarding auditioning for your school?
Show us what you love.

Give Me the Lowdown

Fordham is the best of everything. It's a BA program with an intensive preprofessional track in the heart of New York City—minutes from the Broadway and off-Broadway theatres. We are fervent believers in the BA. We believe in the educated theatre artist and think it's essential to study philosophy, psychology, science, and history—all of the liberal arts in order to question deeply. We are a small program (118 majors), and we are on a first-name basis with all of our students. We are an experiential program. We believe in learning by doing, and we produce four mainstage and 20 studio shows per year so that students are continually practicing their craft. Please visit our website for more information at www.fordham.edu/theatre.

Hofstra University

Hempstead, New York

www.hofstra.edu

Contributor: **David M. Henderson, Chair, Department of Drama and Dance**

Give Me the Facts

Population of College:
12,000 undergrad and grad

Conservatory or Liberal Arts:
Liberal arts

Degrees Offered:
  * BA in drama
  * BFA in theater arts in performance, theater arts in production

Population of Department(s):
About 200

Theatre Scholarships Available:
  * Rosenthal Scholarship for excellence in comedy: $10,000 to a senior
  * Kearsley Scholarship for an incoming stage manager or production major: approximately $3,000
  * Barnes Scholarship for contributions to the department: approximately $3,000
  * Ackerman Scholarship for a senior performance major: approximately $1,000
  * Liebson Scholarship for commitment to the department: approximately $1,500

Popular/Unique/Specialized Classes That You Offer:
  * Popular: Many including Fundamentals of Acting, Stage Makeup, Theater Design Fundamentals
  * Unique: Many including Movement for the Actor 2—Mask, Movement for the Actor 4—Stage Combat, Speech for the Actor (1–4)
  * Specialized: Performing the Plays of Shakespeare, Stage Management, Scenic Art for the Theater

Is an audition required to declare theatre as a major?
BA, no. BFA, yes.

How many students audition versus how many get accepted each year?
20–30 audition, maximum of 16 accepted (for performance)

Do you make cuts after freshman year and subsequent semesters?
No

Can I minor in theatre/musical theatre?
Yes, both

Give Me the Scoop

Would I get a showcase at the end of senior year?
New York City senior showcase for BFA performance and production majors. Student performance has been well received by New York agents, casting directors, and managers.

Will I be able to audition/perform as a freshman?
Yes

What ways can I be involved with the department aside from performing?
* Multiple production opportunities in department shows
* Two students clubs: Spectrum for Drama and Masquerade Musical Theater
* Many department student aide and work–study positions in the scene shop, costume shop, and main office

Say I get a BA rather than a BFA. Will I actually get to perform?
Yes. Auditions are open to BA and BFA majors, and casting is done without preference to BFA. Many BA students are cast every semester.

I love to sing, but I don't consider myself a dancer. Can I still seek a degree in musical theatre at your school?
We have a musical theater minor. A vocal audition is required, but no dance audition is required.

I want to get a BFA in acting, but I also love to sing. Can BFA/BA acting students take voice lessons with top voice faculty?
Yes, private lessons are available through the music department and within the musical theater minor.

Do you discourage or encourage students to audition for theatre outside of the department during the academic year?
It is discouraged during the academic year due to the rigorous production schedule within the department. BFA students are required to get permission for any non-mainstage productions they wish to audition for.

Does your school regularly work in conjunction with any regional theatres?
No

What do students typically do during the summers? Do you actively promote participation in summer theatre auditions?
Yes, we push our students to audition or send production resumes to regional and New York–area theaters. Our large alumni network in New York City helps students find summer work and work after graduation.

How many musicals versus straight plays do you do in a season?
In our mainstage season, one musical and five straight plays (including two Shakespeare). Student clubs produce two more musicals every year.

What are some of your alumni up to? Do you have an active alumni network?
We have a very active alumni network in New York City for recent grads, helping with entry-level jobs, auditioning, and even housing. Many Hofstra Department of Drama graduates have gone on to success in film, television, Broadway, and off-Broadway productions. They have been recognized with Tony, Oscar, and Emmy Awards and nominations.

Give Me the Technical Info

What is the portfolio/interview process for a technical theatre student?
None for incoming students. A portfolio of classwork and outside work is required for the BFA interview process in the sophomore year.

What do you expect to see on a technical theatre resume?
A strong interest and work on at least two productions or a strong art background

I'm interested in lighting, sound design, and stage management. What major should I go for? Can I minor?
You should major in BFA in production. We have a minor in drama that can be focused on production.

Give Me Some Insight

What do you look for in a potential student?
Someone who is hardworking, ready to learn, and considerate to his or her fellow students. A professional, business-like attitude. An actor who knows his or her strengths and is ready to improve on his or her weaknesses.

What are some of the auditors' pet peeves?
Students who arrive late—always come *early* and be ready to go when your name is called.

Students who dress in a sloppy or unprofessional way. *Always* dress as you would for a job interview.

Students who want to chat or waste time in the audition room. Remember, the auditors are seeing a lot of people in one day, and there's tremendous pressure to stay on schedule and be fair to everyone. If the auditors ask you a question or invite you to ask questions, be concise and to the point.

Don't use any kind of dialect or affected voice. The point of the audition is to show off who *you* are. Pick audition material that is appropriate to your age and type.

After I audition, is there a good way to follow up?

It's a good idea to send a thank-you note or email. That gives the auditors the opportunity to reply at their convenience. Avoid phone calls unless there is a specific question you need answered (besides "How was my audition"?).

What's one of the best auditions you have ever seen?

I always enjoy auditions in which the students have chosen simple, straightforward material that lets them find a simple emotional connection. If singing is involved, I like students to stay well within their range and do songs that work well within the confines of the audition room. That means you probably want to avoid "blockbuster" material that demands more space and range than you can muster in a two-minute audition.

If there were one thing you never wanted to see in an audition again, what would it be?

Any song from a modern sung-through musical. It's just impossible to get to the point of a 12-minute song in one minute; choose something with a simple melody that stays well within your range and that you can make sense of in six or eight bars.

What's the best advice you can give me regarding auditioning for your school?

We're not just choosing good actors; we're looking for people to be part of our community for the next four years. Be the best colleague you can be. We know you're 17 or 18 years old. Don't try to act like you have more knowledge or experience than you have. And finally:

Be yourself.

Have fun.

Dress comfortably but nicely.

And stand up straight.

Give Me the Lowdown

Each year the department produces three plays, one musical, and the nationally renowned Shakespeare Festival, the second oldest in the country (produced annually for more than 60 years), which includes both a Shakespeare play and a touring production of a Shakespeare adaptation.

In addition, students in the department produce numerous honors thesis and senior practicum and directing class productions, with a host of other opportunities to get involved.

In spring 2008, the Drama Department opened a new Black Box Theatre. The space is a 50-foot, clear square with 20 feet of vertical clearance. It has user-specified seating for 140 to 200 patrons and a technical mezzanine level surrounding the entire space. The lighting system is replete with a state-of-the-art aircraft cable tension grid, primarily ETC fixtures, and an ETC Emphasis console running on EDMX. Sound is controlled either via a manual 32-channel Yamaha mixing console or via SFX or Cue-Lab playback systems.

The John Cranford Adams Playhouse is a 1,105-seat proscenium theater with orchestra and balcony. The facility includes a 42-foot-wide by 35-foot-deep stage, an all-ETC Source-4 lighting inventory, computer-controlled synchronized rigging system, in-house scene shop, LightViper optical audio routing system, in-auditorium audio mixing position, and an extensive and expandable video network.

If you have dreamed about exploring your passion for theater in college, then Hofstra University is the place for you. Whether you are interested in drama, musical theater, directing, designing, or any other aspect of theater, we provide a whole range of exciting opportunities to develop your craft onstage and behind the scenes.

Illinois Wesleyan University

Bloomington, Illinois

www.iwu.edu

Contributor: **Bernadette Brennan, Theatre Recruitment Coordinator**

Give Me the Facts

Population of College:
2,100 full-time students

Conservatory or Liberal Arts:
Liberal arts

Degrees Offered:
* BFA in design and technology, acting, music theatre
* BA in theatre arts

Population of Department(s):
103 majors, 12 minors

Theatre Scholarships Available:
$8,000–$12,000 in talent awards

Is an audition required to declare theatre as a major? For BFA?
All BFAs require an audition or portfolio interview. BAs require an interview only.

How many students audition versus how many get accepted each year?
About 20% accepted for music theatre, approximately 50% or greater acceptance for all other degrees.

Do you make cuts after freshman year and subsequent semesters?
No

Can I minor in theatre/musical theatre?
Minors are offered in theatre arts, theatre dance, and arts management.

Give Me the Scoop

Would I get a showcase at the end of senior year?
No. At this time, our student success rate for securing a contract prior to graduation have not made it necessary for us to hold a showcase. However, we are now starting to bring individual producers to our campus for class workshops so our students are being seen in a more personal setting.

Will I be able to audition/perform as a freshman?
Not in the mainstage or laboratory seasons, but students may participate in the Phoenix Theatre and are required to be performers for student directors enrolled in directing classes.

What ways can I be involved with the department aside from performing?
Work-study, crew and design work, house management/usher, masquers (Theatre Student Organization)

Say I get a BA rather than a BFA. Will I actually get to perform?
Yes

I love to sing, but I don't consider myself a dancer. Can I still seek a degree in musical theatre at your school?
Dance classes are a required part of the degree. Students will participate in a dance audition in order to gain entry. The dance audition is taught like a class and is for our faculty to assess ability for prospective students to be trainable in the four years they are here. We often take students into the program with little to no training in dance.

I want to get a BFA in acting, but I also love to sing. Can BFA/BA acting students take voice lessons with top voice faculty?
Yes, private lessons can be arranged with voice instructors in the School of Music, as available.

Do you discourage or encourage students to audition for theatre outside of the department during the academic year?
Students may pursue summer work only, unless express permission has been granted by the School of Theatre Arts faculty for casting opportunities during the academic year. We rely on our students in order to cast our own productions. It is extremely rare for a student to participate in an off-campus production.

Does your school regularly work in conjunction with any regional theatres?
No, but we have a vast alumni network that often aids in our students finding internships around the country and overseas.

What do students typically do during the summers? Do you actively promote participation in summer theatre auditions?
Yes. We prescreen in the early fall in order to meet the summer stock audition requirements and to have adequate preparation time for our students.

How many musicals versus straight plays do you do in a season?
Two-year rotation:
Fall play, fall musical; spring play, spring musical (mainstage) with two to three additional lab productions
Fall play, fall musical; spring play, spring faculty-choreographed dance concert (mainstage) with two to three additional lab productions
Phoenix Theatre sees an additional 12–30 productions per year

What are some of your alumni up to? Do you have an active alumni network?
Our alumni network is extremely active, with groups who meet regularly in major theatre cities and alumni visiting our campus almost every week of the year. Please see our website and Facebook page for their bios. Our alumni are involved in everything from Broadway to film/television to Disney to producing/directing.

Give Me the Technical Info

What is the portfolio/interview process for a technical theatre student?
A half-hour interview with our full-time faculty in the design/tech area

What do you expect to see on a technical theatre resume?
Any and all relevant crew and production/design experience. Any additional awards, education, or related experiences such as working in summer camps or building houses.

I'm interested in lighting, sound design, and stage management. What major should I go for? Can I minor?
A student who wishes to double major or has time to pursue acting/directing should consider the BA. All other students would be best served by the BFA in design/tech.

Give Me Some Insight

What do you look for in a potential student?
Will they fit in well with the students and faculty who are here? Will they be able to succeed in their academic classes outside of theatre arts? Are they open to receiving training and direction from the faculty?

What are some of the auditors' pet peeves?
A "know-it-all" attitude where a student is resistant to direction from the faculty. We also offer an "overdone" list for music theatre—audition pieces we'd rather not see again.

After I audition, is there a good way to follow up?
We occasionally receive thank-you cards, but mostly we are contacting prospective students after they have received acceptance letters to gauge their level of interest. We are not allowed to tell students how they did in the audition. They may only be notified officially by the admissions office.

What's the best advice you can give me regarding auditioning for your school?
Find audition materials that speak to who you are as a person and best show off your abilities. Be open to re-direction from the faculty and be yourself.

Indiana University

Bloomington, Indiana

www.indiana.edu

Contributor: George Pinney, Professor and Head of Musical Theatre, Department of Theatre and Drama

Give Me the Facts

Population of College:
42,000

Conservatory or Liberal Arts:
Liberal arts

Degrees Offered:
* BA in theatre and drama, stage management
* BFA in musical theatre
* MA
* MFA in acting, directing, lighting design, scenic design, costume design, theatre technology, playwriting,
* PhD

Population of Department(s):
* 200 undergraduates
* 80 graduates
* 45 BFA musical theatre

Theatre Scholarships Available:
A number of scholarships are awarded every year to established students in the department.

Popular/Unique/Specialized Classes That You Offer:
The American Songbook, American Musical Theatre Dance Styles, Musical Theatre Workshop, playwriting, stage combat, and circus techniques to name just a few. The department offers a full array of classes from broad based to the particular.

Is an audition required to declare theatre as a major? For BFA?
An audition is required for admittance into the BFA in musical theatre. Auditioning is not required for the BA. See www.indiana.edu/~thtr/academics/BFA_application.shtml.

How many students audition versus how many get accepted each year?
For the BFA, generally over 200 students apply to the program. A screening process is in place that includes a short performance submitted by DVD or VHS tape. From those applications, 90 students are invited to campus to audition. We accept 10–12 students each year.

Do you make cuts after freshman year and subsequent semesters?
No, we do not. It is our intention to see a student through the four years.

Can I minor in theatre/musical theatre?
A student may minor in theatre and drama but not in musical theatre.

Give Me the Scoop

Would I get a showcase at the end of senior year?
The department sponsors a yearly musical theatre showcase in New York every spring for agents, casting directors, and other professionals in the business.

Will I be able to audition/perform as a freshman?
Yes, all students are allowed to audition for all departmental productions.

If there is a graduate program, will I get the same performance opportunities as an undergraduate?
Yes, based on audition. The graduate acting studio is capped at nine students. The mainstage season offers well over 120 roles each season in both plays and musicals.

What ways can I be involved with the department aside from performing?
University Players is a student-run organization that focuses on all aspects of theatre production, from acting to design to audience development. In addition, this student group sponsors other events to supplement the classroom experience. There are work–study opportunities as well as opportunities in design, construction, research, dramaturgy, and stage management. There are also a number of independent student projects and several professional/amateur theatre and dance venues in the city of Bloomington.

Say I get a BA rather than a BFA. Will I actually get to perform?
BAs are highly involved in the department and are taken very seriously.

I love to sing, but I don't consider myself a dancer. Can I still seek a degree in musical theatre at your school?
Yes, dance classes are a major part of the curriculum, but not every student is expected to become a Broadway dancer.

I want to get a BFA in acting, but I also love to sing. Can BFA/BA acting students take voice lessons with top voice faculty?
Students in the BFA program study voice under a major professor for the entirety of their residences as part of the BFA curriculum. BA students may study voice through the elective program in the Jacobs School of Music or privately.

Do you discourage or encourage students to audition for theatre outside of the department during the academic year?

Students may participate in any department or other productions, provided academic standards and departmental obligations are maintained.

Does your school regularly work in conjunction with any regional theatres?

We are in current collaboration with Bloomington Playwrights Project in producing a new musical. The production was entirely cast from Indiana University musical theatre students. In addition, students have participated in theatre with Cardinal Stage and Windfall Dancers in Bloomington, as well as the Indy Fringe, Phoenix Theatre, and Indiana Repertory Theatre in Indianapolis.

What do students typically do during the summers? Do you actively promote participation in summer theatre auditions?

Some students do stay for the summer to take classes and perform in summer theatre with the department. The Department of Theatre and Drama produces Indian Festival Theatre, a professional-based company with Equity hires and also offers Equity points toward membership. Students are encouraged not to stay every summer, however, in order to expand their theatre experiences and network beyond Bloomington while still a student.

How many musicals versus straight plays do you do in a season?

The department produces two musicals during the academic year—a large-scale production in the spring and a slightly smaller musical in the fall. There are usually six plays produced during the academic year as well. In the summer, there is a fully produced musical and new work produced under the umbrella of Premiere Musicals, developing musical theatre at Indiana University.

What are some of your alumni up to? Do you have an active alumni network?

We have a very active network of alumni, particularly in New York, Chicago, and on the road. This includes graduates and undergrads from the Department of Theatre and Drama as well as the Jacob's School of Music, the IU Ballet Theatre, and the Contemporary Dance Program. Collaboration on professional productions is frequent, often with alums that did not attend IU at the same time.

Give Me the Technical Info

What is the portfolio/interview process for a technical theatre student?

Because we offer a BA, any student in good academic standing can declare a theatre major and design/technology concentration. Entry into the "concentration" is purely by enrolling into the elective classes, and fulfillment is ensuring that they meet the listed requirements for the focus.

That said, we encourage students with design/technical experience in high school and with ambitions in these areas to introduce themselves to the appropriate faculty specialist. A resume stating the productions they have contributed to and their technical roles is helpful in focusing initial conversations. The design and technology faculty are committed to individually mentoring talented undergraduates in our area.

A freshman would major in theatre and drama and fulfill his or her University Division courses before entering then design and technology concentration. The T125 Introduction to Production (previously the Stagecraft course) would introduce them to the faculty, staff, and backstage technical theatre environment.

The design and technology concentration can be focused on lighting design, costume design, sound design, scenic design, theatre technology, and stage management.

I'm interested in lighting, sound design, and stage management. What major should I go for? Can I minor?
Our degree is a comprehensive theatre curriculum for all BA or BFA students. This includes all aspects of technical theatre. As the BFA in musical theatre is in the Department of Theatre and Drama, it would not be possible to get a minor in the same department as your major. However, some electives in tech theatre could be pursued during a BFA residency in accordance with the BFA curriculum.

Does your school specialize in any division of technical theatre?
The Department of Theatre and Drama offers a full complement of design/technical experiences and opportunities. The MFA level offers degrees in scenic design, costume design, lighting design, and technical theatre. All areas may be a focus of concentration on the undergraduate level.

Give Me Some Insight

What do you look for in a potential student?
The underlying factor is the potential for a professional career in theatre. There are many considerations in determining this: talent, high self-motivation, intelligence, determination, a strong and positive self-image, uniqueness, centered with a strong sense of humanity.

What are some of the auditors' pet peeves?
Being rude to the accompanist and others. Not being prepared. Music that is not accompanist-friendly (as in loose photocopies).

After I audition, is there a good way to follow up?
A short note highlighting a particular aspect of the audition is a simple and effective way to keep in communication.

What's one of the best auditions you have ever seen?

With a solid foundation in acting, the best audition is centered in the dramatic action and revelation of character revealed through song and dance.

If there were one thing you never wanted to see in an audition again, what would it be?

A negative attitude

What's the best advice you can give me regarding auditioning for your school?

Be yourself and be prepared.

Give Me the Lowdown

The BFA in musical theatre provides the rigorous curriculum needed to train students in acting, singing, and dancing. In addition to performance technique classes, students will participate in a rich core of theatre, music, and dance classes and professional classes in "careers in professional theatre," as well as enhanced master classes by visiting guest artists. Past artists have included Stephen Sondheim, Michael Feinstein, Martin Sheen, Nicole Parker, and Simon Callow, to name a few. Designed to bring out the best in an individual, the BFA in musical theatre was created within the context of a liberal arts education. Not only will a student receive superior training in performance technique, the student will be better prepared for life by fulfilling all of the general education requirements required by the College of Arts and Sciences. The program will be limited to only 10–14 admissions per year, providing enormous individual attention throughout the student's career at Indiana University. Tony Award–nominated and Emmy Award–winning choreographer George Pinney heads the program.

Ithaca College

Ithaca, New York

www.ithaca.edu

Contributor: **Linda Ellis, Administrative Assistant, Department of Theatre Arts**

Give Me the Facts

Population of College:
7,200 students

Conservatory or Liberal Arts:
Liberal arts

Degrees Offered:
* BFA in acting, musical theatre, theatrical production arts/design or technology
* BA in drama
* BS in theatre arts management

Population of Department(s):
350 students, 36 faculty and staff

Theatre Scholarships Available:
Endowed scholarships

Popular/Unique/Specialized Classes That You Offer:
Mask Workshop, Makeup, Rehearsal and Performance

Is an audition required to declare theatre as a major? For BFA?
BFA acting and BFA musical theatre require an audition. BFA theatrical production arts, BA in drama, and BS theatre arts management require an interview.

How many students audition versus how many get accepted each year?
Approximately 600 audition for musical theatre and approximately 350 for acting; 4% are accepted for musical theatre and 6% are accepted for acting.

Do you make cuts after freshman year and subsequent semesters?
No cuts. The department has a review process the first two years.

Can I minor in theatre/musical theatre?
No. The department only has a theatre minor and a dance minor.

Give Me the Scoop

Would I get a showcase at the end of senior year?
Yes, in New York City.

Will I be able to audition/perform as a freshman?
Yes

What ways can I be involved with the department aside from performing?
Crews, work–study, student-run performances, and student organizations

Say I get a BA rather than a BFA. Will I actually get to perform?
Some BA in drama students are cast in performances, but we give the majority of the opportunities to the BFA acting and BFA musical theatre students.

I love to sing, but I don't consider myself a dancer. Can I still seek a degree in musical theatre at your school?
Yes, the curriculum includes all the dance classes.

I want to get a BFA in acting, but I also love to sing. Can BFA/BA acting students take voice lessons with top voice faculty?
Yes, the professors in the School of Music sometimes take in additional students for voice lessons.

Do you discourage or encourage students to audition for theatre outside of the department during the academic year?
The student must have the permission of the department to perform outside of the department. They have many commitments during the academic year on campus.

What do students typically do during the summers? Do you actively promote participation in summer theatre auditions?
The students are on their own to choose how they spend their summers.

How many musicals versus straight plays do you do in a season?
Always two musicals: one in the fall and one opera in the spring. Any choice of other plays or musicals could be chosen for the academic year.

What are some of your alumni up to? Do you have an active alumni network?
The alumni are very active with the department. There are highlights on the website of the alums at www.Ithaca.edu/theatre.

Give Me Some Insight

What do you look for in a potential student?
Academics, talent, raw talent, experienced talent, all-round student

What are some of the auditors' pet peeves?
Do not do Shakespeare work as a monologue. Shakespeare monologues are very difficult for a 17 year old.

After I audition, is there a good way to follow up?
The students may call the office to see what stage the decisions are in or contact the admissions department via email.

What's the best advice you can give me regarding auditioning for your school?
Do your homework on Ithaca College Department of Theatre Arts. Find out the dates for the auditions, interviews, and the admissions deadlines.

Marymount Manhattan College

New York, New York

www.mmm.edu

Contributor: **David Mold, Chair, Division of Fine and Performing Arts**

Give Me the Facts

Population of College:
1,650

Conservatory or Liberal Arts:
Liberal arts

Degrees Offered:
- BFA in acting
- BA in theatre arts with concentrations in design and technical production, directing, producing and management, theatre performance, theatre studies, writing for the stage
- Also offer minors in musical theatre and arts management

Population of Department(s):
Total theatre arts, 430: BFA (150), BA theatre arts (280), design and technical production (30), directing (30), producing and management (30), theatre performance (180), theatre studies (12), and writing for the stage (24), musical theatre minor (110). Many students have more than one concentration.

Theatre Scholarships Available:
Yes, ranging from $1,000 to $4,000 per year, based on the audition and/or interview.

Popular/Unique/Specialized Classes That You Offer:
Our concentration in directing is unique at the undergraduate level. Daily dance for musical theatre minors and private voice lessons with professional New York City vocal teachers. Beyond Naturalism, an acting course on experimental styles of acting. Solo Performance, how to create a one-person performance. Viewpoints. For our seniors, we offer a Business of Acting course, which includes seminars with headshot photographers, Actors Access/Breakdown Services, Actors Connection, Actors Equity, Screen Actors Guild, and alumni with Broadway, off-Broadway, regional theatre, and film and television credits.

Is an audition required to declare theatre as a major? For BFA?
Yes, for both BFA in acting and BA in theatre arts majors.

How many students audition versus how many get accepted each year?
We audition over 1,000 students annually. Of those admitted to the college based on academics, we make offers to about one in four that interview or

audition. We typically enroll a first-year class of 50 in the BFA in acting, 50 in the theatre performance concentration of the BA in theatre arts, and about 20 students in design, directing, producing and management, theatre studies, and writing for the stage.

Do you make cuts after freshman year and subsequent semesters?

We do not have a cut system, but in our BFA in acting major, we do have an evaluation process to be sure students are progressing properly for the classical acting training of the junior and senior year. If they are not, they can be asked to leave the BFA major but may be allowed to finish their degree in the BA in theatre arts major. Our process is not based on reducing to a specific number but based on how the student can best learn and grow as an actor.

Can I minor in theatre/musical theatre?

Not in performance. But one can pursue a minor in theatre that has an academic focus. To minor in musical theatre, a student must be a theatre major.

Give Me the Scoop

Would I get a showcase at the end of senior year?

You must audition to be in our senior showcase. Our students have been called in by casting directors, producers, and agents, and this has sometimes led to work for them.

Will I be able to audition/perform as a freshman?

Yes

What ways can I be involved with the department aside from performing?

We have numerous students' clubs that focus on theatre, work–study is available, and many students work for the theatre arts.

Say I get a BA rather than a BFA. Will I actually get to perform?

Yes. Our productions are available for both BA and BFA students to audition, and we do not privilege one program over another.

I love to sing, but I don't consider myself a dancer. Can I still seek a degree in musical theatre at your school?

Yes, we admit some students into our musical theatre minor with limited dance training, and they take four year of rigorous dance training with us.

I want to get a BFA in acting, but I also love to sing. Can BFA/BA acting students take voice lessons with top voice faculty?

Only if they are also in the musical theatre minor

Do you discourage or encourage students to audition for theatre outside of the department during the academic year?

You must get permission from faculty to pursue acting work outside of the college.

Does your school regularly work in conjunction with any regional theatres?
No

What do students typically do during the summers? Do you actively promote participation in summer theatre auditions?
Some work as actors; others stay in New York to pursue further training. We encourage students to pursue this.

How many musicals versus straight plays do you do in a season?
One musical is done on our main stage each year and three straight plays. We also produced 6–10 student-directed one-act plays each semester.

What are some of your alumni up to? Do you have an active alumni network?
We do have an active alumni network. Our alumni have appeared on Broadway in *The Lion King, Rent, Little Shop of Horrors, Aida, The Vertical Hour, The Lieutenant of Inishmore, Rock'n'Roll, Legally Blonde, Hairspray, Wicked, Mary Poppins, Tarzan, American Buffalo,* and *Spring Awakening;* at Lincoln Center; off-Broadway; in films such as *Sex and the City, Pride & Glory,* and *Get on the Bus;* and on television in *Law & Order, The Good Wife, ER, One Tree Hill, The Riches, The Fugitive Chronicles, Over There, 100 Centre Street,* and *Glee.*

Give Me the Technical Info

What is the portfolio/interview process for a technical theatre student?
Students present a portfolio and discuss the portfolio and their ideas about theatre.

What do you expect to see on a technical theatre resume?
Some minimum levels of experience, but we realize this may be limited in high school, so we use the resume and portfolio to have a discussion about the art of theatre.

I'm interested in lighting, sound design, and stage management. What major should I go for? Can I minor?
Our BA in theatre arts with a concentration in design and technical theatre

Give Me Some Insight

What do you look for in a potential student?
The ability to reveal something about themselves through the audition monologue. Some facility with language. A passion to express themselves. The ability to take direction.

What are some of the auditors' pet peeves?
Monologues that are just a recitation of words with no clear objective or action

After I audition, is there a good way to follow up?

We follow up with letters, emails, and phone calls to students we offer admission.

What's one of the best auditions you have ever seen?

A student that personally connected to the audition monologue, expressed a point of view about the human condition of that character, took time, used humor, and used language well.

If there were one thing you never wanted to see in an audition again, what would it be?

Anything from Christopher Durang. He is a wonderful playwright, but few 17 or 18 year olds know how to personalize the characters.

What's the best advice you can give me regarding auditioning for your school?

Come to have fun. Be relaxed and share with us who you are.

Give Me the Lowdown

The major difference between our BA in theatre arts and our BFA in acting is that the BA focuses on contemporary styles of acting and the BFA focuses on classical styles of acting. We do not believe one program is better than another, but we believe that some students learn and grow better in one program over the other. All of our faculty are working professionals who bring their current professional experiences back into the classroom to help educate our students. Our New York City location offers a unique opportunity to be exposed to many genres and styles of professional theatre from Broadway to gritty downtown experimental works. We maintain a small number (12–14 students) in each class, so students are presenting work in class every week and have a close mentoring relationship with faculty. Recently, John Guare, Craig Lucas, and Paul Scott Goodman all came to speak with our students when we were producing their plays and musicals. We have an ongoing relationship with the Broadway Speakers Bureau of the Broadway League, and Broadway professionals come to speak with our students every year.

Millikin University

Decatur, Illinois

www.millikin.edu

Contributors: **Laura Ledford, Chair, Department of Theatre and Dance; Mary Spencer, Assistant to the Chair**

Give Me the Facts

Population of College:
2,300 undergraduate, 40 graduate (MBA, nursing)

Conservatory or Liberal Arts:
Liberal arts

Degrees Offered:
* BA in theatre
* BFA in musical theatre, theatre (acting emphasis), theatre (design-tech emphasis), theatre (stage management emphasis), theatre (theatre administration emphasis)

Population of Department(s):
187 majors

Theatre Scholarships Available:
Yes (range $500–$3,000)

Popular/Unique/Specialized Classes That You Offer:
Stage Combat, Stage Dialects, Improv

The Art of Entrepreneurship: Pipe Dreams Studio Theatre—a student-run theatre company/business with curricular support in the School of Business and Millikin's Center for Entrepreneurship

The New Musicals Workshop—a development workshop where emergent composer/lyricist teams work with faculty and students on staged readings and performances or works in progress

Is an audition required to declare theatre as a major? For BFA?
None required for BA theatre, although an essay is required. Audition or interview required for BFA.

How many students audition versus how many get accepted each year?
161 performance auditions; 80 accepted for 2010 fall entry.

Do you make cuts after freshman year and subsequent semesters?
BFA "hurdles" are held for all new BFA students in all programs at the end of their first year. Faculty assess students' skills, proficiency, potential, and progress at the end of a year of training. Sometimes students are re-directed into

another major or are placed on probationary status, but we do not have a number or percentage we plan to "cut."

Can I minor in theatre/musical theatre?
Only a theatre minor and a dance minor are available.

Give Me the Scoop

Would I get a showcase at the end of senior year?
We have a different format than most university showcases. Students go to New York or Chicago toward the end of their last semester, where we have set up meetings, auditions, and workshops with casting directors, agents, and other professionals. This format allows students to meet, interact with, and perform for the industry professionals in a more informal/workshop setting. We have found this format to be substantially more valuable both educationally and professionally for our students entering these markets.

Will I be able to audition/perform as a freshman?
Yes, all majors are encouraged to audition. Performance majors are required to audition.

What ways can I be involved with the department aside from performing?
APO
Pipe Dreams Studio Theatre (student-run theatre company)
Internships in business management, production management, marketing, house management, various technical aspects of the productions
Student jobs in scene shop, costume shop, props shop, script library, theatre office

Say I get a BA rather than a BFA. Will I actually get to perform?
Yes

I love to sing, but I don't consider myself a dancer. Can I still seek a degree in musical theatre at your school?
Yes. At your audition, we are considering both proficiency and potential in all three areas (singing, dancing, and acting). Many students are accepted without having training in dance if their talent in the other areas is strong and we see potential for successful training in dance fundamentals.

I want to get a BFA, in acting but I also love to sing. Can BFA/BA acting students take voice lessons with top voice faculty?
Yes. Students can take class voice without extra charge or pay an additional fee for private lessons with the same voice faculty who teach the musical theatre and vocal performance majors.

Do you discourage or encourage students to audition for theatre outside of the department during the academic year?

As long as students are fulfilling the audition and casting requirements for the degree program they are in, they are free to audition wherever they like (although there are limited professional opportunities in Decatur).

Does your school regularly work in conjunction with any regional theatres?

Yes. Although we do not have formal agreements with the theatres, our students audition and are frequently cast in a nearby LORT summer stock company, and our students are often employed or serve as interns there and at other companies with whom we have positive relationships based on previous work with our faculty and alums.

What do students typically do during the summers? Do you actively promote participation in summer theatre auditions?

Students' typical summer activities are listed on our website. Yes, we actively promote participation in summer theatre auditions through weekly postings, SETC, Midwest Auditions, and so on.

How many musicals versus straight plays do you do in a season?

Two musicals and two to three straight plays (plus an opera and a dance concert).

What are some of your alumni up to? Do you have an active alumni network?

Yes, we do in New York, Chicago, and Minneapolis. See our website for more information.

Give Me the Technical Info

What is the portfolio/interview process for a technical theatre student?

The student needs to be accepted to the university before interviewing for the major. Once accepted, the student will schedule an appointment with the department. The student will meet with two design/tech faculty to discuss experiences, expectations of college, academics, and so on. The faculty will view the student's portfolio and ask questions about it.

What do you expect to see on a technical theatre resume?

List your past productions, your responsibility on those productions, and where they occurred. There should be at least three references that can speak about your work, such as theatre faculty, employers, and so on.

I'm interested in lighting, sound design, and stage management. What major should I go for? Can I minor?

We have a BFA theatre design/tech and BFA stage management. In the design/tech BFA, you can do both lighting and sound, and there will be the possibility of stage managing if you are keeping current with other work. In the BFA stage management program, you will get a lot of SM experience and would be able to have positions such as electrician and sound engineer, but most likely would not get a chance to design.

Give Me Some Insight

What do you look for in a potential student?

We want students who have a passion for learning about the world and about the art of the theatre, not just a love of performing or design. We look for strong academic skills; discipline; and an open, collaborative spirit.

What are some of the auditors' pet peeves?

Overcoached auditions and schmoozing

After I audition, is there a good way to follow up?

The best follow up is to pay the refundable advanced tuition deposit to hold your spot in the program and respond promptly to any communication from the university or us after the audition. Since we let students know on the day of their auditions which programs they are accepted into, there really isn't a need to follow up, although a note or an email giving us feedback on the audition experience is useful.

If there were one thing you never wanted to see in an audition again, what would it be?

A Puck monologue

What's the best advice you can give me regarding auditioning for your school?

Keep it simple, and make sure you are comfortably within the time limit. Now is not the time to show us your ability to play King Lear or sing Defying Gravity or do your Irish dialect; we need to see *you* in material that suits you, is well within your technical abilities, and that you connect to honestly. Please prepare, but not to the point that you cannot be flexible or that it goes on autopilot. Don't push. Be honest and show us who you are. We *want* you to succeed.

Give Me the Lowdown

Millikin is a place where you can learn your craft and get a great university education at the same time. We are focused on teaching, teaching, and more teaching. Our faculty are outstanding and well credentialed in their respective fields, but make no mistake: they are here for students. They didn't come to Decatur, Illinois, to advance their own professional careers.

We are focused on helping students discover their niche in the theatre and helping them design, on an individual basis and within industry standards, an education that helps them create their own unique path into the art and the profession. We welcome the students we think we can work with and help to realize their potential. We do not accept students based on what gaps we need to fill in the casting pool, the technical assignments, or even the degree programs.

Not only do our graduates work (just visit our website or follow the trade publications), but they work hard and well. Our graduates are prized in the industry for their preparation, skills, work ethic, and discipline. Our graduates frequently tell us that at any given audition or interview, they are told that they are in a different league than their competition in terms of their skills and professionalism. Our reputation is strong, and our students know this, so they are committed to maintaining the standards they have learned to aspire to and that the industry has come to expect in a Millikin graduate.

The learning goals of all our degree programs are collaboration, analysis, technique, professionalism, and a life of meaning and value. By keeping these goals front and center, we have established a departmental ethos of mutual support, respect for the work of all practitioners, the pursuit of excellence in craft and art, and the application of professional expectations within an educational context.

And yes, there are some *very* cool initiatives and opportunities we've been developing for our students. Check out the New Musicals Workshop and Pipe Dreams Studio Theatre on the Department of Theatre and Dance website, www.millikin.edu/theatre. Both of these initiatives have grown very quickly into nationally recognized and model programs. We frequently bring in guest artists like Kari Margolis and our own alums such as Tim Shew, Sierra Bogess, and Annie Wershing for workshops, as well as alums who have started their own companies in Chicago and Minneapolis. We are proud of their success, and in turn they are proud of the education and training they got at Millikin.

Montclair State University

Upper Montclair, New Jersey

www.montclair.edu

Contributors: **Kim Whittam, Adjunct Specialist, Theatre and Dance, with final review by Eric Diamond, Chair of Department**

Give Me the Facts

Population of College:
Approximately 18,000

Conservatory or Liberal Arts:
We operate as a conservatory program within a larger liberal arts community.

Degrees Offered:
- BFA in dance, musical theater, acting, production/design
- BA in dance education, theater studies
- MA program contains three concentrations: theater studies, production/stage management, and arts management

Population of Department(s):
Department of Theater and Dance: approximately 400

Theatre Scholarships Available:
There are scholarships available in the theater and dance programs, particularly for out-of-state and need-based students.

Popular/Unique/Specialized Classes That You Offer:
BA theater studies offers special courses in creativity and collaboration; dramaturgy and "danceaturgy" provide the study, history, and analysis of scripts and dances, and are very popular; the BFA acting program offers an Acting for Television class.

Is an audition required to declare theatre as a major? For BFA?
All of the programs in the Department of Theater and Dance require an audition or an interview. The audition criteria vary depending on the program.

How many students audition versus how many get accepted each year?
The BFA musical theater program accepts approximately 6%; BFA dance and BFA acting accept approximately 20%; BFA production/design, BA theater studies, and BA dance education accept approximately 50%.

Do you make cuts after freshman year and subsequent semesters?
All students must pass juries to proceed. Most do. Students are not required to re-audition once they are accepted into a program, but they have to maintain a minimum GPA and can be removed from a program due to poor academic achievement or lack of artistic growth.

Can I minor in theatre/musical theatre?
We offer a minor in dance, musical theater, and theater.

Give Me the Scoop

Would I get a showcase at the end of senior year?
We hold a senior showcase for BFA students in New York City in the spring of senior year. Many students receive offers from agents, casting directors, and managers; several students have recently been cast in Broadway shows, national tours, and regional productions.

Will I be able to audition/perform as a freshman?
Yes

If there is a graduate program, will I get the same performance opportunities as an undergraduate?
Students in all programs are welcome to attend auditions for any production.

What ways can I be involved with the department aside from performing?
We offer many work–study opportunities within the department. Students work in the costume and scene shops, in the administrative offices, and assisting faculty.

Say I get a BA rather than a BFA. Will I actually get to perform?
Our BA theater studies program emphasizes collaboratively created, ensemble-based theater education that culminates in a senior project created in collaboration with a professional theater artist and performed as a part of the department's production season. Additional performance opportunities include departmental productions and workshops, directing class scenes, and participation in play-reading series.

I love to sing, but I don't consider myself a dancer. Can I still seek a degree in musical theatre at your school?
Our BFA musical theater program fuses training in acting, dance, and music. All majors take classes in ballet, musical theater dance, tap, and jazz. Some previous dance training is recommended, although not required.

I want to get a BFA in acting, but I also love to sing. Can BFA/BA acting students take voice lessons with top voice faculty?
Yes, private lessons are available through the Cali School of Music's preparatory division.

Do you discourage or encourage students to audition for theatre outside of the department during the academic year?
We strongly encourage our students to audition for summer stock and summer intensives related to their respective major. Students who audition for and are cast in outside projects during the academic year are handled on a case-by-case basis.

Does your school regularly work in conjunction with any regional theatres?
We have a state-of-the-art professional theater on campus, where students are often given opportunities to work with professional artists. We also have ongoing relationships with several regional New York and New Jersey theaters.

How many musicals versus straight plays do you do in a season?
All BFA programs offer at least three fully mounted, mainstage productions per year in any of our six on-campus venues. They also participate in performance workshops, staged readings, operas, off-campus performances, and student-run productions.

What are some of your alumni up to? Do you have an active alumni network?
Our proximity to New York City and our nationally renowned faculty and guest artists provide graduating seniors with unprecedented opportunities to move directly into a professional career in the arts. Contemporary dance companies such as Urban Bush Women, Nikolais-Louis Dance Company, Pilobolus, and the Martha Graham Dance Company regularly employ our BFA dance alumni. They perform on Broadway, in music videos, and on television shows such as *Dancing with the Stars.* Our BFA musical theater and BFA acting alumni have performed nationally and internationally in venues including Broadway, off-Broadway, and regional theater. Our production/design alumni are working in all facets of production around the country as lighting, set and costume designers, makeup artists, technical directors, and stage managers. The BA theater studies alumni are currently working as professional actors, directors, producers, playwrights, and educators. BA dance education alumni teach in schools and dance studios or begin their own dance-related businesses.

Give Me the Technical Info

What is the portfolio/interview process for a technical theatre student?
Students participate in a portfolio review in which they are required to provide materials that best represent their area of interest and previous experience. They also participate in a one-on-one interview with faculty from the Department of Production/Design.

What do you expect to see on a Technical Theatre resume?
A history of participation in their field of study

I'm interested in lighting, sound design, and stage management. What major should I go for? Can I minor?
We offer three concentrations within the BFA production design program: The concentration in design includes the study of scenic design, costume design, lighting, and sound; the management concentration includes stage manage-

ment and production management; there is also a concentration in technical theater that encompasses costume, scenery, and lighting.

Give Me Some Insight

What do you look for in a potential student?
The faculty considers all facets of the potential student, including academic excellence and experience in his or her field of study.

What are some of the auditors' pet peeves?
A lack of previous formal training prior to auditions

After I audition, is there a good way to follow up?
Potential students are notified by admissions and/or program coordinators once their results have been determined. No follow up is necessary.

What's one of the best auditions you have ever seen?
We audition so many potential students each year and find that each audition is considered on an individual basis. The best auditions combine talent, originality, and the confidence and poise that come with preparation.

If there were one thing you never wanted to see in an audition again, what would it be?
Lack of preparation, lack of enthusiasm, a general carelessness in appearance and participation

What's the best advice you can give me regarding auditioning for your school?
Be as prepared as possible and try to enjoy the process.

Give Me the Lowdown

MSU provides exposure to the professional talent and arts activities found in New York City, which is only 12 miles away and accessible via our on-campus train terminal to Penn Station. Our outstanding facilities include the state-of-the-art 500-seat Kasser Theater, the 900-seat Memorial Auditorium, the 100-seat flexible Fox Studio, a 125-seat Dance Theater, and the 275-seat Lebhowitz Recital Hall. We provide students with a nationally renowned faculty and guest artists whose credits include film, opera, television, on and off Broadway, throughout the nation and abroad, who mentor our students in every way. *Forbes* magazine recently ranked MSU as the number one public institution in New Jersey, the third best in the state overall and among the top 15 best buys in the entire northeast. We are nationally accredited by the National Association of Schools of Theater (NAST), the National Association of Schools of Dance (NASD), and the National Association of Schools of Music (NASM).

New York University

New York, New York

www.nyu.edu

Contributors: **Scott Loane, Director of Student Services, Department of Drama; Gretchen Souerwine, Administrative Aide; Liz Bradley, Chair, Department of Drama (Give Me Some Insight and Give Me the Lowdown)**

Give Me the Facts

Population of College:
Over 40,000 (relatively even between undergraduate and graduate students)

Conservatory or Liberal Arts:
The Tisch School of the Arts at New York University combines conservatory training with a curriculum of equally intense liberal arts academics.

Degrees Offered:
* BFA in theater

Population of Department:
Approximately 1,400 students

Popular/Unique/Specialized Classes That You Offer:
http://drama.tisch.nyu.edu/page/home.html

Is there an audition required to declare theatre as a major? For BFA?
An artistic review, consisting of an audition/portfolio presentation and an interview, is required for admission to the department.

How many students audition versus how many get accepted each year?
Approximately 2,200 audition. The first-year class is in the upper 300s.

Do you make cuts after freshman year and subsequent semesters?
No

Can I minor in theatre/musical theatre?
We offer a minor in applied theatre, which requires four relevant theatre studies courses such as Community-Based Theatre, Theatre and Therapy, and Political Theatre, in addition to an applied theatre internship. No minor in musical theatre is offered.

Give Me the Scoop

Would I get a showcase at the end of senior year?
We take advantage of our New York City location to regularly expose our students to industry professionals who are in a position to give our graduates

work. Professionals teach our courses as well as direct and attend our productions. Additionally, we designate three of our annual StageWorks productions as "showcase" opportunities to which we invite casting directors, talent agents, and other decision makers to see our students and recent alumni work. We then facilitate communication between the professionals and any actor with whom they wish to follow up. While the emphasis is on connecting seniors and recent alumni, second- and third-year students are sometimes included in these showcase productions.

Will I be able to audition/perform as a freshman?
Freshmen do not perform in departmental productions or curricular studio shows during their first year; transfers may perform in departmental productions or studio shows during their second semester with their studio's permission. All students must be in good academic standing in order to take part in department-wide productions.

If there is a graduate program, will I get the same performance opportunities as an undergraduate?
The Graduate Acting Department at Tisch School of the Arts is a separate department from the Department of Drama. All of the performance opportunities in our department are for our students only.

In what ways can I be involved with the department aside from performing?
Students can volunteer to serve as crew on productions. There are also work–study opportunities available, mostly working in the production shops. We offer extracurricular workshops and seminars, called Drama Talks, which students can attend. We have a formal mentorship program that connects students with faculty members for in-depth discussions about mutual areas of interest.

Say I get a BA rather than a BFA. Will I actually get to perform?
The Drama Department only offers a BFA degree.

I love to sing, but I don't consider myself a dancer. Can I still seek a degree in musical theatre at your school?
All of our students, from musical theatre performers to stage managers, earn a degree in theatre. Within that degree, if qualified by audition, one can specialize in music theatre training, which certainly includes significant dance training. Nondancing actors can supplement their training with additional voice work and performance opportunities.

I want to get a BFA in acting, but I also love to sing. Can BFA/BA acting students take voice lessons with top voice faculty?
Yes

Can acting students audition for musicals? Can musical theatre students audition for straight plays?

All drama students are eligible to audition for all drama StageWorks productions. However, studio-related curricular projects are only open to students within that studio.

Do you discourage or encourage students to audition for theatre outside of their department during the academic year?

Our students quickly discover that they do not have time to keep up with the rigors of our program while auditioning for professional performance work.

Does your school regularly work in conjunction with any regional theatres?

We regularly work in conjunction with the many professional theatres in New York City.

What do students typically do during the summers? Do you actively promote participation in summer theatre auditions?

This varies tremendously with the interests of the students. Many take summer jobs. Many audition for productions. We encourage both. We also encourage rest.

How many musicals versus straight plays do you do in a season?

The Drama Department's 2010–2011 StageWorks season was comprised of five plays, one musical, and seven cabaret performances. Many more productions took place in the studios or were produced by students.

What are some of your alumni up to? Do you have an active alumni network?

Our alumni act, sing, direct, stage manage, design, and otherwise make art all over New York and around the world. Some become theatre teachers, some teach other subjects theatrically. Some go to law school and occasionally even medical school. For more specific information, check out our alumni website at http://alumni.tisch.nyu.edu/page/home.html. You can also learn more about our very active alumni network there.

Give Me the Technical Info

What is the portfolio/interview process for a Technical Theatre student?

The portfolio presentation will include a conversation about your interests, accomplishments, and ideas about your chosen area(s) of specialization. Prospective students are asked to bring a resume, written statement of purpose, recent photograph, and a portfolio of work (designs, drawings, photos, stage manager prompt books). Applicants are interviewed as part of the portfolio presentation discussion. A professional headshot is not necessary.

What do you expect to see on a technical theatre resume?

A production resume should include your career objective and shows (listed in reverse chronological order) in which you have participated and in what capacity. If you have special skills or have received any awards, those should be listed as well.

I'm interested in lighting, sound design, and stage management. What major should I go for? Can I minor?

Again, all students in our department work toward a BFA in theatre. Only an applied theatre minor is available from our department.

Give Me Some Insight

What do you look for in a potential student?

We look for a combination of aptitudes for professional training. Students interested in the world, who have a broader prospective of viewpoints and are interested in issues and complexities outside of themselves. We have a two-part adjudication, with certain academic standards that have to be satisfied and an artistic review that has to be successfully passed with a recommendation for placement. In both cases, we are looking for potential to improve the actor's instrument and to attain a high degree of mastery over it, and we are looking for a passion for ideas and interpretation. These are the qualities we are looking for throughout the adjudicative process.

What are some of the auditors' pet peeves?

Not having read the play from which the monologue is chosen and thus not being able to converse about the life of the character. Not doing a sufficient amount of research, generally—for instance, why Tisch is a fit for you specifically. We assume you're not coming to spend four years looking at the statue of liberty. Why NYU? Why New York?

After I audition, is there a good way to follow up?

Some students choose to send thank-you notes—this is never wrong, but it doesn't necessarily affect your application in any way (positively or negatively). However, as much as we are choosing you, you are choosing us, and it is certainly helpful for us to know you are still interested after the audition. If NYU remains a student's top choice, it's not a bad thing to send an email to let us know that.

What's one of the best auditions you have ever seen?

Each student's journey into the audition room needs to be independent. We want to see flexibility and openness—emotional/physical/intellectual. We want students who are willing to be spontaneous. Beware of over-coaching (or over-rehearsing). Students can literally get stuck, which makes it hard for them to experiment in the room. The adjudicators don't have time to unlock all of that. We're not expecting to see a huge degree of polish. We want to see how you take direction, how you respond to the unexpected; we want to see you, authentic and willing to be vulnerable.

If there were one thing you never wanted to see in an audition again, what would it be?

I mentioned over-coaching above; with it comes *over-selling.* We hate to see students who feel they have to push to the max and control every moment of the experience. We don't want to see anything forced. We don't want to see nervousness and desperation—these negative emotions get in everyone's way, most especially the student's.

What's the best advice you can give me regarding auditioning for your school?

See as much theatre as you possible can. Think about what pieces of theatre charge and energize you. Physically prepare: students who do yoga, fencing, or some form of relaxation have a physical availability that helps them in the audition room. What we're hoping to do is contribute stimuli, so it helps if you come in with flexibility and openness, physically and otherwise.

Give Me the Lowdown

We had an amazing session with Alan Rickman recently. He was extremely thoughtful about acting as a craft and the navigational challenges. Career Self-Management for artists in development. What skills they might be able to put in place, portability of skills. We're shifting into a more clearly sequenced program and starting it early. You will hear about this at orientation.

Northern Kentucky University

Highland Heights, Kentucky

www.nku.edu

Contributor: **Ken Jones, Lois and Richard Rosenthal Endowed Chair in Theatre**

Give Me the Facts

Population of College:
15,000

Conservatory or Liberal Arts:
Liberal arts

Degrees Offered:
* BA in theatre arts, theatre in world cultures
* BFA in acting, musical theatre, playwriting, dance, technology/design (costume, lighting, scenic), stage management, rock and roll/concert technology

Population of Department(s):
260 majors

Theatre Scholarships Available:
22 Theatre Scholarships (half in-state tuition), 11 Uptown Arts Scholarships ($2,000 per year), 1 Friends of Fine Arts (variable), and Conger Musical Theatre Scholarship ($500)

Popular/Unique/Specialized Classes That You Offer:
One-Person Show, Musical Cabaret, and Comedy Improvisation. Also, NKU offers an undergraduate BFA in playwriting degree and a brand new BFA in rock and roll/concert technology.

Is an audition required to declare theatre as a major? For BFA?
No audition is required for a BA, but audition/interview or portfolio is required for BFA.

How many students audition versus how many get accepted each year?
100 students audition for the BFA each year, and approximately 20 get accepted to BFA programs.

Do you make cuts after freshman year and subsequent semesters?
No mandatory cuts are made.

Can I minor in theatre/musical theatre?
A person can minor in theatre and focus their electives on musical theatre courses.

Give Me the Scoop

Would I get a showcase at the end of senior year?

We do not have a New York showcase; instead we bring Broadway and industry casting directors to campus for private senior BFA auditions each spring.

Will I be able to audition/perform as a freshman?

Yes

What ways can I be involved with the department aside from performing?

1. First-year show: full production for freshman and transfer students only

2. Five touring troupes that perform for over 22,000 regional P–12 children

3. Student-directing series in the Studio 307 production space provides students acting and directing opportunities

4. Work–study available in the theatre office, box office, and costume and scene shops

5. Center Stage Players, student theatre organization

6. Internships at 11 greater Cincinnati theatres.

Say I get a BA rather than a BFA. Will I actually get to perform?

Yes, all theatre majors (BA and BFA) are treated equally during audition process.

I love to sing, but I don't consider myself a dancer. Can I still seek a degree in musical theatre at your school?

Yes, although the musical theatre BFA degree requires a dance class almost every semester.

I want to get a BFA in acting, but I also love to sing. Can BFA/BA acting students take voice lessons with top voice faculty?

Yes, we offer voice lessons taught by theatre faculty as part of the student's tuition. All theatre majors are eligible.

Do you discourage or encourage students to audition for theatre outside of the department during the academic year?

We offer internships with 11 greater Cincinnati theatres in which we encourage students to participate only after they have auditioned for the main NKU theatre season.

Does your school regularly work in conjunction with any regional theatres?

Yes. As stated above, we currently have internships associated with 11 theatres.

What do students typically do during the summers? Do you actively promote participation in summer theatre auditions?

Our students audition at SETC, NETC, and other national auditions each year. We prepare our students for these auditions with a four-week workshop in the fall.

How many musicals versus straight plays do you do in a season?

Typically, we offer two major musicals and four to five straight plays during the academic year, and another two musicals during the summer months.

What are some of your alumni up to? Do you have an active alumni network?

We have an active alumni network in New York, Chicago, and LA. Our alums have appeared in national Broadway tours, regional theatre, theme parks, cruise ships, television, major motion pictures, and graduate theatre programs.

Give Me the Technical Info

What is the portfolio/interview process for a technical theatre student?

A student presents a portfolio of photographs and drawings to a faculty committee for entrance into a design/technology program.

What do you expect to see on a technical theatre resume?

A variety of technical work either from high school, community theatre, or professional work

I'm interested in lighting, sound design, and stage management. What major should I go for? Can I minor?

For designers, the BFA is the best choice. You can minor in a general theatre minor but not specifically design.

Does your school specialize in any division of technical theatre?

We are launching the new rock and roll/concert technology BFA degree. This degree will focus on rock and roll venues, including rigging and pyrotechnics, and is supported by internships at major rock venues in the greater Cincinnati area.

Give Me Some Insight

What do you look for in a potential student?

Talent. Focus. Desire.

What are some of the auditors' pet peeves?

Dress for success. The auditors do not appreciate an auditionee who dresses sloppily or casually. It is, after all, a job interview setting.

After I audition, is there a good way to follow up?
Email to the audition coordinator.

What's one of the best auditions you have ever seen?
A young man walked on stage with complete confidence. He seemed to own the room. He performed a hilarious monologue from a Woody Allen piece and sang Rodgers and Hammerstein's song "Ten Minutes Ago."

If there were one thing you never wanted to see in an audition again, what would it be?
Monologues developed from blogs

What's the best advice you can give me regarding auditioning for your school?
Audition at our December BFA/Scholarship audition. You have a better chance than at our April audition, which is primarily for current theatre majors attempting to move into the BFA.

Give Me the Lowdown

Northern Kentucky University is the newest and fastest growing of Kentucky's state universities. Each fall, NKU welcomes over 15,000 students to our campus. Our students are not only from the Commonwealth and tri-state region but also from all over the United States and around the world.

NKU's location places it in the largest metropolitan area of all the state universities in Kentucky. With a population of about 2 million, this area ranks high on the list of U.S. and metro areas with a high quality of life. The NKU campus is close to nationally ranked cultural and historic attractions, architectural gems, an acclaimed river cityscape, and an international airport.

Theatre students at NKU are 10 minutes from downtown Cincinnati; they have easy access to the Tony Award–winning Cincinnati Playhouse in the Park, as well as other professional theatre companies. Cincinnati is also a frequent stop for many Broadway, concert, and other touring productions, which can provide numerous internship opportunities.

Pace University

New York, New York

www.pace.edu

Contributors: Amy Rogers, Associate Professor, Performing Arts; Gian Marco Lo Forte, Production Manager and Set Designer, Performing Arts Dept. (Technical Theatre)

Give Me the Facts

Population of College:
12,704

Conservatory or Liberal Arts:
Liberal arts

Degrees Offered:
* BFA in acting, musical theatre
* BA in theatre arts with an emphasis in dance, acting, directing, technical
* MFA in acting, directing, playwriting from The Actor's Studio

Population of Department(s):
100 BFA musical theatre, 130 BFA acting, 170 BA theatre arts

Theatre Scholarships Available:
The university offers many scholarships. Among the theatre students, the most common is the Honors College Scholarship. This scholarship awards $15,000/year, a free laptop, and free tickets to Broadway shows/movies.

Popular/Unique/Specialized Classes That You Offer:
Freshman Performance Seminar with the heads of the musical theatre program, Contemporary Ballet, Hip-Hop, Modern, Business of Acting with a well-known casting director, Senior Showcase with casting director Bob Cline, Musical Theatre History and Repertoire, Master Class Series

Is an audition required to declare theatre as a major? For BFA?
An audition is required for entrance into all theatre department majors.

How many students audition versus how many get accepted each year?
For the theatre department freshman class, we take approximately 100 students out of 1,000 applicants.

Do you make cuts after freshman year and subsequent semesters?
No cuts, but we do have intense evaluations every semester.

Can I minor in theatre/musical theatre?
No, but a double major is possible, although not advised. A minor in dance is available and encouraged.

Give Me the Scoop

Would I get a showcase at the end of senior year?
Yes, directed by casting director Bob Cline. Most, if not all, students get many appointments with agents.

Will I be able to audition/perform as a freshman?
Yes, we encourage freshmen to audition in school and generally expect to cast them.

If there is a graduate program, will I get the same performance opportunities as an undergraduate?
The Actors Studio MFA is a completely separate entity from the undergraduate theatre department. For more information, check out their page on the Pace website.

What ways can I be involved with the department aside from performing?
We have many student-run theatre organizations, a theatre coalition, work–study positions, and student-led concerts and benefits, as well as opportunities to be involved in the technical side of all productions.

Say I get a BA rather than a BFA. Will I actually get to perform?
Yes

I love to sing, but I don't consider myself a dancer. Can I still seek a degree in musical theatre at your school?
Yes, we actively seek unique performers of all talents with potential for growth.

I want to get a BFA in acting, but I also love to sing. Can BFA/BA acting students take voice lessons with top voice faculty?
Unfortunately, we cannot offer voice lessons through the university, but we are happy to recommend top teachers in the city for your private lessons.

Do you discourage or encourage students to audition for theatre outside of the department during the academic year?
With the permission of the faculty, we definitely encourage students to audition in the professional world, when they feel ready. We have many students on Broadway, national tours, off-Broadway, and at regional theaters who are able to stay in school while performing.

What do students typically do during the summers? Do you actively promote participation in summer theatre auditions?
We host the National Straw-hat summer stock auditions on our campus. So yes, we do promote participation and help the students prepare for their auditions by holding master classes with the head of the Straw-hat auditions.

How many musicals versus straight plays do you do in a season?

As part of our mainstage season, we do four musicals and four straight plays per school year, although there are over 60 performance opportunities a year for students within the university's different theatrical student organizations.

What are some of your alumni up to? Do you have an active alumni network?

Our program is very young, only in its eighth year. Thus, we have been trying to cultivate an active alumni base that comes to performances and still feels united with current students. Our alums and current students can be seen on Broadway, national tours, international tours, Las Vegas, regional theaters, off-Broadway, off-off Broadway, and in television/film.

Give Me the Technical Info

What is the portfolio/interview process for a technical theatre student?

Students auditioning for BA theatre arts, technical theatre/design focus, at Pace University submit the following documents prior to interview:

* photo
* resume (detailed description of all productions they have worked on and in what capacity if technical and/or design)
* two letters of recommendation from:
    1. directors they have designed for, and/or
    2. technical directors and stage managers they have worked for as backstage crew and specify technical capacity, and/or
    3. designers they have assisted and specify in what capacity as model builders/ scenic painter/construction.
* essay: This is an important part of the audition process. Students applying for the program are highly motivated artists who describe in detail all skills they own in design and technical theater; students specify areas of interest in design and technical theater (lighting design/set design/sound design/costume design/prop design and prop construction, and so on).

The interview process includes the presentation of a portfolio of photos from productions students have worked on and specify in what capacity (as assistant designer, designer, carpenter, lighting technician, programming board, board operator, stage manager, backstage hand, and so on).

In addition, for students in set design and lighting design, it is recommended to include drawings, sketches, thumbnail drafting, and lighting plot, set models photos, and visual images of productions they have designed or assisted on.

What do you expect to see on a technical theatre resume?

A broad range of experience including design and technical experience. For stage manager students, experience on all technical aspects and in specific experience programming lighting board and organizational skills.

I'm interested in lighting, sound design, and stage management. What major should I go for? Can I minor?

BA theatre arts with a focus in technical theater/design. Minors are not available. This is a comprehensive program in design, technical theatre, and stage management. Students accepted to the program are encouraged to participate hands-on on several productions in their specific areas of interest. Motivated students will take additional classes (theatre practicum) to design or assistant design school productions; students are credited for internships at professional theaters in New York City. Pace University has established relationships with several professional theaters in New York City.

Give Me Some Insight

What do you look for in a potential student?

We strive to nurture unique, kind, and curious students with a point of view, who want to use New York City as their campus and take all the resources we have to offer to inform their artistic growth.

What are some of the auditors' pet peeves?

Rather than dressing for a business meeting, dress as if you're going on a first date. When applicants don't read instructions. Rudeness.

After I audition, is there a good way to follow up?

We understand that applicants are eager for a response, but it is not in their best interest to email or call seeking feedback.

What's one of the best auditions you have ever seen?

The ones who stand out are the ones who know who they are and understand how to choose appropriate material.

If there were one thing you never wanted to see in an audition again, what would it be?

"Not For the Life of Me" from *Thoroughly Modern Millie.*

What's the best advice you can give me regarding auditioning for your school?

Be your truest self. If you love singing rock, by all means, sing a rock song as one of your selections. If you have a crazy style, let us see it. Don't change yourself to be accepted by us, because ultimately we will accept you in part because of your skill set but also in large part through the amount of comfortable you we can see in your audition.

Give Me the Lowdown

Many guest artists who have come in to work with our students comment on how different they all look, feel, and sound from each other. We take pride in the diversity of styles and the versatility of skills in the students we have brought together. We have students who give concerts around the city with their rock bands, record voice-overs for Cartoon Network, tour around the world with their acclaimed Irish folk band, create music with some of the biggest names in the music industry, travel to Japan to practice their Japanese, volunteer with orphans in Peru, model in New York Fashion Week, try to get their books published, perform on Broadway, act in feature films, and all this while still being in school and training to pursue a career in the musical theatre. Thus, we call ourselves the "Island of Misfit Toys."

Pennsylvania State University

University Park, Pennsylvania

www.psu.edu

Contributors: Judy King, Administrative Assistant, School of Theatre; Dan Carter, Director, School of Theatre

Give Me the Facts

Population of College:
Approx 40,000

Conservatory or Liberal Arts:
Public university/liberal arts

Degrees Offered:
* BFA in musical theatre, design and technology, stage management
* BA in theatre

Population of Department(s):
Approximately 250 students

Theatre Scholarships Available:
Yes, varies by program

Popular/Unique/Specialized Classes That You Offer:
Theatre 100 is a general studies class that combines education and entertainment for over 700 students each semester. By the end of the semester, students will see over 90 examples of live theatre, from Greek tragedy to musical comedy, acted by a core group of professional actors and directors.

Is an audition required to declare theatre as a major? For BFA?
The stage management and design and technology BFA degrees require submission of a headshot, resume, letters of recommendation, essay, and a portfolio, along with an interview. The BFA in musical theatre requires submission of a headshot, resume, letters of recommendation, and an audition and interview. The BA in theatre requires submission of a headshot, resume, letters of recommendation, essay, and audition.

How many students audition versus how many get accepted each year?
For the BFA in musical theatre, we accept 12–14 students per year. For the BA in theatre, we accept 12–14 students per year. Stage management and design and technology BFA degrees accept 5–10 students per year.

Do you make cuts after freshman year and subsequent semesters?
We do not cut students, but students do have semester evaluations.

Can I minor in theatre/musical theatre?
You can minor in theatre, but not musical theatre.

Give Me the Scoop

Would I get a showcase at the end of senior year?
All seniors in the musical theatre program participate in a senior showcase.

Will I be able to audition/perform as a freshman?
Varies by year, but generally freshmen do not audition for productions their first year.

If there is a graduate program, will I get the same performance opportunities as an undergraduate?
Yes, auditions are open to all students—graduate and undergraduate.

What ways can I be involved with the department aside from performing?
There are several student-run theatre groups on campus, but all students in the department are involved in school productions throughout the course of the year.

Say I get a BA rather than a BFA. Will I actually get to perform?
We have an open casting policy for all productions and encourage students in all programs to audition for all productions.

I love to sing, but I don't consider myself a dancer. Can I still seek a degree in musical theatre at your school?
We encourage students who are strong in two of the three areas of musical theatre (dance, voice, acting) to audition for us.

I want to get a BFA in acting, but I also love to sing. Can BFA/BA acting students take voice lessons with top voice faculty?
Yes, based on availability.

Do you discourage or encourage students to audition for theatre outside of the department during the academic year?
We encourage students to work with faculty to consider and evaluate performance opportunities that may present themselves outside of the department.

Does your school regularly work in conjunction with any regional theatres?
We work with Penn State Centre Stage.

What do students typically do during the summers? Do you actively promote participation in summer theatre auditions?
We encourage students to continue working in the field during their summer break (summer stock, local theatre).

How many musicals versus straight plays do you do in a season?
Varies by year, but always at least two musicals per year in addition to plays.

What are some of your alumni up to? Do you have an active alumni network?
We have a very active alumni network. The Penn State alumni association is the largest dues-paying alumni association in the country, and many of our theatre alums are working in television, on Broadway, and in touring companies across the country.

Give Me the Technical Info

What is the portfolio/interview process for a technical theatre student?
Students are required to submit a headshot, resume, letters of recommendation, essays, and portfolio for review before an interview.

What do you expect to see on a technical theatre resume?
Experiences working in the student's area of interest

I'm interested in lighting, sound design, and stage management. What major should I go for? Can I minor?
We offer a BFA degree in both stage management and design and technology. Students should apply to the major of interest.

Give Me Some Insight

What do you look for in a potential student?
Talent, drive, passion, experience.

All of the above. First and foremost is talent. We need to be assured that with four years of our training, the student will be competitive in the professional musical theatre job market.

What are some of the auditors' pet peeves?
Songs that are the same and show no range and monologues that are out of the student's experience/imagination zone

After I audition, is there a good way to follow up?
With patience. Thank-you notes are in vogue but really have no impact.

What's one of the best auditions you have ever seen?
One in which we really get to know the student

What's the best advice you can give me regarding auditioning for your school?
Be yourself, share your personality, and show us who you are and what experiences you've had. Keep in mind that we aren't casting a show but looking for people we want to spend four intense years with.

Give Me the Lowdown

For more information, please visit:
http://theatre.psu.edu
http://wow.psu.edu

Shenandoah University

Winchester, Virginia

www.su.edu

Contributors: **Thomas Albert, D.M.A. Professor of Music (Composition, Musical Theatre); Charles B. Levitin, Chair in Musical Theatre**

Give Me the Facts

Population of College:
3,500

Conservatory or Liberal Arts:
Conservatory (Shenandoah Conservatory)

Degrees Offered:
* BFA in acting, costume design, musical theatre, scenic and lighting design, technical theatre production, theatre for youth
* BM in musical theatre accompanying

Population of Department(s):
Approximately 150 students (including all majors in theatre)

Theatre Scholarships Available:
A limited number of Conservatory Awards are designated for incoming theatre students.

Popular/Unique/Specialized Classes That You Offer:
Recognizing that more than half of the current and planned musical theatre productions in the United States (including Broadway, regional, tours, and stock) are pop or rock oriented, Shenandoah has its musical theatre voice students include two semesters of pop-rock repertoire study in the senior year. To support this study, the Conservatory's Voice Division hired a pop-rock specialist as a member of the faculty, beginning in fall 2010.

Acting Through Song (sophomore-level, one-semester requirement for musical theatre) and Advanced Acting Through Song (senior-level, two semesters); Preparation for the Theatre Profession (required of acting and musical theatre majors)

Is an audition required to declare theatre as a major? For BFA?
Yes

How many students audition versus how many get accepted each year?
Out of approximately 400 auditions each year, we accept 24 in musical theatre and 12 in acting.

Do you make cuts after freshman year and subsequent semesters?
No. We do, however, see the students annually in a jury, where each student presents a short audition-like performance for a panel of faculty, who then

spend 5–10 minutes chatting honestly with the student about past performance and future prospects.

Can I minor in theatre/musical theatre?

There is a general theatre minor offered for students in the university whose curriculum requires a minor (such as nonconservatory students in liberal arts degree programs). Conservatory students who are enrolled in professional programs in music, theatre, and dance do not take curricular minors.

Give Me the Scoop

Would I get a showcase at the end of senior year?

Yes, but not the traditional "go to New York and do a 40-minute revue for invited guests" type of showcase. Rather than joining the scores of schools vying for New York agents' and casting directors' attention in April and May every year, we invite industry professionals to campus, where they spend a day with our students. Each senior presents an audition-like performance, and then gets immediate feedback from the guest (or guests) in a masterclass environment. Our innovative approach has been quite successful; it is attractive to agents and casting directors, and other schools are beginning to emulate our model for the on-campus showcase.

Will I be able to audition/perform as a freshman?

Yes, all theatre performance students are required to audition (and perform, if cast) for all productions, beginning with the first semester of the freshman year.

What ways can I be involved with the department aside from performing?

Alpha Psi Omega, National Honorary Theatre Society; work–study opportunities in the box office and some assignments to individual faculty; technical work in the shops and crewing productions beyond course requirements; stage management opportunities beyond course requirements; assistant director/assistant choreographer/assistant music director.

Say I get a BA rather than a BFA. Will I actually get to perform?

We offer only the BFA.

I love to sing, but I don't consider myself a dancer. Can I still seek a degree in musical theatre at your school?

We require a three-part audition demonstrating skill and/or potential as an actor, singer, and dancer. Dance is an integral and required part of the degree program.

I want to get a BFA in acting, but I also love to sing. Can BFA/BA acting students take voice lessons with top voice faculty?

Nonmusical theatre students may take elective study in voice, which requires an extra fee; noncredit voice study is also available through the Shenandoah Conservatory Arts Academy.

Do you discourage or encourage students to audition for theatre outside of the department during the academic year?

We actively discourage outside work during the academic year, as it invariably interferes with the students' work in the conservatory.

Does your school regularly work in conjunction with any regional theatres?

Yes. During the current academic year (2010–2011), we are doing a new musical project with Tony Award-winning Signature Theatre of Arlington, Virginia; Signature's artistic director, Eric Schaeffer, is directing a workshop of the new musical with a cast comprised entirely of Shenandoah students. Rehearsals and performance are scheduled for March 2011.

What do students typically do during the summers? Do you actively promote participation in summer theatre auditions?

We do actively encourage our students to seek summer employment, and many of them do so every year, both for our own summer company as well as many others throughout the country. Since 1984, we have offered Shenandoah Summer Music Theatre, which presents four fully mounted musicals each summer (each with a two-week run), all performed with a full orchestra. It is a non-Equity company, and our students get first chance to audition. Equity and non-Equity guest artists augment the company as well.

How many musicals versus straight plays do you do in a season?

The academic year season consists of three mainstage productions (two musicals and one play), three second stage productions (two plays and one musical), and three youth theatre productions (two plays and one touring production).

What are some of your alumni up to? Do you have an active alumni network?

Many of our alumni are currently or have been recently in Broadway shows, including J. Robert Spencer (*Jersey Boys, Next to Normal*—Tony nominated), Aaron Galligan-Stierle (*Ragtime, Dr. Seuss's How The Grinch Stole Christmas*), Laura Woyasz (*Wicked*), Jason Wooten (*Hair, Grease, The Times They Are A-Changin', Dance of the Vampires, The Rocky Horror Show, Jesus Christ Superstar, Footloose*), Kathy Voytko (*The Pirate Queen, The Frogs, Nine, Oklahoma!*), Kris Koop (*The Phantom of the Opera*), and Gregg Goodbrod (*Thoroughly Modern Millie*). Alumni have been or currently are in national tours such as *Legally Blonde, Hair, A Chorus Line,* and *Hairspray* and are frequently seen in regional theatres throughout the country. We have a very active alumni network, utilizing both Facebook and LinkedIn to keep current students in touch with alums.

Give Me the Technical Info

What is the portfolio/interview process for a technical theatre student?

The candidate submits a portfolio, either hard copy or digital, and meets with the interviewer to discuss background and basic knowledge of technical theatre. The portfolio/interview process is a one-on-one meeting with the candidate to determine area of interest, understanding of level of commitment to a BFA design program, artistic and aesthetic potential, and problem-solving abilities. The candidate is expected to have documentation of previous shows he or she has been involved with, drawing and sketching abilities, drafting experience, carpentry or painting skills, experience with hanging and focusing lights, programming light boards, stage management experience, back stage run experience, costume or makeup design, and project or realized work they may have completed in high school or community college. It is not expected that every applicant will have experience in every area; they should emphasize their areas of strength.

What do you expect to see on a technical theatre resume?

We ask the candidate to submit a reverse chronological listing of any experience he or she has in technical theatre. This can include work within any theatrical venue, schools, church groups, or community or professional theaters. We also ask for letters of reference for the program.

I'm interested in lighting, sound design, and stage management. What major should I go for? Can I minor?

You should major in the area in which you have the most interest or select a program that allows for lateral movement when you have decided what area of specialization you want to pursue. Our program is a sceneographic degree that concentrates on set design, lighting design, and technical theatre production. We have secondary emphasis in sound design. Most technical students specialize in one area over another; however, they must cross over and experience all areas of technical theatre. We offer a separate degree in stage management that has a strong technical emphasis. We also offer a separate BFA in costume design. Our majors do not typically have a minor since we are a BFA program; however, the conservatory does offer an arts management degree with emphasis in technical theatre.

Give Me Some Insight

What do you look for in a potential student?

Besides academic preparation, evidence of talent, and potential for growth, we consider how an auditionee will fit as a person in our community.

What are some of the auditors' pet peeves?

Slick, presentational performances that lack honesty and directness (like *American Idol*); songs that are presented with no acting values; "story" monologues; failure to comply with published requirements (usually relating to age-appropriateness and duration of monologues).

After I audition, is there a good way to follow up?
A thank-you email within a day or so of the audition is always a good idea. Email follow up after a couple of weeks is fine.

If there were one thing you never wanted to see in an audition again, what would it be?
Monologues about rape, suicide, disease, and other such morbid subjects that require emotional breakdowns; also over-the-top stand-up routine monologues

What's the best advice you can give me regarding auditioning for your school?
Read the guidelines and stick to them.

Give Me the Lowdown

Shenandoah Conservatory's musical theatre degree, well established as one of the oldest in the nation, is also one of the country's most up-to-date programs. We review the curriculum regularly to ensure that we are providing the education and training an aspiring professional needs to work in the modern world of theatre.

Our innovative approach to the senior showcase brings industry professionals to campus for intensive personal interaction with our students and has yielded very positive results.

In the fall of 2011, we hired a new member of the voice faculty who has extensive training and background in both classical and commercial voice and performance, making Shenandoah the first school to include a year of study in pop-rock techniques and repertoire for the BFA in musical theatre.

Shenandoah is also on the leading edge of modern singing training teachers and professionals. Our CCM Vocal Pedagogy Institute was created to meet the demand for training grounded in voice science, voice medicine, and tested methods of contemporary commercial music (CCM) vocal pedagogy. We continue to be the first and only institution to include courses in CCM vocal pedagogy for academic credit in a graduate degree program. The best and the brightest voice professionals from all vocal disciplines worldwide have been drawn to the CCM Vocal Pedagogy Institute for the past seven summers. World-renowned teacher Jeannette LoVetri, creator of Somatic Voicework, guides the institute.

In Spring 2011, Shenandoah and Tony Award–winning Signature Theatre co-produced a workshop of a new musical, *Crossing*, with book by Grace Barnes and music and lyrics by Matt Conner. Eric Schaeffer, artistic director of Signature Theatre, directed Shenandoah students in the workshop production.

Shorter University

Rome, Georgia

www.shorter.edu

Contributor: **David Nisbet, Chair, Department of Theatre**

Give Me the Facts

Population of College:
1,500

Conservatory or Liberal Arts:
Liberal arts

Degrees Offered:
* BA in theatre
* BFA in acting
* BFA in musical theatre

Population of Department(s):
50

Theatre Scholarships Available:
Theatre Department, Friends of Theatre

Popular/Unique/Specialized Classes That You Offer:
Film Acting Technique, Stage Combat, Intense concentration in music for BFAMT

Is an audition required to declare theatre as a major? For BFA?
Audition required for BFA and BFAMT

How many students audition versus how many get accepted each year?
50–60% are accepted

Do you make cuts after freshman year and subsequent semesters?
There are reviews every year; cuts are rare.

Can I minor in Theatre/Musical Theatre?
Yes

Give Me the Scoop

Would I get a showcase at the end of senior year?
Yes, in New York and Atlanta.

Will I be able to audition/perform as a freshman?
Yes

What ways can I be involved with the department aside from performing?
We offer work–study that allows the students to participate in the everyday workings of the theatre department. There are numerous theatre groups run by students.

Say I get a BA rather than a BFA. Will I actually get to perform?
Yes

I love to sing, but I don't consider myself a dancer. Can I still seek a degree in musical theatre at your school?
Students must complete a dance audition. If accepted, dance training will be part of the curriculum.

I want to get a BFA in acting, but I also love to sing. Can BFA/BA acting students take voice lessons with top voice faculty?
Yes

Do you discourage or encourage students to audition for theatre outside of the department during the academic year?
Encourage

Does your school regularly work in conjunction with any regional theatres?
We do not work with a regional theatre per se, but yearly, The Milwaukee Rep comes to campus to audition students for their intern program.

What do students typically do during the summers? Do you actively promote participation in summer theatre auditions?
Yes. We participate in GTC and SETC and have theatres come to Shorter to audition the students.

How many musicals versus straight plays do you do in a season?
Two musicals, three or four straight shows

What are some of your alumni up to? Do you have an active alumni network?
We do. The vast majority of our alumni are working in the acting profession; 75% of our alumni are employed in theatre within three months after graduation.

Give Me the Technical Info

What is the portfolio/interview process for a technical theatre student?
An interview is required for the BA program in technical theatre (with the technical director). There is no portfolio requirement.

What do you expect to see on a technical theatre resume?
We expect to see all stage management credits, design credits, and all other experience dealing with technical theatre (sound design, work with specialized materials, and so on).

I'm interested in lighting, sound design, and stage management. What major should I go for? Can I minor?

We offer lighting and scene design tracks along with stage management tracks. These are all BAs.

Give Me Some Insight

What do you look for in a potential student?

Desire to work hard and learn their craft

What are some of the auditors' pet peeves?

Songs and monologues that go on forever

After I audition, is there a good way to follow up?

You may contact the chair at any time.

What's one of the best auditions you have ever seen?

"I Am Adolfo."

If there were one thing you never wanted to see in an audition again, what would it be?

Elard from *The Nerd*

What's the best advice you can give me regarding auditioning for your school?

Be prepared, be brief, and be confident.

Give Me the Lowdown

* Faculty Achievement Awards in Directing, Dialect/Text Coaching, and Scenic Design
* Outstanding Achievement Award in Direction, Fight Choreography, Musical Direction, and Scenic Design for *Jekyll and Hyde: The Musical*
* For the past seven years, Shorter University musical theatre and theatre students have represented over one-third of all college and university students chosen to represent the state of Georgia at SETC; over 60% of students who audition at GTC are passed onto SETC; a Shorter student has been selected top female performer (2009, 2010)
* Multiple alumni have already completed or are now on national tours (including *The Sound of Music*, *The Full Monty*, *Beauty and the Beast*, *Grease*, and *The Little Mermaid*) or are working off-Broadway or on Broadway (including *Forbidden Broadway* and *Jersey Boys*)
* Nearly 85% of our alumni earn their primary paycheck from working in the theatre within three months of graduation

- Graduates are currently working in a number of diverse theatre productions at numerous theatres, including Actors Express (including the Artistic Director), Dad's Garage Theatre, Atlanta Lyric, Alliance Theatre Company, Orlando Shakespeare Festival, Harry Potter Theme Park, 14th St Playhouse, Disney, Theatre in the Square, Zudzu Playhouse, and the Village Playhouse
- Two interns accepted to the prestigious Milwaukee Repertory Theatre (2010)
- Multiple professional workshops yearly with casting directors, agents, directors, and choreographers
- Student-directed mainstage productions community service and professional development projects
- Raised $5,000 for the DeSoto Theatre Restoration Project with the 2004 Fall Musical, *West Side Story*
- Organized and participated in fundraisers for victims of Hurricane Katrina, St. Judes Children's Hospital, a local domestic violence shelter, and more
- Multiple invitations by such organizations as the Southeastern Theatre Conference, Georgia Theatre Conference, and Georgia Thespian Festival

Syracuse University

Syracuse, New York

www.syr.edu

Contributor: **Leslie Noble, Administrative Specialist and Part-Time Instructor, Drama**

Give Me the Facts

Population of College:
College of Visual and Performing Arts: approximately 1,800

Conservatory or Liberal Arts:
Conservatory-style training in a university setting in direct partnership with a professional LORT theater (Syracuse Stage)

Degrees Offered:
* BFA in musical theater, stage management, acting, theatre design and technology
* BS in drama with concentrations in acting or theatre design tech

Population of Department(s):
Approximately 250 majors

Scholarships Available:
* Merit scholarship: Department of Drama currently has two at $1,000 each
* Other merit scholarships: Founder's, Chancellor's, and Dean's scholarships offer up to $12,000 per year

Popular/Unique/Specialized Classes That You Offer:
* Clown Technique
* Back Story (Solo Creation)
* Musical Theatre Cabaret
* Conflict Resolution & Crisis Management
* Computer-Assisted Design
* Stage Combat
* Stage Rigging
* Advance Scene Study: Poetics
* On-Camera Acting
* Art in Action
* Theater Dance Styles

Is an audition required to declare theatre as a major? For BFA?
Yes. All performance students must currently enter as BFA candidates. After their first or second year, they may choose to move to a BS in drama or they may be asked to move to the BS after their second-year evaluation.

How many students audition versus how many get accepted each year?
Approximately 700 audition; approximately 100 get accepted

Do you make cuts after freshman year and subsequent semesters?
For performance students, the second-year evaluation determines whether or not they can continue in the BFA. This is not a quota system; if the student passes the evaluation, he or she moves on to upper-level classes. If they don't pass, they may be asked to repeat certain classes and re-evaluate the following term or move to the BS degree.

Can I minor in Theatre/Musical Theatre?
You can minor in drama but not musical theater.

Give Me the Scoop

Would I get a showcase at the end of senior year?
Our current senior classes are too large for all to attend the showcase. Currently, we select students on the basis of an audition and the faculty's determination that they are ready to enter the profession.

Will I be able to audition/perform as a freshman?
Freshman year is focused on building foundational skills and self-awareness. It's also a time for students to have a chance to bond with their classmates. For these reasons, freshmen don't perform, design, or stage manage. Since we audition for our productions the semester before they're scheduled, freshman performance students audition in April for the following fall's shows.

What ways can I be involved with the department aside from performing?
Work–study opportunities at Syracuse Stage (with whom we share a building)
   * Crew assignments as part of Introduction to Theater
   * Black Box Players: an entirely student-run, theater-producing organization
   * Freshmen can be production assistants on department shows
   * Community arts practice opportunities through Community Artists Workshop
   * Opportunities to assist with prospective student auditions and give tours

Say I get a BA rather than a BFA. Will I actually get to perform?
Students who pursue the BS in drama have the same opportunity to audition and perform in Drama Department productions.

I love to sing, but I don't consider myself a dancer. Can I still seek a degree in musical theatre at your school?

Not at present. Musical theater students must have potential in acting, singing, and dancing.

I want to get a BFA in acting, but I also love to sing. Can BFA/BA acting students take voice lessons with top voice faculty?

They may on a space available basis, and there may be an additional cost.

Do you discourage or encourage students to audition for theatre outside of the department during the academic year?

With the exception of freshmen, students are permitted to participate in outside productions, with the understanding that their commitment to class work is their first priority.

Does your school regularly work in conjunction with any regional theatres?

Yes, our program is in partnership with Syracuse Stage and students are cast each year in our annual drama/stage coproduction and sometimes also in age-appropriate roles in other Syracuse Stage shows. We share a building complex with Syracuse Stage, and several of their professional technical staff teach in our stage management and theater design and technology programs.

What do students typically do during the summers? Do you actively promote participation in summer theatre auditions?

We promote summer theater auditions and internships, and many of our students participate in these activities. We also encourage students to rest, renew, and seek experiences apart from the theater that will help them grow as individuals.

How many musicals versus straight plays do you do in a season?

Two musicals—a big book and a small cast musical

What are some of your alumni up to? Do you have an active alumni network?

We have a very active alumni network, Syracuse University Drama Department (SUDO), which works with our Alumni Affairs office to share news and opportunities. Very visible people such as Aaron Sorkin, Arielle Tepper, Jerry Stiller, and The Araca Group have provided programming support over the years. Others, such as Vanessa Williams, Vera Farmiga, and Taye Diggs, stay in contact with former teachers and have returned to work with students. We have active alumni in theatre design, production stage management, and casting, who return every year to see our senior showcase and provide contacts to graduating students.

Give Me the Technical Info

What is the portfolio/interview process for a technical theatre student?
An interview appointment with theater design and technology faculty includes a review of the student's portfolio and a conversation about his or her interests and how he or she might intersect with what our program has to offer.

What do you expect to see on a technical theatre resume?
Some high school and/or community theater experience is always useful.

I'm interested in lighting, sound design, and stage management. What major should I go for? Can I minor?
BFA in theater design and technology or BFA in stage management. The minor is in the more general "drama" offering, but some design classes are open to minors.

Give Me Some Insight

What do you look for in a potential student?
Some combination of accomplishment and potential

What are some of the auditors' pet peeves?
Very high heels, constricting clothing, disorganized sheet music

After I audition, is there a good way to follow up?
Not necessary. Our Admissions Department keeps students updated in a timely manner.

What's one of the best auditions you have ever seen?
It's different for every student, but the best auditions are those that are well prepared and presented with inventive ideas lived out truthfully.

If there were one thing you never wanted to see in an audition again, what would it be?
Slow Dance on the Killing Ground (overdone)
Laramie Project (more narration than acting)

What's the best advice you can give me regarding auditioning for your school?
Remember: We're looking for people to invite; we're not looking for people to eliminate. Bring yourself, not the person you think we're looking for. "To thine own self be true."

University of California, Irvine

Irvine, California

www.uci.edu

Contributor: **Eli Simon, Chair, Drama Department**

Give Me the Facts

Population of College:
17,000 total at UCIrvine

Conservatory or Liberal Arts:
Liberal arts BA, with a BFA in musical theatre

Degrees Offered:
- BA, BFA, MFA in acting, directing, stage management, scenic, costume, lighting, sound
- Doctoral studies

Population of Department(s):
370 undergraduates, 70 graduates

Theatre Scholarships Available:
Drama-specific
Steve Lyle Memorial Scholarship
Bette and Steven Warner Scholarship [shared with the Music (voice)]

Schoolwide
Kris and Linda Elftmann Scholarship
Elizabeth and Thomas Tierney Scholarship

Popular/Unique/Specialized Classes That You Offer:
Clowning, Acting for Camera, Audition Techniques, Movement for Actors (based on Contact Improv), Shakespeare, Improvisation, sound/lighting/costume/scenic design; full complement of courses in theory, history, and criticism.

Is an audition required to declare theatre as a major? For BFA?
No

How many students audition versus how many get accepted each year?
Nobody has to audition to gain entrance to our department. Once accepted at UCIrvine, you can simply declare drama as your major.

Do you make cuts after freshman year and subsequent semesters?
No. We do not cut students.

Can I minor in theatre/musical theatre?
There's no minor in MT.

Give Me the Scoop

Would I get a showcase at the end of senior year?
Yes, if you are in the musical theatre BFA. No, if you are in the drama BA.

Are showcases successful?
Our BFA showcases in New York City and is very successful. It is well attended by agents and managers who are looking to represent our students. Most of our BFA alums are working on Broadway, regionally, or in national tours.

Will I be able to audition/perform as a freshman?
Auditions are open to everyone in the department. Most freshmen that audition for all faculty- and student-directed productions and workshops in the season wind up on stage. But not everyone does. It is competitive and roles are not guaranteed; they are earned. This is one way that our department mirrors the "real world." If you find that you are not being cast, year after year, it may be possible that your talents lie in directing, design (lighting, sound, costume, scenic), stage management, or theory and criticism. There are a myriad of opportunities awaiting our undergraduates in all of these areas.

If there is a graduate program, will I get the same performance opportunities as an undergraduate?
One way we assure more equal casting is by offering three produced all-undergraduate shows a year. These are fully produced and one is a faculty- or guest-directed musical. There are also all-undergraduate workshops produced throughout the year. And undergraduates can audition for all shows that graduate actors are eligible for.

What ways can I be involved with the department aside from performing?
We have a very active Undergraduate Student Council. These students oversee special theatre projects, seminars with faculty and special guests, fundraising efforts, and much, much more. Many undergraduates at UCIrvine wind up working on productions as directors, designers, or in stage management.

Say I get a BA rather than a BFA. Will I actually get to perform?
Yes, if you are talented and right for a role. I just directed *Into the Woods*, and it was open to graduate and undergraduate actors. There were four graduate actors, 15 BA actors, and two BFA actors in the cast. The graduate-directed workshops this quarter were cast with BA students. So there are ample opportunities to audition for shows, but it is competitive and you have to win your roles through auditions.

I love to sing, but I don't consider myself a dancer. Can I still seek a degree in musical theatre at your school?
Yes. Our BA and BFA training begins with acting and singing. We do teach dancing as well, but it is not mandatory that you leave as a triple threat.

I want to get a BFA in acting, but I also love to sing. Can BFA/BA acting students take voice lessons with top voice faculty?
Yes, many of our BA students study singing—in groups and privately—with our musical theatre faculty.

Do you discourage or encourage students to audition for theatre outside of the department during the academic year?
BA students can audition wherever they like, and sometimes they do land roles in professional theatres. If they can manage the rehearsal and performance schedule without diminishing attendance at classes or schoolwork, we have no problem with this. It's up to the student to decide what route to take.

Does your school regularly work in conjunction with any regional theatres?
Not officially, but we do have close ties to South Coast Repertory, a nearby Tony Award–winning regional theatre.

What do students typically do during the summers? Do you actively promote participation in summer theatre auditions?
There are many summer companies that audition directly on our campus. We allow BFA, Honors in Acting, and other select BA students to audition for these casting directors.

How many musicals versus straight plays do you do in a season?
We produce about eight shows in a season. Two or three of these are musicals. We also produce our Festival of New Musicals, which features between two and four new musical works.

What are some of your alumni up to? Do you have an active alumni network?
We work to stay in close touch with our alums. Please see our alumni newsletter at http://drama.arts.uci.edu/alumni.html. As you will see, our alums work across the country as actors, directors, designers, artistic directors, and stage managers, in theatre, film, television, and themed entertainment. Our alumni played starring roles in the Broadway/off-Broadway *Hair, South Pacific, Spring Awakening, Mamma Mia, Jersey Boys,* and *The Marvelous Wonderettes* in 2008–2009.

Give Me the Technical Info

What is the portfolio/interview process for a technical theatre student?
Our technical theatre students are not preselected. Here's the process:

1. Get accepted at UCIrvine.
2. Declare drama as your major.
3. Choose the aspect in drama that you are most interested in studying.
4. Get to work.

I'm interested in lighting, sound design, and stage management. What major should I go for? Can I minor?

You can specialize in any of these areas under our BA degree.

Give Me Some Insight

What do you look for in a potential student?

BA students do not need to audition. BFA students begin on the BA track and then advance to the audition for the BFA. Our BFA students are selected from top BA candidates, usually in their junior year.

Give Me the Lowdown

One of the most special undergraduate programs we have is the New York Satellite Program. This is a four-week residency in New York City, specifically focused on musical theatre. Our students work with top professionals in the Big Apple, see dozens of Broadway and off-Broadway shows, and get a taste of what it would be like to live and work in New York City. Many of our undergraduates, especially in musical theatre, move directly to New York City upon graduation. They have made professional contacts there through the Satellite Program and often wind up with representation or cast in productions right out of school.

Another stellar program is our Festival of New Musicals, in association with the Acadamy for New Musical Theatre (ANMT), in LA. ANMT writes musicals for our students. We give readings, workshops, and/or full productions of these plays (in LA and on campus).

Our faculty is comprised of working professionals. We regularly act, direct, design, and dramaturge at professional theatres across the country.

Our acting faculty has published more books on acting than any other department in the country. Want to study acting? We wrote the books. Authors include Robert Cohen, Richard Brestoff, Eli Simon, and Annie Loui.

I would also like to highlight our location, which is an hour and a half's drive to LA or San Diego, two cities which host first-rate theatres. Our campus is suburban in feel, hosts six theatres, and is close to some of the most spectacular beaches in the country.

In terms of feel, we are a large department. This is good and bad for undergraduate students. If you aren't sure what you want to study, or if you need more hand holding, you might be well advised to pick a smaller department. If you want lots of choices and a place that feels like a microcosm of the real world, UCIrvine is probably more what you're looking for. There's a wide range of courses, productions, and special programs to engage in, but you have to be ready to work, work, work. Those students who really put their heart and soul into departmental activities wind up being leaders in our universe.

University of California, Los Angeles

Los Angeles, California

www.ucla.edu

Contributor: **Richard Rose, Vice Chair, Undergraduate Theatre Program**

Give Me the Facts

Population of College:
37,000

Conservatory or Liberal Arts:
Liberal arts

Degrees Offered:
- BA in theater
- MA in theater
- MFA in acting, design for theater and entertainment media, directing, playwriting
- PhD in theater and performance studies

Population of Department(s):
Theater Department: 392 (309 undergrad, 83 grad)
Film/Television/Digital Media Department: 331 (62 undergrad, 269 grad)

Theatre Scholarships Available:
50

Popular/Unique/Specialized Classes That You Offer:
Acting for the Camera, Auditioning Techniques for the Actor, Auditioning Techniques for Musical Theater, Theater Walt Disney Imagineering, AutoCAD/ Vectorworks

Is an audition required to declare theatre as a major? For BFA?
Audition and interview for MT and acting (again, both are BAs). Interview required for all other specializations.

How many students audition versus how many get accepted each year?
Approximately 1,000 audition. Freshman class = 70; junior transfer class = 20.

Do you make cuts after freshman year and subsequent semesters?
We do not have a cut system. We have a "seat" in the senior year for every freshman that we take in. However, students may be asked to leave their specialization (but not the major) due to poor progress.

Can I minor in theatre/musical theatre?
The BA degree is a *major* in *theatre*. The diploma says *theatre* and does not list a specialization. However, all applicants choose a specialization when they apply. All students take the same liberal arts core courses throughout their

four years. But each specialization has its own conservatory-style course progression that begins in the sophomore year following a "freshman experience" year. The major is thus like a standard liberal arts BA/conservatory-style "hybrid" of sorts.

The specializations are acting, design/production, Ray Bolger Musical Theater program, playwriting, teaching artists program, and general theater studies (sort of a "design your own major"). In addition, students can, after taking two introductory directing courses, interview for a select few seats in a two-year directing specialization.

Give Me the Scoop

Would I get a showcase at the end of senior year?
No

Will I be able to audition/perform as a freshman?
Yes, after the first quarter

If there is a graduate program, will I get the same performance opportunities as an undergraduate?
Graduate and undergraduate productions have, for the most part, separate and discreet grad or undergrad casting pools. The two rarely, if ever, are mingled in the same cast. The seasons average an equal amount of graduate versus undergraduate productions.

What ways can I be involved with the department aside from performing?
There are several student-producing organizations within the department as well as on campus. There are some work–study opportunities for students who qualify.

Say I get a BA rather than a BFA. Will I actually get to perform?
Again, all actors at UCLA are in a BA program. The acting classes are *only* for the acting and musical theater specialization students. The actors in the productions are BA students (both theater majors and minors).

I love to sing, but I don't consider myself a dancer. Can I still seek a degree in musical theatre at your school?
Yes, if we determine you have raw potential and that you are trainable in dance at the time of your audition.

I want to get a BFA in acting, but I also love to sing. Can BFA/BA acting students take voice lessons with top voice faculty?
Only MT students (all BA students) can take the departmental group singing and the individual voice lessons.

Do you discourage or encourage students to audition for theatre outside of the department during the academic year?

Neither. But we do take roll every day and have severe grading consequences for absences. It is up to each individual student to determine whether or not he or she has the time management skills necessary for outside activities—be it acting, designing, or working.

Does your school regularly work in conjunction with any regional theatres?

No. But UCLA owns the Geffen Theater across the street. It is one of the leading professional theaters (LORT B) in LA. Our students (design, directing, stage management) regularly intern and assist when the artists are in residence. Acting opportunities are very rare but have occurred from time to time.

What do students typically do during the summers? Do you actively promote participation in summer theatre auditions?

Many take general education classes at junior colleges or other schools in order to have a more open schedule during the year. Many go abroad for a summer abroad educational experience. And many perform, design, and so on. We do not actively promote nor discourage any summer activity.

How many musicals versus straight plays do you do in a season?

One major musical versus at least six major straight plays. There are more lower tier plays as well.

What are some of your alumni up to? Do you have an active alumni network?

Alumni run the gamut of postgraduation life activities: grad school, Broadway, regional theater, film, television, waiting tables, designing, playwriting festivals, and so on. We have an active "unofficial" alumni network.

Give Me the Technical Info

What is the portfolio/interview process for a technical theatre student?

Present a portfolio (if they have one) or list of experiences at the interview. All is covered in the interview.

What do you expect to see on a technical theatre resume?

The whole range—practically nothing (may have some stage crew experience but a real drive and need and want to do it) to "you name it" (has been a technical director, stage crew heads, builds scenery, and so on). We are looking for the desire as much as the experience.

I'm interested in lighting, sound design, and stage management. What major should I go for? Can I minor?

All our specializations are in the theater major. UCLA allows minors in another department (even film).

Give Me Some Insight

What do you look for in a potential student?

Number one is intellectual curiosity—a hunger for learning about their world. We seek out applicants with a strong interest in things outside of theater; and of course, talent and experience *or* raw talent even without much experience.

What are some of the auditors' pet peeves?

- Scenes from a monologue book with its attendant not understanding the play or even the moments leading up to that scene. One cannot "work" with the actor at the audition if they can't answer questions about plot, intention, and so on.
- Not knowing anything about the playwright.
- Not knowing lines because it is obvious the scenes were learned a week before at most—easy to spot.
- Doing scenes—accompanied by the blocking—from a show the student was in.
- Applicants who are overly "done up" or applicants who look sloppy, as in "I-just-rolled-out-of-bed-and-made-it-over-here."
- Playing accents or playing outside of a believable age range (an old person).

After I audition, is there a good way to follow up?

Yes, we give applicants who audition (and/or interview) a card with a follow-up email address just for them. We are glad to answer any sort of questions via email. However, we do not give critiques or reasons for acceptance or denial. The university will notify the applicant either way in mid-March (freshmen) or mid-April (junior transfers).

What's one of the best auditions you have ever seen?

A young woman did an obscure male monologue from *Cymbeline,* an obscure Shakespeare play. But it wasn't the material or the fact that she took a man's part. It was the specificity of detail, the layers of intention and character choice, the confidence, and above all the sheer *joy* of performing the piece. The monologue was way too long, but I let her go because I loved watching her enjoy the opportunity to act.

—JM

If there were one thing you never wanted to see in an audition again, what would it be?

It's never good to do an ill-prepared rendition of an overdone piece. For example, the "tuna fish" monologue from Durang's *Laughing Wild* or the "Mr. Cornel I have tried to be neighborly" monologue from Neil Simon's *Star Spangled Girl.*

What's the best advice you can give me regarding auditioning for your school?

In addition to heeding the warnings in the pet peeves above, show that you are pleased to be there. Smile during your dance and singing auditions; show enthusiasm and charm.

Know your material. Who is the playwright? Know who your character is. Be able to answer questions about the plot and your character's intentions.

Work on your auditions well in advance of the auditions.

Give Me the Lowdown

Our program is a BA but acts like a BA/BFA hybrid. Its focus is academic (half of a student's units are in general elective courses, like a typical BA) but students specialize at the beginning of the sophomore year (acting, musical theater, design/production, directing, playwriting, teaching artists program, general theater studies) like a BFA. We feel that this produces a smarter, better-educated, more well-rounded undergraduate.

University of Central Florida

Orlando, Florida

www.ucf.edu

Contributors: **Christopher Niess, Chair/Artistic Director, UCF Conservatory Theatre; Mark Brotherton, Associate Professor, UCF Conservatory Theatre; Earl Weaver, Coordinator of Musical Theatre, UCF Conservatory Theatre; Bert Scott, Production Manager, UCF Conservatory Theatre**

Give Me the Facts

Population of College:
56,000+ students; 10,000+ faculty and staff

Conservatory or Liberal Arts:
Conservatory-minded program in a liberal arts environment

Degrees Offered:
* BA in theatre studies
* BFA in acting, musical theatre, design/tech, stage management
* MA in theatre studies
* MFA in acting, theatre for young audiences
* Degrees on hiatus: MFA in musical theatre, MFA in design

Population of Department(s):
400 theatre majors (grad and undergrad), 75 theatre minors, 75 dance minors

Theatre Scholarships Available:
Department Talent grants, Disney scholarships, Out-of-State Tuition Waiver Scholarship (undergraduate), several privately funded scholarships

Popular/Unique/Specialized Classes That You Offer:
BFA acting and BFA musical theatre—Professional faculty certified in major actor/training techniques, including Meisner, Linklater, Fitzmaurice, Skinner/Lessac, Contact Improv, and so on. Students are encouraged to learn about a variety of techniques and find the common ground necessary to anchor a strong process. Classes include Acting for the Camera, Shakespeare, Period Movement, Stage Violence, Circus Arts, and so on.

Proximity to partner organizations including Walt Disney World, Universal Studios, Orlando Shakespeare Theatre, and the Orlando Repertory Theatre provide easy audition opportunity. Companies who have come to campus to audition UCF students include Actors Theatre of Louisville, RWS and Associates, Stage Entertainment, Inc., and the Hangar Theatre.

BFA stage management—Gene Columbus, former manager of Entertainment Staffing for Walt Disney Entertainment and executive director for Orlando Repertory Theatre, teaches all levels of the stage management program. Many classes involve site visits to and guest lectures from the substantial local entertainment industry.

BFA design tech—Course and production work in costumes, scenery, lighting, and sound within well-staffed costume and scene shops. Many classes involve site visits to and guest lectures from the substantial local entertainment industry.

BA theatre studies—Among the many opportunities within a diverse curriculum are the student one-act festivals, featuring work entirely by students.

Is an audition required to declare theatre as a major? For BFA?

All candidates will undergo an audition/interview (all acting/musical theatre tracks), portfolio review (design/tech and stage management tracks), or entrance interview (MA and BA theatre studies).

How many students audition versus how many get accepted each year?

Approximately 500 students interview at auditions in New York, Chicago, Southeastern Theatre Conference, Florida Theatre Conference, Florida Thespians Conference, and at four auditions on the Orlando campus.

* Maximum of 20 BFA acting, musical theatre, design/tech, and stage management accepted per year
* Maximum number of MA and BA theatre studies students admitted is open and dependent on interviews.
* MFA acting and MFA theatre for young audiences programs accept classes every other year—currently eight for the acting MFA and four for the MFA-TYA.

Do you make cuts after freshman year and subsequent semesters?

MFA and BFA candidates receive oral interviews each semester to monitor progress in the program. There are no scheduled mandated cuts.

Can I minor in theatre/musical theatre?

Minors available in theatre and dance

Give Me the Scoop

Would I get a showcase at the end of senior year?

All students are required, after classes on interviewing and auditioning, to obtain a professional internship in order to graduate with a BFA or MFA degree.

Are showcases successful?

Internship requirement (for BFA/MFA) was established in 1998. Placement is consistently 100%.

Will I be able to audition/perform as a freshman?
All BFA/MFA acting and musical theatre candidates are required to audition each semester. However, casting for the performance season is open to all University of Central Florida students. Freshmen have performed in a variety of roles.

If there is a graduate program, will I get the same performance opportunities as an undergraduate?
University of Central Florida Conservatory Theatre produces eight productions during the academic year and two to three during the summer. Academic year productions use primarily a student cast and faculty and guest artists in special circumstances. No roles are reserved for graduate/undergraduates. Summer shows use a combination of faculty, guests, and student performers.

What ways can I be involved with the department aside from performing?
UCF Conservatory Theatre has a productive Alpha Psi Omega chapter, various work–study opportunities, and students are encouraged to create material to present at theatre workshops on the regional and national level (SETC, ATHE, USITT, and so on).

Say I get a BA rather than a BFA. Will I actually get to perform?
See the above note on open casting. There is an expectation that if a student is involved in more studio classes, then he or she is more likely to be cast. This tends to hold true, although there are many instances of BA theatre studies majors being cast. Additionally, the student one-act festival provides additional performance opportunity that focuses on the actor's craft (above technical theatrical elements).

I love to sing, but I don't consider myself a dancer. Can I still seek a degree in musical theatre at your school?
Every instrument (actor) is unique. However, dance and movement are an integral part of the training of a musical theatre artist. Realistically, not everyone will reach the level of a polished Broadway dancer but can benefit physically from movement/dance training.

I want to get a BFA in acting, but I also love to sing. Can BFA/BA acting students take voice lessons with top voice faculty?
Musical Theatre Voice class is in the BFA acting curriculum. Musical Theatre Voice class is available as an elective to BA theatre studies students.

Do you discourage or encourage students to audition for theatre outside of the department during the academic year?

The students' primary responsibility is to their program of study (classes) and performance responsibilities (the laboratory). It is required that students consult their advisor and area coordinator before auditioning/interviewing for an outside job or role to determine if there is any conflict with their studio classes or performance responsibilities.

Many students participate in part-time positions, acting jobs with minimal time commitments (such as commercial and film work), and occasionally a role at one of the many area professional venues and entertainment companies, including Walt Disney World, Universal Studios, Sea World, Orlando Shakespeare Theater, Orlando Repertory Theatre, Mad Cow Theatre, and so on.

Does your school regularly work in conjunction with any regional theatres?

UCF Conservatory Theatre enjoys active partnerships with the Orlando Shakespeare Theater and the Orlando Repertory Theatre that spawn valuable student participation in projects such as PlayFest!, Writes of Spring, and so on.

What do students typically do during the summers? Do you actively promote participation in summer theatre auditions?

UCF Conservatory Theatre produces an active summer season of two to three shows, using a greater concentration of faculty and guest artists. This provides opportunity to work with faculty in a more concentrated fashion in a more professional timeframe. Many students also attend Southeastern Theatre Conference and other national auditions and procure work in summer theatres and entertainment venues.

How many musicals versus straight plays do you do in a season?

Two musicals, five plays, and one dance concert

What are some of your alumni up to? Do you have an active alumni network?

To see recent alumni activity, please visit http://theatre.ucf.edu/alumni_spotlight.php.

Give Me Some Insight

What do you look for in a potential student?

Commitment, discipline, and a strong work ethic. Also, a willingness to reach beyond past ideas and an excitement about exploration of new techniques.

What are some of the auditors' pet peeves?

When the audition is not treated professionally in all areas—dress, attitude, poise, and audition preparation. Lack of preparation is probably the most avoidable. One should simply read and follow the audition guidelines set forth by the department. Also, not having music properly prepared for the accompanist, not wearing appropriate dance clothing or the correct shoes for a dance call, or not having audition material memorized can instantly sabotage your audition. Allotting enough time to get to the audition so that you don't arrive late is essential, as well as being fully warmed up and prepared to audition.

After I audition, is there a good way to follow up?

An email is the simplest way to let the department know you are interested in the program. A simple letter or card expressing this interest is a personable way to follow up as well. Oftentimes, decisions on offers must be delayed, and knowing whether you are serious about the program can help speed the process. If you have not heard from the department by the deadlines for decisions that are given at the audition, *do* send an email to check your status.

What's one of the best auditions you have ever seen?

Several in which the actor's choices were truthful, honest, and clear—and yet not safe. By the end of an audition piece, it is much better for the audience (auditors) to be left seeing a character who is not quite sure of what will happen next, which creates a slightly dangerous situation for the character. It also makes the monologue more active. In too many auditions, actors tackle a character as if that character knows everything that has, is, and *will* transpire. All that is left to do is to herald decisions that have already been made—there is no present action.

Along those lines, some of the best auditions witnessed have been ones in which the actors have a strong sense of *why* they and their character are there. For the actor with great potential, there always seems to be an empathy with the character; an enjoyment in playing; a passion in pursuing the objective, that goes far beyond individual ego. The monologue should go well beyond a sense of whether the actor looked good or gave an attractive delivery.

As far as the character is concerned, the best auditions have the clearest sense that the character is fighting for something *important* (simply put, high stakes, strong objectives, and driven tactics) and leave us with the impression that the character will continue to fight or seek resolution after the monologue is finished.

On a more basic level, we witness the best auditions from students who are confident in their dance audition (even if they make mistakes) and have fun; who have prepared quality, age-appropriate audition material (contrasting songs that show a full vocal range/monologue that shows depth of acting technique and stakes). Most important, students who obviously relish the chance to audition and show us who they really are tend to command our attention.

If there were one thing you never wanted to see in an audition again, what would it be?

An unprepared student. It is worth repeating. Preparation includes much more than memorizing the lines, a series of gestures, and facial expressions. It includes choosing material appropriate for your age and "type." Appropriate material is more important than worrying about whether the material is "overdone." If you choose a popular piece and make it your own, it can be successful.

Make sure the material allows your character to be active as opposed to reflective or passive. A character is engaging when he or she is working toward something (an objective) rather than reporting or telling a story about something that has already happened (exposition). Gratuitous emotion can have the same effect. A momentary emotional reaction can be effective, but then it is important to see what the character *wants to do next.* A monologue that serves only to demonstrate that the actor can cry or be angry for two minutes is not effective.

What's the best advice you can give me regarding auditioning for your school?

Research the program(s) you are interested in attending. It's important to feel that the program(s) is a good fit. If you are not excited at the possibility of working in this program, it will be evident.

Then, rehearse, rehearse, rehearse. Get coaching from your instructors and directors before you audition. The auditors want to see the honesty and truthfulness in your monologues. They want to see you breathe freely and enjoy performing and interviewing. It is your chance to let loose and shine for us. The auditors do not want to see the labor or the anxiety or the trauma of auditioning. They honestly want you to be the best person they see all day.

Give Me the Lowdown

The first line of our mission statement reads: We provide a competitive edge to undergraduate and graduate students seeking to achieve excellence as professional theatre practitioners and creative intellectual leaders while inspiring them to be aware and enlightened human beings. Our focus is to provide as much as possible to give that "competitive edge" and to produce graduates who work within the industry as well as in related disciplines.

Aiding us in that mission are our professional partnerships with the Orlando Shakespeare Theater and the Orlando Repertory Theatre. Graduate students receive hands-on training onstage and backstage, through outreach programs, and in management as well. Undergraduates benefit from guest lectures, classes, and programs such as the Harriett Lake Festival of New Plays, which utilizes the skills of many department students. Additionally, Walt Disney World continues to provide a wealth of support through scholarships, visitations, and lectures. A committed professional advisory board brings a wealth of knowledge and mentoring to the student body from a large number of entertainment industry leaders. The high degree of placement of UCF graduates into the area entertainment industry is indicative of their focused support as well as the resultant talent of our graduates.

On campus, students work with a talented faculty and staff in an ample performance season (11 productions including summer). Production work covers a broad range of theatrical material encompassing the contemporary and classical, the cutting edge and traditional. Productions have included Shakespearean, devised, commedia, farce, historical and contemporary musical theatre, and many more styles and genre. UCF Conservatory Theatre is an active participant in the Kennedy Center–American College Theatre Festival, having had productions invited to compete in Region IV for the past eight years. UCF has been fortunate to have a consistent roster of finalists at the regional competition and several finalists at the national level in both the Irene Ryan and Barbizon competitions.

Students are also encouraged to participate in regional and national theatre conferences by preparing and presenting workshops and scholastic presentations. This engagement has proven valuable not only for those interested in further work in theatre theory and education but for developing artists and designers as well.

University of Central Oklahoma

Edmond, Oklahoma

www.uco.edu

Contributors: **Greg White, PhD, Director of Music Theatre; Daisy Nystul, Chair, Department of Theatre Arts; Christopher Domanski, Head of Theatre Design (Technical Theatre)**

Give Me the Facts

Population of College:
17,000

Conservatory or Liberal Arts:
Liberal arts

Degrees Offered:
* BFA in performance
* BFA in design technology
* BFA in theatre/communication education

Population of Department(s):
125

Theatre Scholarships Available:
Yes, $1,000

Popular/Unique/Specialized Classes That You Offer:
Lessac Certified Trainer teaches voice, movement, and acting; play production—capstone project in which students direct their own one-acts; career advancement course, where students develop their own one-person show. Free guest artist series—guests such as Meisner teacher Larry Silverberg.

Is an audition required to declare theatre as a major? For BFA?
No, but must pass sophomore juries to continue in the program.

How many students audition versus how many get accepted each year?
We give students the opportunity to explore theatre arts as a career but hold sophomore juries as a barrier.

Do you make cuts after freshman year and subsequent semesters?
Sophomore year

Can I minor in Theatre/Musical Theatre?
We offer a minor in theatre, but we do not offer a minor in music theatre.

Give Me the Scoop

Would I get a showcase at the end of senior year?
A capstone project of directing a one-act

Will I be able to audition/perform as a freshman?
Yes

What ways can I be involved with the department aside from performing?
APO—theatre fraternity.

Say I get a BA rather than a BFA. Will I actually get to perform?
We only have a BFA.

I love to sing, but I don't consider myself a dancer. Can I still seek a degree in musical theatre at your school?
We accept students with strong individual potential in all three areas. If a student has no dance training but has the drive and determination, I am confident our faculty can provide solid training.

I want to get a BFA in acting, but I also love to sing. Can BFA/BA acting students take voice lessons with top voice faculty?
Unfortunately, our voice studios stay pretty full with School of Music students. However, we are in the process of transforming our BM in music theatre to a BFA degree.

Does your school regularly work in conjunction with any regional theatres?
Yes

What do students typically do during the summers? Do you actively promote participation in summer theatre auditions?
Yes

How many musicals versus straight plays do you do in a season?
The Theatre Arts Department puts on four major productions, 20 senior-directed, one-act plays, and two improvisational shows per year, and the School of Music produces two mainstage musicals each year, as well as two revue shows.

What are some of your alumni up to? Do you have an active alumni network?
Professional work in acting, design, directing, and so on. Yes, we have a Facebook page.

Give Me the Technical Info

What is the portfolio/interview process for a technical theatre student?
There is no formal interview process to start in the program. Once in, however, we have a yearly (January) portfolio review which all technical theatre students are required to display. The second time the student displays, he or she must present it as in an interview. Faculty and staff score on a rubric and, if successful, the student is invited to enroll in the upper level courses to complete the degree program. The student's last display must also be presented

in his or her Exit Portfolio. This is a display that encompasses all of his or her best work as for a graduate school or URTA interview.

What do you expect to see on a technical theatre resume?
Name, area of interest or how they define themselves, past and current education, description of work related to how they define themselves, any skills they might have that relate to their area of interest, references, and a means to contact the individual.

I'm interested in lighting, sound design, and stage management. What major should I go for? Can I minor?
Our design and technical degree program serves as a basis for all areas of design (scenery, lighting, costume, sound, hair and makeup, and properties) and all areas of technical (costume construction, scene painting, sound engineering, technical direction, master electrician, master carpenter, and stage management). Students enrolled in the degree program will have training in all of the areas listed above. Within this program, you can specialize in the upper-level requirements and focus the degree to your interests. There is no specific design and technology theatre minor, but the foundation courses are open for anyone to enroll.

Give Me Some Insight

What do you look for in a potential student?
A hard worker, good attitude

What are some of the auditors' pet peeves?
Don't apologize

After I audition, is there a good way to follow up?
Email the chair, Daisy Nystul

If there were one thing you never wanted to see in an audition again, what would it be?
Indicating and overacting

What's the best advice you can give me regarding auditioning for your school?
Have fun and be yourself.

University of Cincinnati College–Conservatory of Music

Cincinnati, Ohio

www.ccm.uc.edu

Contributor: **Richard Hess, Chair, CCM Drama**

Give Me the Facts

Population of College:
780 undergraduate and 710 graduate

Conservatory or Liberal Arts:
Conservatory

Degrees Offered:
* Nine degrees: BA, BM, BFA, MFA, MM, MA, AD, DMA, PhD in over 100 possible majors

Population of Department(s):
Varies: CCM Drama holds a population of 45–50

Theatre Scholarships Available:
Yes

Popular/Unique/Specialized Classes That You Offer:
The entire CCM Drama program is unique in that it is one of the few BFA curriculums in the country sans an accompanying MFA program. Without adhering to one sole acting approach, CCM Drama comprehensively utilizes Suzuki, Viewpoints, Meisner, Cohen, and Chekhov. With one of the nation's premiere voice teachers, CCM Drama offers voice training in IPA, Dialects, and Alba Emoting. Stage Combat and the opportunity to test for the Society of American Fight Directors is offered the third year. Involving the entire department, there is a festival weekend of student-created performances (conceived, produced, written, designed, and performed) that occurs every winter. Audition Techniques, Acting for the Camera, and Business Skills are offered to prepare the actor for the theatrical and film/television industries, while focused artistic and critical thinking courses such as The Artist in Society grooms our actors toward becoming meaningful contributors. Bi-coastal showcases in New York and LA culminate the program.

Is an audition required to declare theatre as a major? For BFA?
CCM Drama offers only BFA training, and yes, an audition is required.

How many students audition versus how many get accepted each year?
15 to 1. We will take in a first-year class of 15–18 from nearly 200 applicants.

Do you make cuts after freshman year and subsequent semesters?
CCM Drama does not have a cut program, but it does have a retention policy. Students are evaluated twice a year during their first and second years: Grades, performance, and overall academic/artistic health are measured.

Can I minor in theatre/musical theatre?
No

Give Me the Scoop

Would I get a showcase at the end of senior year?
Yes (two). Over 100 agents, casting directors, managers, and industry personnel attend our showcases on both coasts each year.

Will I be able to audition/perform as a freshman?
No. However, every student performs every day in each of the core classes. We present our first-year students to the rest of the department and CCM community through our freshman showcase every spring.

If there is a graduate program, will I get the same performance opportunities as an undergraduate?
CCM Drama has no graduate program.

What ways can I be involved with the department aside from performing?
We have an Ambassador program, where our students meet with prospective students, take them on tours, answer financial aid questions, and overall be our number-one recruitment tool. Their joy and enthusiasm for where they study and train is something our students love to share. CCM Drama offers a series of masterclasses; past invitees are Anne Bogart (SITI Company), Geoff Soffer (ABC Casting), Brian Crowe (New Jersey Shakespeare), Bill Lengfelder (Kitchen Dog Theater), Sandy Logan (ABC Casting), Gary Krasny (The Krasny Office), and Cindi Rush (Cindi Rush Casting). Our students founded a university club called The Theater Project, which devotes its resources to securing even more masterclasses; invitees include Theater Mitu, the SITI Co., Andre' Gregory, and Studio 6.

I love to sing, but I don't consider myself a dancer. Can I still seek a degree in musical theatre at your school?
More information about musical theater degrees and opportunities at CCM can be found at www.ccm.uc.edu/musical_theatre.

I want to get a BFA in acting, but I also love to sing. Can BFA/BA acting students take voice lessons with top voice faculty?
CCM has one of the highest regarded voice faculties in the United States. Principal students from all over the world come to study with our professors of voice, and our dramatic performance students have opportunities to train with these professional pupils.

Do you discourage or encourage students to audition for theatre outside of the department during the academic year?
Encourage. We not only support our students' work outside the department; we require it. Professional experiences are expected. We also encourage our students' success beyond theatre. Many have working relationships with local talent agencies and unions doing film and television, voice-over, and industrials. (Currently, a third-year student is vice president of the local chapter of AFTRA.)

Does your school regularly work in conjunction with any regional theatres?
Though CCM Drama does not have any contractual relationships with regional professional theaters, our students have performed with The Cincinnati Playhouse in the Park, The Ensemble Theater of Cincinnati, The Human Race Theatre, The Know Theatre, New Stage Collective, New Edgecliff Theater, Covedale Center for the Performing Arts, the Showboat Majestic, The Carnegie Theater, and the Cincinnati Fringe Festival.

What do students typically do during the summers? Do you actively promote participation in summer theatre auditions?
We encourage our students to train and perform during the summer months. Many go to New York and LA (and around the world) for internships and performance opportunities. Several joined summer acting conservatories, took classes, or interned with the following: the SITI Company, the Society of American Fight Directors, Royal Academy of Dramatic Art, Second City, Steppenwolf, The Atlantic Theatre, The Groundlings, The Dell' Arte International School of Physical Theater, the Hangar Theatre, DC Improv Comedy School, the Shakespeare Festival of St. Louis, and the Edinburgh International Festival. A group of students created their own theater company for the summer months—Cincinnati Outdoor Classics. Now in its third season, these performances have become a significant event for the city of Cincinnati and the region.

How many musicals versus straight plays do you do in a season?
An equal amount

What are some of your alumni up to? Do you have an active alumni network?
We have a very strong community of alumni, all over the country, who support and encourage our young graduates. We have actors, producers, directors, writers, musical directors, visual artists, musicians and singers, voice-over artists, models, stunt people, magicians, clowns, and comediennes amongst our alums. From Broadway to motion pictures, from television to Las Vegas and the White House, CCM Drama is there. Our alums regularly return to campus to share stories, news, and advice with the entire department. For more specific information about the professional activities of our graduates, we encourage you to peruse the website at www.ccm.uc.edu/drama.

Give Me the Technical Info

Please visit www.ccm.uc.edu/tdp for more information about technical and design degrees and opportunities at CCM.

Give Me Some Insight

What do you look for in a potential student?

A great deal of our evaluation concerns who you are. Therefore, be proud of who you are, share with us honestly, and work hard on your preparation. We look for students who have big hearts and who feel passionately about their lives and life around them. We look for their acting to be organic and seemingly natural—unbound and free of being too planned. We look for students who sincerely connect with their characters' hearts and issues.

What are some of the auditors' pet peeves?

On the CCM Drama website, we offer advice and guidelines for our audition process. A pet peeve would be evidence that the auditionee did not do his or her homework and follow directions, such as going over the allotted time or choosing monologues from the banned monologue list or not from a high-quality, full-length play. Good writing produces good acting.

After I audition, is there a good way to follow up?

Always. Feel free to write/email the head of recruiting for CCM Drama, Professor K. Jenny Jones. Links can be found on the website at www.ccm.uc.edu/drama.

What's one of the best auditions you have ever seen?

A good audition is when you fall in love. When time stands still. When we knew we wanted to spend the next four years of our lives with this young person.

If there were one thing you never wanted to see in an audition again, what would it be?

We ask you to avoid climactic material that requires great depth or intensity. It is too difficult to be truthful and can lead to overacting.

What's the best advice you can give me regarding auditioning for your school?

Check out our website at www.ccm.uc.edu/drama, do your homework, and be proud of who you are, your work, your dreams, and your future—and have fun.

Give Me the Lowdown

We pride ourselves that CCM Drama graduates do not walk, talk, nor look alike. We cultivate all students' voices as an artist's while preparing them for the realities of a demanding industry. We are a physically rigorous training program for the serious young actor. We foster generous actors who understand the power of the ensemble, the force of a good story, and the strength of creative expression. Indeed, we are ensemble based, knowing that "stardom" relies more upon fate than talent.

We have a faculty of professional teaching artists, each of whom continues to work professionally throughout the country. The facilities at the conservatory are not only state of the art but also the best to be found in the country. CCM was one of only 14 recipients, from among 421 submissions, of the 2000 National Honor Award for Outstanding Architecture by the American Institute of Architects.

Our graduates seek ways to make a difference through their chosen mediums, the stage, film, television, music, and special events—and even in Dadaab, Kenya, where two of our graduates are creating theater with locals. With Department Chair Richard E. Hess, five students will travel to Nairobi, Kenya, in June to join our alums and work alongside refugees from the Dadaab Refugee Camp on leadership, communication, storytelling, and theatre, culminating in a presentation together on World Refugee Day in Nairobi.

At CCM Drama, we imagine the possibilities.

University of Memphis

Memphis, Tennessee

www.memphis.edu

Contributor: **Robert Hetherington, Chair, Theatre & Dance**

Give Me the Facts

Population of University:
23,000

Conservatory or Liberal Arts:
Conservatory-like training within a comprehensive university setting

Degrees Offered:
- BFA in theatre: performance, musical theatre, design technology
- MFA in theatre: directing or design technology

Population of Department(s):
Undergraduate students: 105
Graduate students: 16
Faculty/staff: 17

Theatre Scholarships Available:
Each spring, usually the final Saturday in February, three full in-state tuition, departmental talent scholarships are awarded to incoming freshmen or transfer students who compete for them in an audition. These may be awarded to performance or design students.

In addition, there are also musical theatre talent scholarships of varying amounts to award to students auditioning for entry into the musical theatre concentration within the theatre program. As we are preparing to do Andrew Lloyd Webber's *Phantom of the Opera* in February 2012, we will be increasing the number of musical theatre scholarships in the upcoming year to support the new students joining us for musical theatre training in the fall of 2011.

The theatre program also gives financial awards each spring, known as merit awards, to students within the program. These awards vary in amount, and students apply to win these monies, awarded on an annual basis.

Popular/Unique/Specialized Classes That You Offer:
Directing Experiments, Playwriting, Mask, Asian Theatre, Narrative Theatre, Musical Theory, Stage Combat, African-American Theatre, Mime, Acting for TV and Film, and laboratory experience in all aspects of production.

Is an audition required to declare theatre as a major? For BFA?
No, we do not require auditions to declare a theatre major, but BFA students are required to audition to remain in the program. Design tech students present a portfolio each year.

Do you make cuts after freshman year and subsequent semesters?
No, we do not have a cut policy.

Can I minor in theatre/musical theatre?
Yes

Give Me the Scoop

Would I get a showcase at the end of senior year?
No

Will I be able to audition/perform as a freshman?
Yes

If there is a graduate program, will I get the same performance opportunities as an undergraduate?
We do not have an MFA in acting, so undergraduates have ample performance opportunities.

What ways can I be involved with the department aside from performing?
There are three student organizations in the department. There are work-study opportunities in all of the production shops as well as in the box office and the design lab.

Say I get a BA rather than a BFA. Will I actually get to perform?
We do not offer a BA degree.

I love to sing, but I don't consider myself a dancer. Can I still seek a degree in musical theatre at your school?
Yes, and as a musical theatre student, you will be required to take movement classes.

I want to get a BFA in acting, but I also love to sing. Can BFA/BA acting students take voice lessons with top voice faculty?
Yes

Do you discourage or encourage students to audition for theatre outside of the department during the academic year?
The first priority is the department, but when opportunities arise, we encourage our students to work outside for other theatres.

What do students typically do during the summers? Do you actively promote participation in summer theatre auditions?
Our students are typically doing summer stock and internships during the summer. We do actively promote and support participation in regional theatre auditions (SETC, TTA, UPTAS). We also have internship partnerships with several Memphis area theatres.

How many musicals versus straight plays do you do in a season?
Two musicals and four straight plays plus many graduate directing projects

What are some of your alumni up to? Do you have an active alumni network?
We have a very active alumni network. Our alums are working in regional theatres across the country. Several are currently working in New York, Chicago, LA, Minneapolis, and Seattle. We also have alums teaching in colleges and universities across the country.

Give Me Some Insight

What do you look for in a potential student?
In addition to raw talent, the potential student should share an audition or a portfolio that indicates time has been devoted to the development and refinement of the overall craft displayed in the work. The successful student will also display a sense of professionalism and maturity and a familiarity with the program when conversing during an interview. A sense of ease and confidence are highly regarded. Curiosity and creativity and an ability to collaborate with others are vital to the success in the discipline.

What are some of the auditors' pet peeves?
Lack of preparation. Lack of knowledge about the program, so readily available on the website.

After I audition, is there a good way to follow up?
A brief thank-you email or letter is a very professional gesture.

What's one of the best auditions you have ever seen?
We see excellent auditions every year. Preparation is key, as well as the ability to loosen up and take direction if an auditor decides to coach an actor's piece in a different direction. When presenting portfolios, the most successful students are able to talk about the developmental and creative process behind the drawings or photographs they decide to share. Thoughtful questions about the program are welcome.

If there were one thing you never wanted to see in an audition again, what would it be?
Three things come to mind, actually: Lack of preparation is certainly linked to lack of success in an audition. It is also discouraging when a potential acting student displays the inability to try a new approach on the material, should the occasion arise. Finally, auditionees should treat each other with collegiality and respect.

What's the best advice you can give me regarding auditioning for your school?

Make sure all application materials are turned in on time, work with a good coach on your portfolio or pieces, and find the "fun" in approaching the challenge of auditioning. Having the ease and confidence to be yourself throughout the process is very helpful in letting the auditors get a sense of who you are as a person as well as a potential artist.

Prepare your audition by doing it fully (in audition clothes) in front of a group of people who are not your family and friends.

University of Miami

Coral Gables, Florida

www.miami.edu

Contributor: **Lowell Williams, Lecturer, Department of Theatre Arts; with collaboration from other Theatre Arts Department faculty**

Give Me the Facts

Population of College:
10,000 undergraduates

Conservatory or Liberal Arts:
Both

Degrees Offered:
* BFA in musical theatre, acting, design/technology, stage management, theatre management
* BA in theatre arts

Population of Department(s):
Approximately 250 majors

Theatre Scholarships Available:
Yes

Is an audition required to declare theatre as a major? For BFA?
For the conservatory musical theatre and acting BFA degrees, yes. An interview is required for BFA in design production management (DPM).

How many students audition versus how many get accepted each year?
400 apply, 18 are accepted in the conservatory program

Do you make cuts after freshman year and subsequent semesters?
No, we do not have a set cut system.

Can I minor in Theatre/Musical Theatre?
You can minor in theatre in the BA program.

Give Me the Scoop

Would I get a showcase at the end of senior year?
In the conservatory program, yes, both in New York City and LA.

Are showcases successful?
Very. Our graduates are working in all areas of the business based on these contacts. Last year, a 2010 graduate went straight to Broadway and is starring in *West Side Story.*

Will I be able to audition/perform as a freshman?
No. The BFA freshman students do have a performance project that is an in-house production.

If there is a graduate program, will I get the same performance opportunities as an undergraduate?
There is *no* graduate program in our department. Our undergraduates do it all.

What ways can I be involved with the department aside from performing?
There are numerous ways to be involved with our department. Our student-run organization, TAG (Theatre Action Group), is the student-advisory arm of the department.

Say I get a BA rather than a BFA. Will I actually get to perform?
Absolutely; our BA students routinely get cast in our mainstage productions. The BA degree is not a performance degree.

I love to sing, but I don't consider myself a dancer. Can I still seek a degree in musical theatre at your school?
Our philosophy in musical theatre is to train a triple-threat performer, someone who can be employed and sing, dance, and act. Acting is the focus of our program.

I want to get a BFA in acting, but I also love to sing. Can BFA/BA acting students take voice lessons with top voice faculty?
We offer a Singing for the Actor class for all of our BFA acting students. Private voice lessons are available once the musical students are assigned.

Do you discourage or encourage students to audition for theatre outside of the department during the academic year?
Encourage summer work as long as students' work in the department is their first priority.

What do students typically do during the summers? Do you actively promote participation in summer theatre auditions?
Working professionally in the summer is very important. We promote such summer theatre auditions as SETC, NETC, and Strawhat.

How many musicals versus straight plays do you do in a season?
50/50

What are some of your alumni up to? Do you have an active alumni network?
Our alumni are working on Broadway, off-Broadway, in TV, film, and every other area of entertainment industry.

Give Me the Technical Info

What is the portfolio/interview process for a technical theatre student?
For all BFA design, stage management, and theatre management majors, an interview is required to be accepted into the program.

What do you expect to see on a technical theatre resume?
Depends on the area of interest. High school level experience is fine.

I'm interested in lighting, sound design, and stage management. What major should I go for? Can I minor?
We have BFAs in design (lighting, scenic, costumes), stage management, and theatre management majors. You could also get a general BA degree or minor in theatre—and focus in backstage work.

Give Me Some Insight

What do you look for in a potential student?
To be themselves. Ability to train. Have a little talent.

After I audition, is there a good way to follow up?
Email is the most efficient way to follow up.

If there were one thing you never wanted to see in an audition again, what would it be?
Insincerity

What's the best advice you can give me regarding auditioning for your school?
Find material that you relate to, work hard to make it real for you, and be yourself in the audition.

Give Me the Lowdown

The University of Miami's Department of Theatre Arts is located in the warm and tropical breezes of South Florida. We offer our students one-to-one training in their area of interest. Our conservatory program focuses on quality of student rather than quantity of students. Our incoming musical theatre/acting class is 18 students. It is impossible to get lost in such a small program. We *do not have graduate* programs, so all of our attention is on our undergraduate education. Our faculty have backgrounds as working professionals in their area of specialization.

University of Michigan

Ann Arbor, Michigan

www.umich.edu

Contributors: **Brent Wagner, Chair of Musical Theatre; John Neville-Andrews, Chair of Performance**

Give Me the Facts

Population of College:
Approx 43,000

Conservatory or Liberal Arts:
A conservatory-based program within an academic institution

Degrees Offered:
- BFA in performance: acting and directing concentration, musical theatre, design and production: scenic, lighting, costume design, and stage management, interarts performance: joint degree with School of Art and Design
- BTA (bachelor of theatre arts)
- Minor in African-American theatre

Population of Department(s):
BFA in performance, approximately 68 (directing, approximately 14)
BFA in musical theatre, 80–85
BFA in design and production, approximately 30
BFA, interarts performance, approximately 9
BTA, approximately 43
Minor in African-American theatre, unknown

Theatre Scholarships Available:
Yes, named scholarships and merit funding awarded by the Department of Theatre and Drama

Most Common Academic/Need-Based/Miscellaneous Scholarships:
All, through the University Financial Aid programs

Popular/Unique/Specialized Classes That You Offer:
Stage Combat, Directing, Clown, La Coq, Tai Chi, Arts Administration, Professional Theatre Preparation, and involvement/workshops with renowned visiting professional theatre companies, such as Royal Shakespeare Company, Maly Drama Theatre, and Propeller Theatre Company. Visiting industry professionals workshops.

Is an audition required to declare theatre as a major?
Yes.
   BFA in performance: audition; directing: interview, portfolio review

BFA in musical theatre: audition
BFA in design and production: interview
BFA interarts performance: audition, interview, portfolio review
BTA bachelor of theatre arts: writing samples

How many students audition versus how many get accepted each year?
BFA in performance: 250–350 audition to yield an incoming freshman class of approximately 16
BFA in musical theatre: About 4–6% of those who apply are admitted

Do you make cuts after freshman year and subsequent semesters?
No

Can I minor in theatre/musical theatre?
No

Give Me the Scoop

Would I get a showcase at the end of senior year?
BFA in performance: No
BFA in musical theatre: Yes

Are showcases successful?
Yes

Will I be able to audition/perform as a freshman?
BFA in performance: Yes; however, the first semester it's optional; after that, all students must audition for the mainstage shows and accept any casting.
BFA in musical theatre: With restrictions.

What ways can I be involved with the department aside from performing?
Possible work–study, independent study, assist on shows, lab requirements, assist in specialized classes, volunteer work, PR/marketing, take specialized classes in such topics as Performing Arts Management and Business of Theatre. Tech and production work. Direct for the student-run theatre—Basement Arts, Musket, or The Rude Mechanicals.

Say I get a BA rather than a BFA. Will I actually get to perform?
No BAs offered by either the theatre or musical theatre departments.

I love to sing, but I don't consider myself a dancer. Can I still seek a degree in musical theatre at your school?
Yes, depending on movement potential.

I want to get a BFA in acting, but I also love to sing. Can BFA/BA acting students take voice lessons with top voice faculty?
Yes, BFA students can, within the School of Music, Theatre & Dance. May not be with top voice faculty, but highly qualified faculty and GSIs.

Do you discourage or encourage students to audition for theatre outside of the department during the academic year?

BFA in performance: We don't encourage it or discourage it. It's very difficult to perform outside of the theatre department, considering the demands of the BFA degree, mainstage shows, and other theatre projects taking place during the semester.

BFA in musical theatre: Students should plan to be in residence for four years. Other local opportunities may exist, but most of the focus is within the department.

Does your school regularly work in conjunction with any regional theatres?
No, though many work at major summer theatres.

What do students typically do during the summers? Do you actively promote participation in summer theatre auditions?
Students audition and get summer stock work, internships in theatre, with agents and casting directors, and go abroad to study. Some also return home, get traditional jobs, and so on. It varies. Yes, we promote and encourage summer theatre work.

How many musicals versus straight plays do you do in a season?
Theatre department: No musicals. Five plays.
Musical theatre department: Three musicals; one play; and many, many more opportunities for special event performances.

I also like to play sports. Do you encourage musical theatre/acting students to pursue other interests?
Most definitely. The discipline and teamwork required by being involved in sports is most valuable to actors.

Give Me the Technical Info

What is the portfolio/interview process for a technical theatre student?
Interviews and a portfolio reviews are held on campus four times a year.

What do you expect to see on a technical theatre resume?
Evidence of technical and production work at high school, community theatre, or other such performance venues.

I'm interested in lighting, sound design, and stage management. What major should I go for? Can I minor?
BFA in design and production. No minor at present; however, it is in the works for the future.

Give Me Some Insight

What do you look for in a potential student?
The ability to respond to the methodology and required curriculum and a student who will make a significant contribution to the program

What are some of the auditors' pet peeves?

Not being well prepared, poor choice of material, not dressing or conducting yourself professionally

After I audition, is there a good way to follow up?

A thank-you card or email is always nice.

If there were one thing you never wanted to see in an audition again, what would it be?

Actors getting too close to the adjudicator's table

What's the best advice you can give me regarding auditioning for your school?

Relax; be yourself. Come well prepared, with the best contrasting material you can find, and be open to, and ready for, anything. Also, read the website very carefully. We don't have high regard for applicants who haven't done their homework.

Give Me the Lowdown

Our students regularly appear and are sought after for work in theatre, television, and movies. For example, Daren Criss, recurring roles on *Eastwick* and now a regular on *Glee;* James Wolk, lead roles in *Lonestar* and the Hallmark Hall of Fame show, *Front of the Class;* Zachary Booth appears as Glen Close's son on *Damages;* Sophina Brown, recurring role on *Shark;* Miriam Shor, lead role in *Swingtown* and appeared in the original production and the movie *Hedwig and the Angry Inch.* These are a smattering of the successes that some of our graduates have obtained.

We also encourage students to develop and present their own material for production. One group, while at the U of M, created the musical version of a Harry Potter book, called *A Very Potter Musical,* which was seen by over 11 million people on YouTube. This led to Universal Pictures commissioning them to write a follow-up show, *A Very Potter Sequel,* for the Harry Potter Theme Park in Florida. Since then, the students have formed their own production company, Starkid Productions, and have just completed a new musical, *Starship,* which played in Chicago.

For information on visiting guest artists, go to www.music.umich.edu/departments/theatre/guests.htm.

The thorough training that students receive in the Department of Theatre & Drama at the University of Michigan, combined with their own creativity and ingenuity, puts them in an ideal position upon graduation to get work in the professional entertainment industry. We don't have a showcase because we don't need one. Our students are the showcase—one that attracts the attention of agents, producers, casting directors, and directors in every area of theatre, television, and film.

University of Nevada, Las Vegas

Las Vegas, Nevada

www.unlv.edu

Contributor: **Kim Hobbs, Administrative Assistant, Theatre**

Give Me the Facts

Population of College:
Approximately 30,000 students for the 2010–2011 scholastic year

Conservatory or Liberal Arts:
Liberal arts

Degrees Offered:
* BA in theatre (specific area of study not listed)

Population of Department(s):
Department of Theatre currently (Spring 2011) has 315 students

Theatre Scholarships Available:
DeVos Drama, Jim Brennan Design, CSUN Scholarship, and multiple scholarships and awards available online

Popular/Unique/Specialized Classes That You Offer:
Women Playwrights, Black Drama/Performance, Gay Plays, Stage Combat, Musical Theatre, Design/Technology, Costume Design, Scenic Design, Lighting Design, Theatre for Senior Adults, Voice & Movement for the Actor, Acting for the Camera, Oral History Theatre, Entertainment Fine Arts Law

Is an audition required to declare theatre as a major? For BFA?
Yes, for the stage and screen acting emphasis; no, for general theatre studies or design/technology, for the minor in theatre, or for senior adult theatre. A BFA is not offered.

How many students audition versus how many get accepted each year?
Probably 100 audition and 50–60 are accepted as freshmen

Do you make cuts after freshman year and subsequent semesters?
Yes

Can I minor in theatre/musical theatre?
A minor in theatre is offered. No degree or minor in musical theatre at UNLV

Give Me the Scoop

Would I get a showcase at the end of senior year?
SSA and D/T students have a showcase at the end of each year.

Will I be able to audition/perform as a freshman?

In some of the second season or one-act plays in the Black Box or Paul Harris Theatres; probably not on the Main Stage Judy Bayley Theatre

If there is a graduate program, will I get the same performance opportunities as an undergraduate?

Yes, there is, and probably not fully the same opportunities, although you may audition for any production.

What ways can I be involved with the department aside from performing?

Students set up their own acting and performing groups. Your emphasis as a freshman is to get through the general core requirements and learn the craft before trying to exhibit your ability.

I want to get a BFA in acting, but I also love to sing. Can BFA/BA acting students take voice lessons with top voice faculty?

This is not a conservatory on the undergraduate level; there are many performances that require singing parts, and there is a very good relationship with the music department for singing lessons as a class or as an individual.

Do you discourage or encourage students to audition for theatre outside of the department during the academic year?

Students are encouraged to participate in all productions. It is part of the requirements to be a student of theatre.

Does your school regularly work in conjunction with any regional theatres?

Individuals within the Department of Theatre do. The department as a whole does not.

What do students typically do during the summers? Do you actively promote participation in summer theatre auditions?

There are internship possibilities.

How many musicals versus straight plays do you do in a season?

There are 13 productions each year. It is a combination of musicals and non-musical plays; there are period pieces and current ones; there is a Shakespearean play each year.

What are some of your alumni up to? Do you have an active alumni network?

There are lists of what graduates do and where they work. Most all find work quite easily. There is an active alumni association and the area heads within the department as well as fellow students keep in contact with one another.

Give Me the Technical Info

What is the portfolio/interview process for a technical theatre student?

None on the undergraduate level

What do you expect to see on a technical theatre resume?

The portfolio is prepared and finalized during the four-year course of study. The student usually does not have need for such a document as a freshman.

I'm interested in lighting, sound design, and stage management. What major should I go for? Can I minor?

Design/technology would be the best. Minoring would not be to your best advantage.

Give Me Some Insight

What do you look for in a potential student?

Accepted students are individuals interested in learning and capable of learning.

What are some of the auditors' pet peeves?

Accreditation shows UNLV Theatre to be well rounded on the undergraduate level of study.

After I audition, is there a good way to follow up?

You can call or email.

What's one of the best auditions you have ever seen?

The auditioning students who follow the directions and try not to embellish their performance with fluff

If there were one thing you never wanted to see in an audition again, what would it be?

Total inability

What's the best advice you can give me regarding auditioning for your school?

Be prepared.

Give Me the Lowdown

Consider that the faculty is made up of highly qualified individuals, well trained and well honed in their craft. Brackley Frayer, USA, is our chair but is a highly sought lighting director; Joe Aldridge, USA, is a technical director who worked with Electric Engineering, and they designed Entertainment Engineering; Robert Brewer, AEA, was a director on Broadway and teaches performance; Nate Bynum, AEA, is stage/screen actor (*Walker, Texas Ranger, Benjie*); Glenn Casale, SDC, is a Tony Award–winning director; Rayme Cornell, AEA, is a stage and screen actress; Clarence Gilyard, AEA, is a stage and screen actor (*Walker, Texas Ranger* and many more worldwide); Judy Ryerson, USA, is head of costume (formerly with PCP); Shannon Sumpter, USA, has stage managed throughout the USA; Michael Tylo, AEA, actor in *Guiding Light, All My Children,* and many more). The depth and sharing of these people serves as a training base students are eager to have.

The production list each year is diverse, and all productions are well attended. The production arm is the Nevada Conservatory Theatre.

University of Tennessee

Knoxville, Tennessee

www.utk.edu

Contributor: **Casey Sams, Assistant Professor of Theatre/Head of Undergraduate Studies**

Give Me the Facts

Population of College:
Approximately 27,000

Conservatory or Liberal Arts:
Liberal arts

Degrees Offered:
  * BA in theatre
  * MFA in acting, scenic design, costume design, lighting design

Population of Department(s):
14 faculty, full professional staff, approximately 80 undergraduate students, 24 graduate students

Theatre Scholarships Available:
Yes

Most Common Academic/Need-Based/Miscellaneous Scholarships:
50/50 academic and need based

Popular/Unique/Specialized Classes That You Offer:
Acting, musical theatre, stage combat, ensemble (a "by-audition-only" acting class), Shakespeare

Is an audition required to declare theatre as a major? For BFA?
Not for the undergraduate program; yes for the MFA

Do you make cuts after freshman year and subsequent semesters?
No

Can I minor in theatre/musical theatre?
You can minor in theatre.

Give Me the Scoop

Would I get a showcase at the end of senior year?
No

Will I be able to audition/perform as a freshman?
Yes

If there is a graduate program, will I get the same performance opportunities as an undergraduate?

Two shows each year are primarily undergraduate shows, assuring that undergraduates have the opportunity to play leads as well as supporting roles.

What ways can I be involved with the department aside from performing?

Student organizations include All Campus Theatre and Strange Fruit. Work-study opportunities are available in all the shops.

Say I get a BA rather than a BFA. Will I actually get to perform?

No BFA offered

I love to sing, but I don't consider myself a dancer. Can I still seek a degree in musical theatre at your school?

Our program doesn't focus on musical theatre, but we do produce a musical every year, with many roles available to undergraduates, both dancers and nondancers.

I want to get a BFA in acting, but I also love to sing. Can BFA/BA acting students take voice lessons with top voice faculty?

Students can major in theatre and minor in vocal performance, or vice versa.

Do you discourage or encourage students to audition for theatre outside of the department during the academic year?

Discourage

Does your school regularly work in conjunction with any regional theatres?

The Clarence Brown Theatre, a LORT D theatre, is housed on the UT campus. All students work on or perform in Clarence Brown productions during their time on campus.

What do students typically do during the summers? Do you actively promote participation in summer theatre auditions?

We provide audition coaching for SETC and summer theatre auditions. Summers for students vary wildly.

How many musicals versus straight plays do you do in a season?

Usually one large musical and seven straight plays

What are some of your alumni up to? Do you have an active alumni network?

UT alumni are working in theatres across the country. We have an alumni network that is just getting established.

Give Me the Technical Info

What is the portfolio/interview process for a technical theatre student?

None for entry to the program

What do you expect to see on a technical theatre resume?
No resume required for acceptance into the program. Your resume is developed during your time at UT.

I'm interested in lighting, sound design, and stage management. What major should I go for? Can I minor?
Theatre. Students specialize by selecting electives in their specific discipline.

Give Me the Lowdown

Theatre, at its best, is a mirror through which an individual or group can re-examine themselves, their beliefs, and behaviors. At the University of Tennessee, Knoxville, we strongly believe that a theatre artist must have a well-rounded liberal arts education in order to create theatre that reflects the world around them. We teach our students to think critically and communicate fully, creatively, and effectively through the art and practice of making theatre.

Our educational program is deeply integrated with the professional production season of The Clarence Brown Theatre, a LORT D theatre located on the UT campus. All theatre majors participate in Clarence Brown productions, working directly with nationally recognized directors, designers, and actors. (Recent guest directors: Paul Barnes, Bill Jenkins, Risa Brennin, and Ron Himes. Recent guest designers: Beverley Emmons, Jenifer Tipton, and Scott Bradley. Recent guest actors: Dale Dickey, David Keith, Jonathan Daly, and Carol Mayo Jenkins.) While not every student can be guaranteed a role in a Clarence Brown production, all eight shows that are produced each year have roles for undergraduates, and two of the eight are specifically chosen to provide leading roles for undergraduate students.

UT students get first-hand exposure to the demands and challenges they can expect from the theatre profession. They develop collaborative and practical skills in problem solving that are essential to success in theatre, as well as providing the foundation for a wide range of career paths.

Wagner College

Staten Island, New York

www.wagner.edu

Contributors: **Dr. Felicia Ruff, Chair of Theatre; David McDonald, Head of Voice; Jean-Claude Darne, Graduate Assistant**

Give Me the Facts

Population of College:
2,000

Conservatory or Liberal Arts:
Liberal arts

Degrees Offered:
* BA in theatre and speech with concentrations in performance, design/technology/management, and theatre studies
* BS in arts administration, dual major in theatre and education

Population of Department(s):
240

Theatre Scholarships Available:
Yes

Popular/Unique/Specialized Classes That You Offer:
Oscar Wilde seminar; Modern Commedia dell'Arte taught in Amsterdam; Acting V, a senior-year course where industry reps are brought in weekly

Is an audition required to declare theatre as a major? For BFA?
Yes. We hold auditions for high school students in February, and accepted student are invited to join our BA program in theatre performance.

How many students audition versus how many get accepted each year?
Of 250 auditions, 50 are accepted (of which, approximately 34 begin in the performance concentration)

Do you make cuts after freshman year and subsequent semesters?
No

Can I minor in theatre/musical theatre?
Yes

Give Me the Scoop

Would I get a showcase at the end of senior year?
Yes. Our senior showcases are produced in major off-Broadway houses such as the York Theatre or Playwrights Horizons. Many industry reps along with

department alumni and faculty. Many students secure meeting, representation, and/or work from our showcase.

Will I be able to audition/perform as a freshman?

Yes

What ways can I be involved with the department aside from performing?

Our Theatre Advisory Board (T.A.B.) is our liaison between the department faculty and student body, with a full cabinet and class officers. T.A.B. organizes productions, benefits, and master classes in addition to its assistance with student issues and season selection. There is also the Dance Club, which sponsors workshops and events, as well as student membership in USITT. Student organizations like Completely Student Productions produce student-written plays as well as musicals such as *Sweeny Todd* and *Hair.* There are numerous class-related performance opportunities, including directing and choreography classes, independent studies, and senior honors projects.

Say I get a BA rather than a BFA. Will I actually get to perform?

Ours is a BA program at Wagner, but our production calendar is extensive. All students, freshmen included, have the opportunity to audition for eight seasonal productions, in addition to a robust student-driven production environment.

I love to sing, but I don't consider myself a dancer. Can I still seek a degree in musical theatre at your school?

Yes, but know that the dance portion of our audition is graded the same as the acting and singing portions.

I want to get a BFA in acting, but I also love to sing. Can BFA/BA acting students take voice lessons with top voice faculty?

All of our students are able to take weekly voice lessons with our music department faculty.

Do you discourage or encourage students to audition for theatre outside of the department during the academic year?

We encourage students to audition as much as they like, provided it doesn't interfere with their classroom attendance or production responsibilities. Students who obtain work are allowed to take a leave of absence from the school and are welcomed back when they want to return.

Does your school regularly work in conjunction with any regional theatres?

No

What do students typically do during the summers? Do you actively promote participation in summer theatre auditions?

Yes, and many of our students work in theatres up and down the east coast and throughout the country every summer.

How many musicals versus straight plays do you do in a season?

Every season we produce four musicals, three plays, and the annual Dance Project or Dance Concert.

I also like to play sports. Do you encourage musical theatre/acting students to pursue other interests?

Yes

What are some of your alumni up to? Do you have an active alumni network?

Many have gone on to work on Broadway, regional theatre, national tours, film, and television. Many keep in contact with Wagner through our alumni network and theatre support group, Friends of the Theatre. This year alone we have had numerous alums performing on Broadway, including two in *Westside Story, the Book of Mormon, Memphis, La Bete* (technical), *How to Succeed* (technical), *Mama Mia, Sister Act,* and *Wonderland.* Many are on cruise ships and on tour, including the first national of *South Pacific* and *West Side Story,* as well as the current *Spamalot, Fiddler,* and numerous other non-Equity tours.

Give Me the Technical Info

What is the portfolio/interview process for a technical theatre student?

Apply through the admissions department. Once you have received academic clearance, schedule an audition/interview. Await decision.

What do you expect to see on a technical theatre resume?

The resume should list any shows you have worked on, special skills, and relevant classes you have taken such as art, theatre, music, industrial arts, history, literature, drafting, and so on.

If you have a portfolio, bring it along. A portfolio might include examples of your skills in drawing, sketching, and painting; any theatre design work; prompt books or examples of other stage management work; photographs of productions; items that you feel might be helpful in getting to know you. The portfolio is to help jump-start the interview; please bring whatever you have.

I'm interested in lighting, sound design, and stage management. What major should I go for? Can I minor?

BA in theatre with a DTM concentration. One can minor.

Give Me Some Insight

What do you look for in a potential student?

Attitude, preparation, confidence, poise, talent

What are some of the auditors' pet peeves?

Lack of preparation, poor attitude, overdone monologues and songs

After I audition, is there a good way to follow up?

Best to send a general thank-you note to the department if you enjoyed your experience.

If there were one thing you never wanted to see in an audition again, what would it be?

Poor preparation

What's the best advice you can give me regarding auditioning for your school?

Be prepared to demonstrate your best work, have a good attitude, and go for it. Be auditioning us as well: "Is this school and program where I want to be?"

Give Me the Lowdown

Our location on top of a scenic hill overlooking the city skyline in one of the boroughs of New York City allows our students to audition in the city, attend shows, and do internships. Indeed, students often do several internships at places as far ranging as the Met, MTV, Carnegie Hall, Paul Taylor Dance, the Dramatist Guild, Disney, and so on. It also means our faculty often work in New York City and Broadway; our stage management professor is currently the PSM on *Memphis,* our resident costumer works regularly on *Mama Mia,* our wigs/makeup professor just closed *La Bete,* and the professor who teaches our Acting V: The Professional Actor and our Showcase is a Tony Award–winning actress who just starred in a new play at Playwright's Horizons.

We also have a tradition of success, which includes well over two dozen alums that have performed on Broadway, several of whom have won Tony and Drama Desk awards. Because we are a bachelor of arts program, we often see students become lawyers, teachers, casting directors, talent managers, MBAs, Air Force pilots, PhDs in social justice, critics, arts administrators, concessions managers, missionaries, ministers, chiropractors, and so on. That is to say, students successfully apply their theatre education from Wagner in pursuit of any number of theatre, theatre-related, and other kinds of professional opportunities.

Webster University

St. Louis, Missouri

www.webster.edu

Contributors: **Lara Teeter**, Head of Musical Theatre; **John Wylie**, Head of Design/Tech (Technical Theatre)

Give Me the Facts

Population of College:
8,500

Conservatory or Liberal Arts:
Conservatory

Degrees Offered:
* BFA in acting, musical theatre, scene design, costume design, lighting design, sound design, wig and makeup design, scene painting, costume construction, technical production, stage management
* BA in directing

Population of Department(s):
225

Theatre Scholarships Available:
There are various scholarships that are based on contributions to the program and the community along with GPA.

Is an audition required to declare theatre as a major? For BFA?
Yes and yes

How many students audition versus how many get accepted each year?
For BFA in acting and musical theatre, 600+ audition for the two performance degrees. On average, we accept about 60 students in hopes of getting a class of about 25.

Do you make cuts after freshman year and subsequent semesters?
No

Can I minor in theatre/musical theatre?
No

Give Me the Scoop

Would I get a showcase at the end of senior year?
Yes

Will I be able to audition/perform as a freshman?
No

What ways can I be involved with the department aside from performing?
There is work–study. The students are extremely busy between their class time, crew time, and performance time.

I love to sing, but I don't consider myself a dancer. Can I still seek a degree in musical theatre at your school?
Yes

I want to get a BFA in acting, but I also love to sing. Can BFA/BA acting students take voice lessons with top voice faculty?
Yes

Do you discourage or encourage students to audition for theatre outside of the department during the academic year?
Yes

Does your school regularly work in conjunction with any regional theatres?
Yes. The St. Louis Repertory Theatre shares our main stage space with us. Our students do all of the running crew assignments for all of the shows, and they are required to audition and be considered for the Rep's season.

What do students typically do during the summers? Do you actively promote participation in summer theatre auditions?
They do summer stock. We have a strong study abroad, as we have 10 international campuses, including our London campus.

How many musicals versus straight plays do you do in a season?
We do four plays and two musicals (one large and one small) a year. This does not include the St. Louis Theatre Repertory casting possibilities along with our senior directing students' "Capstone" plays/musicals, which are small in terms of cast/production value.

What are some of your alumni up to?
Jerry Mitchell's (*Broadway, Hairspray, Legally Blonde, La Cage*) *Catch Me if You Can* on Broadway starred one of our esteemed alums, Norbert Leo Butz.

Do you have an active alumni network?
Yes. Hunter Bell (Broadway, *Title of Show*) is very involved with our senior showcase and hosts a yearly get-together for our performance and tech theatre alums.

Give Me Some Insight

What do you look for in a potential student?
At Webster, we look for a strong connection to the "other" imaginary partner in both the songs (two contrasting) and the monologues (two contrasting), along with material that is appropriate for the actor/singer.

What are some of the auditors' pet peeves?

Not being truly prepared. It's a national market and the competition is too steep not to be fully invested in this defining moment in one's young artistic life.

After I audition, is there a good way to follow up?

Sure. Email, call, and always send a handwritten thank-you card.

What's one of the best auditions you have ever seen?

One in which the personality, the material, the execution, the "vibe" was exactly in line with the type of company member we hope to train.

If there were one thing you never wanted to see in an audition again, what would it be?

We are not interested in seeing someone who is not fully prepared and/or invested in the audition itself. We are not interested in seeing someone who makes the audition and their interpretation of the material *all about them*. We are looking for team players.

What's the best advice you can give me regarding auditioning for your school?

Be well prepared and well coached. Do the research. Know who's in the room and what they do. Relax. Have fun. Be yourself because we are really interested in you. Be yourself and be that well.

Give Me the Lowdown

Our program is an *acting-based* program. Webster is a Stanislavski-based program. One glance at our curriculum, and one can see that the focus is on acting. This is really excellent news for our musical theatre majors, as they take the four-year sequence of our core acting classes (acting, voice and speech, movement) right alongside the acting majors. When it comes to casting our conservatory season, our acting majors are cast in our musicals and our musical theatre majors are cast in our plays, and visa versa. The musical theatre majors also have four years of musical theatre song study (musical theatre styles class), along with their voice lessons, music theory classes, piano, and choir requirements housed in the music school, as well as their dance requirements housed in the dance department. The focus of any young artist should be on self-discovery. We encourage our students to find their "authentic voice," and we hope to train the future visionaries of the theatre arts.

Wright State University

Dayton, Ohio

www.wright.edu

Contributor: W. Stuart McDowell, PhD, Chair/Artistic Director, Department of Theatre, Dance & Motion Pictures

Give Me the Facts

Population of University:
17,000

Conservatory or Liberal Arts:
Liberal arts

Degrees Offered:
* BFA in acting and acting/musical theatre, scenic design, costume design, lights, sound, stage management, technology, dance, theatre studies, motion picture production
* BA in film history, theory and criticism

Population of Department(s):
300

Theatre Scholarships Available:
Numerous: Tom Hanks & Rita Wilson Scholarship; Martin Sheen Scholarship; Rising Star Scholarship; Merit Scholarship; ArtsGala Scholarship; over $300,000 given away each year in all areas combined

Popular/Unique/Specialized Classes That You Offer:
Conservatory-style courses

Is an audition required to declare theatre as a major? For BFA?
Yes for acting/musical theatre, dance, and design/technology. None for BAs including BFA in motion pictures.

How many students audition versus how many get accepted each year?
Over 300 for 30 positions in acting/musical theatre. Over 100 for 20 positions in dance.

Do you make cuts after freshman year and subsequent semesters?
Yes. Juries in acting/musical theatre; portfolio reviews in design/technology

Can I minor in Theatre/Musical Theatre?
No, strictly four-year full-time.

Give Me the Scoop

Would I get a showcase at the end of senior year?
In acting/musical theatre, there is a major senior showcase in New York, attended by over 50 agents, managers, directors, and so on in the spring of each year. In 2010, 12 senior acting/musical theatre majors all got callbacks and offers for work.

Will I be able to audition/perform as a freshman?
Yes

If there is a graduate program, will I get the same performance opportunities as an undergraduate?
No graduate program; no competition for roles, facilities, or funds.

What ways can I be involved with the department aside from performing?
Some students do internships in leading professional theatres across the country; some students write, compose, direct, act, and/or produce in the unique, student-run Directing Lab (seats 100) throughout the entire year.

Say I get a BA rather than a BFA. Will I actually get to perform?
Yes, many BA students perform in shows.

I love to sing, but I don't consider myself a dancer. Can I still seek a degree in musical theatre at your school?
Yes. Many double threats get into the BFA program and then have four years of training in the other area (acting, singing, dancing).

I want to get a BFA in acting, but I also love to sing. Can BFA/BA acting students take voice lessons with top voice faculty?
Yes, across the board. Our voice faculty are leading professionals, many of them with extensive professional performance experience.

Do you discourage or encourage students to audition for theatre outside of the department during the academic year?
Yes, but they must always also audition for the WSU Theatre productions and "play as cast." However, permission is sometimes given in advance for outside professional performance work in certain circumstances, and we encourage it.

What do students typically do during the summers? Do you actively promote participation in summer theatre auditions?
Most actors work in regional, summer stock, and internships. Virtually all design/tech students have work in their chosen areas.

How many musicals versus straight plays do you do in a season?
Currently, four plays and four musicals in two theatres, not including around 20 plays and musicals produced by students in the Directing Lab.

What are some of your alumni up to? Do you have an active alumni network?
Nicole Scherzinger: *Dancing with the Stars* winner and leading singer; Andrea Bendewald, working actress on numerous shows and series in LA. Numerous actors and dancers on cruises, regional theatres, and on Broadway.

Give Me Some Insight

What do you look for in a potential student?
Substantial talent, ability, focus, and a great passion for their work

After I audition, is there a good way to follow up?
Be prepared *before* the audition and be on time, organized, make a good first impression, and have all the relevant information and a decent representative headshot. Follow up for a university audition is not appropriate, except to finish the application thoroughly and get it in on time, especially for scholarship applications.

What's one of the best auditions you have ever seen?
The one where the material was appropriate and right on—and the actor wore the material like a glove, and then went on to surprise me with passion.

If there were one thing you never wanted to see in an audition again, what would it be?
The ring speech from *Twelfth Night*

Appendix A
Additional Programs to Consider

American Academy of Dramatic Arts

New York, New York/Los Angeles, California

BA in theatre (in conjunction with a number of other colleges); Certificate of advanced studies in acting (3 year program); Associates of Arts in acting (LA), Associates of occupational studies (NYC) (2 year programs)

American Musical and Dramatic Academy

New York, New York/Los Angeles, California

BFA in acting, musical theatre, dance theatre, and performing arts; Certificates in acting, musical theatre, and dance theatre

*AMDA has two campuses and two types of "programs." The four-year BFA programs are new and are only available through the LA campus (although students can spend up to two of their four years at the New York campus). The Certificates offered by AMDA are not degrees. The Certificate programs are only two years in length and have no general studies component. Students who have already completed a Certificate program can go back for their BFA in two years, but must spend both years in LA.

Belmont University, Department of Theatre and Dance

Nashville, Tennessee

BFA in directing, performance, production design, theatre education and musical theatre (through the School of Music); BA in theatre & drama; BM (Bachelor of Music) in musical theatre (through the School of Music)

Birmingham-Southern College, Department of Theatre & Dance

Birmingham, Alabama

BA in theatre and musical theatre

Boston Conservatory, Theater Division

Boston, Massachusetts

BFA in musical theater

Catholic University, Department of Drama

Washington, DC

BA in drama and musical theatre (through the School of Music)

Central Washington University, Theatre Arts Department

Ellensburg, Washington

BFA in performance, design & production, musical theatre; BA in theatre generalist, teaching theatre K–12

Circle in the Square School

New York, New York

Certificates in acting and musical theatre

*A Certificate is not a degree. Circle in the Square is an accredited conservatory that offers 2-year intensive training programs. It is affiliated with the Broadway theatre Circle in the Square Theatre.

Coastal Carolina University, Department of Theatre

Conway, South Carolina

BFA in musical theatre, theatre/acting, theatre/physical theatre, theatre/design & technology; BA in dramatic arts

Duke University, Department of Theater Studies

Durham, North Carolina

BA in theater studies

Harvard University, Office for the Arts, Committee on the Dramatic Arts

Cambridge, Massachusetts

No degrees offered in theatre; Secondary Concentration (minor) in dramatic arts

*Harvard does not offer a "Concentration" (a major) in theatre. There is now a minor available through the Committee on Dramatic Arts, which is a group of professors who help students pursue theatre through coursework and extracurricular performances and projects. There is an active student-run theatre scene at Harvard, and funding is available for projects through the Office for the Arts.

James Madison University, College of Visual & Performing Arts, School of Theatre & Dance

Harrisonburg, Virginia

BA in theatre and musical theatre

The Juilliard School, Drama Division

New York, New York

BFA in drama; Certificate in drama (available to students who already hold an undergraduate degree)

Louisiana State University, Department of Theatre

Baton Rouge, Louisiana

BA in theatre (with concentrations in performance, design/technology, theatre studies, literature/theory/history and arts administration)

Middlebury College, Department of Theatre

Middlebury, Vermont

BA in theatre (with concentrations in acting, directing, playwriting, and design)

Northwestern University, School of Communications, Department of Theatre

Evanston, Illinois

BA in theatre; Certificate in music theatre

Ohio Northern University, Getty College of Arts & Sciences, Fine Arts Division

Ada, Ohio

BFA in musical theatre, international technical production; BA in theatre

Oklahoma City University, School of Theatre

Oklahoma City, Oklahoma

BFA in acting and theatre design & production; BA in theatre performance; BM in music theatre (through the School of Music)

Otterbein University, Department of Theatre & Dance

Westerville, Ohio

BFA in acting, musical theatre, musical theatre with concentration in dance, and design & technology; BA in theatre

Ouachita Baptist University, School of Fine Arts, Department of Theatre Arts

Arkadelphia, Arkansas

BA in theatre arts, musical theatre, and theatre arts & speech communication education

Pepperdine, Fine Arts Division, Theatre Department

Malibu, California

BA in theatre arts, theatre & television, theatre & music

Roosevelt University, Chicago College of the Performing Arts, Theatre Conservatory

Chicago, Illinois

BFA in acting, musical theatre

Sam Houston State, Department of Theatre and Dance

Huntsville, Texas

BFA in musical theatre, acting & directing, and design & technology

Southern Methodist University, Meadows School of the Arts

Dallas, Texas

BFA in theatre studies and acting

Southwest Missouri State, Department of Theatre & Dance

Springfield, Missouri

BFA in acting, musical theatre, and design, technology & management; BA in theatre studies; BSed (Bachelor of Science in education) for theatre and speech

SUNY at Buffalo, College of Arts & Sciences, Department of Theatre & Dance

Buffalo, New York

BFA in music theatre, theatre performance, and design & technology; BA in theatre (with concentrations in acting, design/technology, history/ literature and directing)

University of the Arts

Philadelphia, Pennsylvania

BFA in acting, musical theatre, theatre design and technology, directing, playwriting and production

University of Florida, College of Fine Arts, School of Theatre & Dance

Gainesville, Florida

BFA in theatre performance (acting), musical theatre and design & technology; BA in theatre

University of Hartford, The Hartt School

West Hartford, Connecticut

BFA in acting and music theatre

University of Evansville, Department of Theatre

Evansville, Indiana

BA in theatre performance, theatre design technology, theatre generalist, theatre management, theatre education; BS in stage management

University of Minnesota Duluth, Department of Theatre

Duluth, Minnesota

BFA in acting, musical theatre, design/tech, and stage management; BA in theatre

University of Mississippi, Department of Theatre Arts

University, Mississippi

BFA in acting, musical theatre, and theatre design & technology; BA in theatre

University of North Carolina at Chapel Hill, Department of Dramatic Arts

Chapel Hill, North Carolina

BA in drama

University of North Carolina School of the Arts, School of Drama

Winston-Salem, North Carolina

BFA in acting

University of Oklahoma, College of Fine Arts, School of Drama

Norman, Oklahoma

BFA in acting, costume technology, design, dramaturgy, scene technology, stage management and musical theatre performance (through the School of Musical Theatre)

USC, School of Theatre

Los Angeles, California

BFA in acting, design (scenic, lighting, costume), technical direction, stage management; BA in theatre

University of Tampa, Department of Speech, Theatre & Dance

Tampa, Florida

BA in performing arts (musical theatre) and theatre

University of Tulsa, Department of Theatre and Musical Theatre

Tulsa, Oklahoma

BA in theatre and musical theatre

Valdosta University, College of the Arts, Department of Communication Arts

Valdosta, Georgia

BFA in theatre (with emphases in traditional theatre performance, technical theatre production, and musical theatre)

Viterbo University, Theatre Department

La Crosse, Wisconsin

BFA in acting, design, music theatre, technical production, and stage management; BA in theatre arts; BS in theatre arts education

Western Kentucky University, Potter College of Arts & Letters, Department of Theatre & Dance

Bowling Green, Kentucky

BFA in performing arts; BA in theatre

Yale University, Department of Theater Studies

New Haven, Connecticut

BA in theater studies

*Yale's reputation for outstanding theatre comes from its graduate program at the Yale School of Drama. The undergraduate theatre degree is a relatively new liberal arts program that has gained in credibility and quality over the past few years, but does not share the fame or prestige of the Master's program. Additionally, while there is some interaction between the programs that might benefit a Yale undergraduate student's development, a Bachelor's degree from Yale does not offer any advantage when applying to the Master's program.

About the Authors

Chelsea Cipolla is a New York-based actress, acting coach, and career consultant. Chelsea graduated from Emerson College in Boston, MA with a BA in acting and theatre education. After graduating, Chelsea returned to Emerson to help teach their Summer Arts Academy for three years. Chelsea can be found on-stage in the city and on-screen in numerous print ads and commercials. Chelsea resides on the Upper East Side with her King Charles Cavalier puppy, Cooper.

Chelsea is the founder of My College Audition (www.mycollegeaudition .com)—a resource for high school juniors and seniors looking to obtain a degree in theatre, musical theatre or music at the collegiate level. My College Audition students are coached in monologue selection/preparation, song selection/preparation, dance preparation, resume/headshot/self marketing, and general audition preparation. Past acceptances include: University of Michigan, Emerson College, Boston University, Syracuse University, Ithaca College, Fordham University, Pace University, Boston Conservatory, Marymount Manhattan College, New York University, and many more.

John West is an actor and college consultant who has appeared in leading roles in New York, on national tours, and regionally. John attended the Tennessee Governor's School for the Arts and holds a BFA in musical theatre from Northern Kentucky University. While touring for three years, he cultivated his passion for mentoring high school students in theatre by conducting workshops across the United States and Canada on the college selection process. He has accrued an extensive knowledge of the theatre programs and faculty across the country through active participation in national conferences and frequent visits to countless schools. He now serves as a proud staff member of the Open Jar Institute (founded by director Jeff Whiting)—New York City's most Broadway-integrated actor training program in Musical Theater.

Chelsea and John also serve on the staff of New York Vocal Coaching, where Chelsea is the monologue coach (www.newyorkmonologuecoach. com) and John heads the speech division (www.newyorkspeechcoaching .com).

New York Vocal Coaching Inc. www.newyorkvocalcoaching.com was founded in 2005 by Justin Stoney, one of New York's most sought after voice teachers and vocal coaches. Since its founding, New York Vocal Coaching has helped thousands of artists from over 20 countries to achieve success in all areas of the performing arts.

CPSIA information can be obtained at www.ICGtesting.com
Printed in the USA
BVOW041541031212

307111BV00005BA/14/P